us!

US!

CHRIS BACHELDER

BLOOMSBURY

First published in Great Britain 2006
This paperback edition published 2007

Copyright © 2006 by Chris Bachelder

The moral right of the author has been asserted

I, Candidate for Governor: And How I Got Licked (1934-35) and *The
Autobiography of Upton Sinclair* (1962): Copyright © 1934, 1935, 1962
by Upton Sinclair. Reprinted with permission of John and Jeffrey Weidman.
The photograph of picketing children was taken by Allen Bachelder

Bloomsbury Publishing Plc,
36 Soho Square,
London W1D 3QY

www.bloomsbury.com

A CIP catalogue record for this book
is available from the British Library

ISBN 978 0 7475 8595 4

10 9 8 7 6 5 4 3 2 1

Printed in Great Britain by Clays Ltd, St Ives plc

Bloomsbury Publishing Plc, London, New York, Berlin

All papers used by Bloomsbury Publishing are natural,
recyclable products made from wood grown in well-managed
forests. The manufacturing processes conform to the
environmental regulations of the country of origin

For Jenn

Do anything but ignore me.
—UPTON SINCLAIR
LETTER TO H. L. MENCKEN

Contents

An old, mad, blind, despised, and dying King;
Princes, the dregs of their dull race, who flow
Through public scorn,—mud from a muddy spring;
Rulers who neither see nor feel nor know,
But leechlike to their fainting country cling
Till they drop, blind in blood, without a blow.
A people starved and stabbed in th' untilled field;
An army, whom liberticide and prey
Makes as a two-edged sword to all who wield;
Golden and sanguine laws which tempt and slay;
Religion Christless, Godless—a book sealed;
A senate, Time's worst statute, unrepealed—
Are graves from which a glorious Phantom may
Burst, to illumine our tempestuous day.

—PERCY BYSSHE SHELLEY
"ENGLAND IN 1819"

PART ONE!

Resurrection
Scrapbook

My God is an experimental God.
                    —UPTON SINCLAIR

Hope and Shovels Forever, Upton

As far back as I can remember,
my life was a series of
Cinderella transformations.
—*THE AUTOBIOGRAPHY OF UPTON SINCLAIR*

Tony was driving—he had his father's old four-door Plymouth Valiant—so it was me in the backseat with Upton Sinclair. He slouched away from me, against the door, and as far as I could tell, he still wasn't breathing. He smelled overpoweringly of the earth—metallic, elemental, potted. I stared at the back of Tony's head for a few miles, then closed my eyes. The strong, near-rotten smell in the car made me remember the way the summer rains would bring up long, knotty earthworms in the streets of my childhood neighborhood. It occurs to me now that I haven't seen worms like that in years. Perhaps the earthworm is a bellwether, a coal-mine canary, yet another harbinger of planetary doom. No doubt there will soon be a book, called *The Missing Tiller,* perhaps, or *Dearthworm,* blurbed as "quite possibly the best of the disappearing animal books." And the books about disappearing frogs, disappearing dolphins, and disappearing eagles will disappear to the discount table, three for ten dollars.

Tony said, "What about now? Is he moving? Is he breathing?"

I opened my eyes and looked over at Upton. "No," I said, reaching across the seat to lock his door. "I don't think so. Not yet."

Tony said, "Are we supposed to *do* anything? Are we supposed to help?" We were both starting to panic, pretending not to. We were so young.

"No," I said. "Not really. It just sort of happens naturally."

"We could do CPR or something."

"Slow down. Don't speed."

"It's been over an hour."

"Relax."

"Maybe I should open the window."

The winter night rushed in through the cracked window, loud and cold and rather too blatantly suggestive that the world is inhospitable to human life. "Roll that up," I said. "Now he's just dead and cold."

I stared at the slumped figure beside me, which was briefly illuminated as we passed under streetlights or caught the headlights of oncoming cars. He was wearing his funeral suit, the one, I think, that he wore later on the cover of *Rolling Stone*. It was already, at this time, too large for him. It may have fit at one point, but death was making him smaller, frailer. His gaunt face was creased and collapsed; lines ran from his eyes and the corners of his mouth like the spoked flight paths on an airline hub map. His skin was mottled with spots and scars, and coated with a thin film. Dirt or dust. Time, maybe. Or death. There was something lodged in his left ear—it might have been a hearing aid, but it looked more like a mushroom. Despite the ugly red smile across his throat and the small black hole in his temple, he looked peaceful. I felt guilty and silly for bringing him back in cold December. Our intentions were good, I still believe that, but they were hardly pure. Some of our political anger had to do with missing the '60s, feeling cheated by history. We had been tying knots with the Boy Scouts during the love-ins and demonstrations, and by the time we joined the cause, there was no more nudity or tear gas. It is true that we wanted to be class heroes, that we hoped to get laid by our beautiful, serious, kerchiefed comrades. We longed for the revolution, but we also longed to hold these girls in the night and breathe in their strong, unwashed scent and to confess to them our fears in such a way that made us seem stronger and less vulnerable. They were hairy and sexually frank and brimming with political theory, the history of ideas. They were profane, tough-minded egalitarians with delicate fingers and long necks.

"Tony," I said. "Maybe this is wrong."

"What?"

"We should turn around."

"What are you talking about?"

"I think maybe we should put him back."

And it was then, as if at the prospect of leaving this troubled world and returning to the grave, that Sinclair began stirring beside me.

Tony said, "We're not putting him back."

"Wait," I said. "Hold it. I think he's living."

Tony turned around to look in the backseat and the Valiant veered onto the washboard grid of the shoulder. Upton began twitching and jerking, lightly at first but then violently. We had not read or heard anything about this.

Tony said, "What's going on? Make him stop that."

I put my hand on Upton's shoulder and his convulsions just grew worse. I was afraid his bones would break.

"Sir," I said. "Mr. Sinclair."

His eyes rolled in his head. He pulled his arms up to his chest. His fingers—nine, I noticed—were spread out and curled arthritically. It was a difficult birth; it looked every bit as bad as dying.

"Mr. Sinclair," I said. "It's OK. You're with friends."

His spasms continued, as did Tony's erratic driving and my hapless nursing. This went on for five minutes, maybe longer. Eventually Sinclair's convulsions subsided to trembling and he tried to say something. Tony said, "What did he say?"

I said, "Mr. Sinclair?"

He tried the word again and this time I could make it out. *Cold*. I told Tony to turn up the heat. "Heat, OK," Tony said. The heater fan in the old Valiant had the same rattling volume, the same noise-to-air ratio, as fans in gas station bathrooms. Upton hugged himself and rocked back and forth in the seat. His heavy breathing occasionally burst into coughing fits that sprayed small pebbles and clods onto the floor of the car. I could hear them popping the vinyl floor mat like sleet on a window. The seat, too, was covered with a fine layer of dirt and dust, flakes of dead skin.

Here beside me, frail and ancient, retching dry dirt, was the last best hope of the American Left.

Upton squinted up in my direction. "Glasses."

"Glasses," I repeated, before realizing that I had been holding his glasses and dentures. We had removed them from his suit pocket, as we had been told to do. We had also removed the old letter from Einstein; we couldn't help it. We had read it, though we already knew it by heart, and then carefully replaced it in the pocket. "I'm sorry," I said, and handed him his glasses and dentures. "There's some water in the seat pouch. And some Dr Pepper." An article in an underground newspaper had said that Sinclair liked Dr Pepper, but this turned out to be a hoax. Later we found out that he is opposed to all dark colas.

Sinclair put on his glasses and placed his dentures in his coat pocket. He took the bottled water from the seat pouch and held it up right in front of his eyes.

"It's water," I said.

"They sell this?" he asked. "You buy this?"

"Yes," I said. He looked at me as if to ask another question, but he remained silent. I could not tell if he was impressed or disgusted.

He struggled to twist the cap off the bottle of retail water. His eyes were squeezed shut and his arms trembled with the effort. I offered to help him but he ignored me, he wouldn't give in. Finally he broke the safety seal, removed the cap, and sniffed at the water. It did not occur to me to offer to take a drink of the water first. Years later, of course, Sinclair employed a series of tasters, one of whom died and one of whom killed him. They both kept interesting Web logs.

He took a few small sips and then leaned once more against the door, staring out the window at the passing night. Tony looked at me in the rearview mirror. He clearly wanted me to do something, say something.

I said, "Mr. Sinclair?"

He turned slowly from the window. "It's Upton." He cleared his throat again. "Call me Upton."

"Upton," I said. "Are you OK?"

He looked at me. "These resurrections are killing me." He coughed again, cleared his throat. "It's not easy coming back. Not at my age."

I said, "Can we get you anything else? Are you hungry?"

"Sometimes I wish you all would just let me be."

What could I possibly say? I said, "I'm sorry. We have sandwiches."

Tony said, "We have two different kinds." It was true, we did have two different kinds. I had insisted.

Upton shook his head and I shook my head to Tony. The heater was beginning to work and I took off my jacket, a thick navy peacoat that had belonged to my great-grandfather, the alcoholic Wobbly. Upton still shivered and rubbed his hands together. He said, "Is this a Ford?"

I said, "No, it's a Plymouth."

"It's nice."

I nodded.

He said, "Tell me something." I just kept nodding, like a puppet, while Tony's face hovered in the mirror. "Are we Socialist yet?"

I said, "We?"

"The United States."

"No."

"I see."

I had thought I was breaking bad news, but I realize now that Sinclair must have been relieved. He would not have wanted it to happen without him.

"Are we metric?"

"You mean the metric system?"

He leaned toward me. "Yes."

"No," I said. "We don't use that."

He was agitated now. "It's just like Prohibition. The people want it, but the capitalists don't." He cleared his throat. He took off his glasses and cleaned them with his dirty coat sleeve. "Well, we've got a lot of work to do."

Tony said, "Mr. Sinclair, what's it like being dead?"

I reached around Tony's seat to try to jab him, but my hand got caught in the seat belt and I couldn't reach him.

Upton said, "Pen?" He made a writing motion with his hand. I didn't have one, but Tony handed one back. I searched the seat pouch and found a small notebook that Tony's father had used years earlier to calculate his gas mileage. I tried to find an empty page but couldn't. Each page, front and back, was filled with rows and columns of data—DATE, # GAL., $/GAL., MILES, MPG—all written in a small, precise hand. I held the notebook up to Tony. "Can he use this?"

Tony frowned. "There's not anything else?"

I said, "I'll check."

Upton said, "That will do just fine."

"Go ahead," Tony said. "Just go ahead."

I handed the notebook to Upton. He flipped it open and began writing slowly in the spaces around Tony's father's neat figures. His hand trembled and he had a difficult time making the letters and the words, but he kept at it. Tony didn't turn on the dome light. Upton filled several pages in the dark and then closed the notebook and put it into his coat pocket.

He asked me my name and age. He asked me the month and year. He asked me where we were and where we were going. He asked me who the president was, and when I told him who would be inaugurated in January, he wouldn't believe me.

"You shouldn't have a laugh at the expense of an old man."

"It's true," I said. "You'll see."

"It can't be."

"It is true," Tony said. "He's not joking around."

"Well, I suppose it's fitting," Upton said, "that we turn to Hollywood."

He asked me who had won the U.S. Open and I said I couldn't remember.

"McEnroe," Tony said.

"Ack," Sinclair said. "I dislike the man."

"Do you want a sandwich?" I was beginning to feel bold and useful, historically relevant.

"Tell me, my boy. Is capitalism still stampeding unchecked over the bodies and lives of the workers?"

I said that as far as I could tell, it was.

"Listen," he said, "you mustn't let me just rot down there. You mustn't just leave me in the ground when there's so much to be done."

Tony said, "Cop. Duck."

Upton was down in a flash, but then Tony said, "No, it's not a cop. Looked like one. Sorry."

Upton rose slowly. Without actually providing any help, I put my hand on his shoulder and guided him upward, back to a sitting position. His suit jacket was so large that I could not feel his body beneath the baggy, wrinkled fabric. He stared out the window. By leaning forward I could see, just off the interstate, a long outdoor mall, store after store like cars on a train, each of them empty, gang-painted, for rent. Upton said, "Three years ago they probably had a big thing here with balloons. Cut the ribbon with a huge pair of scissors. You understand?"

"Like a ceremony," I offered.

"Took a lot of photographs. The men in suits with yellow hard hats on? You know? Shovels? Pushing the shovels into a mound of dirt with their shiny shoes."

I nodded. "Like a ground-breaking thing, sure."

"Talking about the dawn of a new day with huge scissors." He turned back toward the night. "And now look at it."

I of course couldn't look at it, because by that time we were a kilo-meter past the strip mall. But there were others just like it that I could look at, and I've seen plenty of them since.

"Terrible," I said.

Then nobody said anything for a while and Tony turned on the radio. We heard the end of a folk song that imagined the world living as one, and when Tony changed the station, we heard the song again, from the beginning. Perpetual revolution! The song was nearly ten years old at that point, hardly in heavy rotation, but the radio, like the rest of the world, seemed to exist for us. The universe was acknowledging us and I, for one, was not surprised. I had no notion of coincidence. I felt that this was one in a long series of meaningful nodes that constituted the wake-ful life. I thought that the world, day to day, got either better or worse, and that we could make it better. I thought we could make people listen and care. The economy was bad, I thought we had a shot. Like I said, I was young. When the song ended the second time and the DJ told us that the singer had been shot outside of his upscale New York apartment building, I didn't dare look over at Upton. Tony turned off the radio. Tony's father was dead too.

Without turning from the window, Upton said, "What do you want with me? Why have you brought me back?"

I caught Tony's eyes in the mirror and I knew he wasn't going to help me. It was clear that I was on my own. I said, *"Why?"*

Upton said, "Yes. Why. I trust it's not a prank of some kind."

"It's not a prank."

"So tell me."

"Well," I said. "What we—" Upton turned toward me. "The reason is that..." His glasses gleamed and I could not see his eyes. I thought of the serious girls, the way they would cherish the opportunity to an-swer this question. I thought of all the statistics and theoretical force they would marshal, their sense of the specific historical moment. Di-alectics. "Things," I said finally, "aren't fair." Upton stared at me in the dark. "Things aren't fair is why."

I felt my face fill with red heat. Tony kept his eyes on the road. He had abandoned me. Upton leaned his head back against the seat and closed his eyes. The car was hot and pungent, and I considered throwing myself out the door.

Tony said, "Is that a cop?"

Upton said, "You must be careful, young man." He kept his head back and his eyes closed, but he was smiling now. His knees bounced nervously, his fingers twitched in his lap. "That idea is quite likely to get us killed."

Our Nodding Scheherazade
(Review of *Pharmaceutical!*)

Pharmaceutical!
Upton Sinclair
352 pages
Red Shovel Press

> *The job of the artist is to deepen the mystery.*
> —FRANCIS BACON

Apparently, being dead has done little for the artistry of Upton Sinclair (though being alive, it must be said, was hardly propitious). One might have hoped that a few months of cemetery rest would have reinvigorated Sinclair's literary project, but this is sadly not the case. *Pharmaceutical!*, Sinclair's 107th novel and his first in two years, is an embarrassment, the kind of formulaic, simplistic Socialist screed this country has not seen since, well, Upton Sinclair.

Sinclair, readers may need reminding, was once considered a mildly important figure in American literature and politics. In his first lifetime (1878–1968), the muckraker wrote scores of so-called novels illustrating the plight and sordid working conditions of the poor, and the evil machinations of the bosses. The novels were motivated, it has often been suggested, less by a sympathetic bond with the poor than by a fierce hatred of the wealthy. His most well-known and successful book, *The Jungle* (1906), portrayed life in the Chicago stockyards with, as an editor who refused the book put it, "gloom and horror unrelieved." The novel was celebrated internationally as a major work of realism and as a catalyst for significant reform in the meatpacking industry (as if better sausage were the purpose of literature). In a clear admission of his poor artistic marksmanship, Sinclair would later say of *The Jungle*, "I aimed at the public's heart, and by accident I hit it in the stomach." In 1943, at which time he was already old, the muckraker won the Pulitzer Prize for a novel whose title is now known only to professors and teenage criminals.*

More activist than artist, Sinclair even ran for governor of California in 1934 under a baldly Socialist scheme called EPIC (End Poverty in California). He proposed that the state turn over the farms and factories to the workers, and allow them to keep what they produce. Sound familiar? Sinclair, running as a Democrat, was defeated by the Republican candidate, Frank Merriam. That Sinclair received over 875,000 votes speaks more to the desperation of the Depression years than to the legitimacy of his EPIC platform, which was mocked by opponents as "Empty Promises in California."

Today, the oft-resurrected and oft-assassinated leftist is known more as a cultural figure or a folk hero than as a writer. Predictably, his standing in the literary canon has slipped steadily through the years. The work has not stood up to time—Sinclair's novels today seem vulgar, tendentious, hysterical. It isn't simply that his ideas are extreme, outdated, and irrelevant (though they are; no serious thinker today takes Socialism seriously). The issue, rather, is aesthetic: Sinclair has

---

* The novel is called *Dragon's Teeth*, one of eleven long-forgotten (and out-of-print) books in Sinclair's Lanny Budd series.

never understood that art and polemic do not mix, that great and lasting art has no authorial agenda. Novels are not tracts or pamphlets; they do not serve to convince readers of anything. A novel may ask questions, but a good one never supplies an answer. In the long history of Western literature, in the Natural Selection of Great Books, we can clearly see that the survivors are those that aspire to a timeless and organic Beauty and not those that are written to support an autoworker's strike.

Let us be clear that the above complaint is not an anachronistic imposition of contemporary critical fashions on the literature of a bygone era. Sinclair's peers took him to task far more harshly than the current review. In 1916, Sherwood Anderson wrote in a letter to Sinclair, "There is something terrible to me in the thought of the art of writing being bent and twisted to serve the end of propaganda. My conception of an artist's attitude toward life about him is that he shall at all costs keep himself open to impressions, that he shall not let himself become an advocate." Ten years later, Edith Wharton wrote Sinclair a similar letter. Of his novel *Oil!*, Wharton scolds: "It seems to me an excellent story until the moment, all too soon, when it becomes a political pamphlet. I make this criticism without regard to the views which you teach, and which are detestable to me. Had you written in favor of those in which I believe, my judgment would have been exactly the same. I have never known a novel that was just good enough to be good in spite of its being adapted to the author's political views." Sinclair would have been wise to heed the words of his contemporaries. Decades later, we find that Anderson's and Wharton's high standing in the American canon is secure, while Sinclair is remembered only as a tireless pamphleteer and a "polymaniac" (to borrow Ezra Pound's memorable epithet).

Pharmaceutical!, as the reader might easily imagine, is an extended, criminally unbalanced tirade against the pharmaceutical industry. The plodding, predetermined plot follows Harold, a virtuous and hardworking young man who is—you guessed it—*poor*, and who is, yes, *struggling to support his family*, including his *infirm grand-mother*, who needs a certain prescription drug to keep from knocking off. Harold, he just can't seem to get ahead, no matter what, and his desperation leads to desperate acts. As Harold attempts to secure the drug for his grandmother, he finds—well, suffice it to say that he finds injustice everywhere! As in scores of Sinclair's other novels, the wealthy are evil and Machiavellian, and competition and corporate greed are the diabolical forces that daily crush the likes of Harold and his sick Meemaw. The great solution, we are led to believe, is that we should all share. In the final thirty pages, Harold, having suffered spectacularly, disappears into the global, good-hearted mass of inter-national workers and exclamation points. One does end up sympathiz-ing with Harold, though not for the reasons that Sinclair intends. Harold's great conflict is not that he is trapped within a ruthless eco-nomic system, but that he is trapped within a ruthless novel, a struc-ture infinitely more dehumanizing, rigid, and predetermined than the capitalism it denounces. The wonderful thing about America is that you always have a shot, while the dreadful thing about a Sinclair novel is that you don't. Poor Harold, he was born into a Socialist novel. Kid never had a chance.

Quite aside from the naïveté and artistic bankruptcy of his narra-tive mode, Sinclair proves himself, on nearly every page, to be woe-fully out of touch with contemporary culture, as when he calls a fax machine a "Telepaper Device" or when he describes one of the vehi-cles in a high-speed chase as a "Vanette," which this reviewer can only surmise to be a minivan. And frankly, I just have no idea what a "Belted Phototalker" might be. This oblivion is perhaps to be ex-pected from an ancient writer who has recently been dead, but it is the dear reader who suffers.

As of the time this review went to press, Mr. Sinclair had not yet been reassassinated. By any way of reckoning his age, he is a very, very old man, and the fact is, Sinclair was missing his target even when he was a young writer at the height of his powers (nearly a century ago!). If he will not be deterred from writing even more books like *Pharmaceutical!* by the bad reviews and bullets that seem to follow him everywhere, perhaps a comrade might suggest to him, gently, that most artists tend to lose their touch by age 120 or so.

I Regret That I Have but One Anonymous Phone Tip to Give to My Country: Partial Transcript of Calls to the Toll-Free U.S. Tip Line (1-800-US-Watch) May 13, 1993

FROM: Perlis, VA
LINE: Cell phone
TIME: 9:04 A.M. EST
TIP: I just saw Upton at the Shoney's breakfast buffet. The one on Clifton, not the one out by the interstate. That one's disgusting. He's wearing a mesh baseball cap that says, "Fish tremble at the mention of my name." He's got on one of those sweaters with the buttons. What are they called? You put them on like a shirt. Like a button-down shirt. They're sort of like a jacket but they're a sweater for old men. Oh. You know what I mean. Not an *ottoman,* but a . . . um . . . It's green. He ate three plates of fruit! He left before I did. I hurried up and finished my breakfast so I could call. Thank you.

FROM: Salina, KS
LINE: Domestic
TIME: 9:17 A.M. EST
TIP: Sinclair is in my shed. Repeat: Sinclair is in my shed. It's a blue and white aluminum structure behind the house. If you

storm the premises, I ask only that you please watch out for my wife's flower beds back there.

FROM: Huntsville, AL
LINE: Business
TIME: 9:58 A.M. EST
TIP: I've called every day for a week and have yet to get a response. I'm going to say this one more time. Upton is working as a greeter in the Huntsville Wal-Mart. He's going by the alias of William Farley. That's William Farley. His nametag says "William," not "Upton." He's very slippery. I've got my eye on him, but I could sure as hell use some backup.

FROM: Rogers, IA
LINE: Cell phone
TIME: 10:22 A.M. EST
TIP: I just saw him! I just... He was here! He was on a bus! He... [inaudible]... in the window. I know it was him. I turned around, but then I got stuck at a railroad crossing. Shit! When the train passes, I'm going to catch up to that bus. I'll trail him and... [inaudible]... my shotgun.

FROM: Perlis, VA
LINE: Cell phone
TIME: 10:32 A.M. EST
TIP: *Cardigan* is what I was trying to think of before. Thank you.

FROM: Santa Fe, NM
LINE: Domestic
TIME: 11:19 A.M. EST
TIP: Upton is here. He is in the earth and in the rocks. He is in the wind and in the sky. He is in the grains of desert sand. As

a part of the life force, he is inside me and inside you and
inside the white-tailed rabbit. But most of all, he is in a light
blue Dodge Neon heading north on I-25.

FROM: Portland, OR
LINE: Domestic
TIME: 11:38 A.M. EST
TIP: Um, yes, I was just wondering if you had Prince Albert in
a can? ... *Dude*, shut up. *Dude.* Dude, shut *up*. OK, yes,
um, I was wondering if I could speak to a Mr. Freely?
Pass it here. A Mr. I. P. Freely? ... Stop it. Stop *doing* that.
Hello?

FROM: Houston, TX
LINE: Pay phone
TIME: 12:02 P.M. EST
TIP: This one's called "U.S. Watch." Sing along if you know the
words. Sorry about my guitar. Can't keep it tuned right in
this humidity. Here we go: Well I saw Upton Sinclair in the
grocery store / The one that stays open all night / He spent
thirty minutes with the desserts / Everything so sweet and so
bright / Walt was with the pork chops unseen / Hey blue and
yellow make green / But maybe it was just a weather
balloon / Yeah maybe it was just a weather balloon / I saw
Upton Sinclair in the meatpacking district / He was taking
notes for a pamphlet / I saw him go home to the apartment /
He shares with the chimp who typed Hamlet / Monkey and
Upton eating dinner on the floor / They had a bad feeling it
had all been done before / But maybe it was just a weather
balloon / Yeah could have been a trick of the light / I saw
Upton Sinclair in the Russian tearoom and his hair was
perfect / But it could have been a weather balloon / Yeah
could have been atmospheric disturbance / Could have

been secret weapon testing or Fata Morgana / Might just
have been the northern lights or a spaceship in the
night / Probably best to assume that what I saw was a
weather balloon

Bulldawg Country

Sinclair takes a lifetime to cross the makeshift stage. The tepid applause has long since died by the time he shuffles up to the podium. There is coughing and whispering, there is chatter from electric hand-held devices whose use has not been discontinued. Programs are fans in the heat.

Championship banners hang in the high ceiling, a long record of wrestling excellence. A dynasty, according to the local *Standard*. The lights in the gymnasium hang and flicker. Metal grates cover the bulbs, protect them from arcing balls. The effect, Sinclair feels without noticing, is that the very light, in this venue, is caged. The bleachers fold into the walls, fold out of the walls, fold into the walls. There are messages and pictures painted high on the cinder block walls. BULLDAWG PRIDE. WELCOME TO BULLDAWG COUNTRY. The school saved money by using art students instead of professional painters. The bulldog looks more like a pug with a spiked collar. They were not art students per se, since there is no art program. They were students interested in climbing ladders. There are more than sixty painted stars in the teal field of the American flag—either an error or an edgy comment on manifest destiny and imperialism. A slippery aesthetic question. The old muckraker, it must be said, prefers a less oblique mode of political art.

The podium gives Sinclair a nasty splinter in the loose leather

21

webbing between thumb and forefinger—a tiny spear lost in his dry wrinkled hand and not coming out. The hands tell a long story: nine fingers, mottled and bent, knuckles like walnuts.

Sinclair clears his throat, tastes the damp dirt in his mouth. Not many people are taking photographs. There are white worms in his pantcuffs and he feels his energy returning. Through thick glasses Sinclair squints out at the audience in their plastic chairs. This could be, he thinks, the cradle of American Socialism. This could be where the revolution starts. Members of the wrestling team sit together off to Sinclair's right—red-faced, open-mouthed, their blue gowns draped over chemical bulk. Elsewhere, many of the graduates have used masking tape to construct lewd and ungrammatical messages on their mortarboards. The youth are not clever and many, it seems, are intoxicated. Their younger siblings are ill-behaved and seething along the sticky hardwood floor. Their parents and grandparents wear clothes that Sinclair has not witnessed in several lives. Knit ties and pleats, waves and waves of ruffles. The school does not have an auditorium and the plants have all shut down.

There is nothing like hope in this place and a red-haired child is already booing. In the inside pocket of his funeral jacket Sinclair has a brittle, yellowed letter from Albert Einstein and a copy of his address to graduating seniors. Einstein's letter, dated November 1934, begins in analogy: "My son, when he was about five years old, attempted to split wood with my razor. You can be sure that it was less bad for the wood than the razor." The speech to graduating seniors is about the triumphant march of science and technology and free markets. It's about the will to succeed. It touches lightly on the threat of nuclear annihilation, and it uses the terms *capitalism* and *democracy* more or less interchangeably. Sinclair didn't write it.

He ignores the thick speech in his pocket. He says, "Greetings, Class of '89."

Members of the Class of '87 scream out a correction, and Sinclair patiently waits for their exuberance to subside.

"Members of the Class of '89, let me begin my address with an analogy." The gymnasium vibrates with an unhappy groan. The audience regards analogies, like college professors or foreign automobiles, with suspicion, if not contempt. Sinclair says, "When six men go out into a field to catch a horse, it makes all the difference whether—"

Someone in the back yells, "Louder, Gramps!" This is regarded, in the gymnasium, as a comment of slicing wit. The collapsed bleachers rumble in the laughter.

Sinclair attempts to adjust the microphone, but it won't move. He leans forward, using both hands to pull it down. His grunting is amplified. From the floor it appears that he is locked in a battle to the death, and the audience grows quiet. Sinclair won't surrender and finally he wrangles the microphone down to his dry lips. He catches his breath and looks out at the audience once more. These faces are the faces he saw in California in '34. He says, "When six men go out into a field to catch a horse"—the squealing feedback makes the audience members fidget and complain and make fists in their laps—"it makes all the difference whether they spend their time catching the horse or keeping one another from catching the horse."

Sinclair pauses here, notes the sudden silence. The analogy hangs over the gym like a weather system. These people have caught their share of horses. Chairs creak and the caged lights hum. There is a great deal of old chewing gum stuck to the podium.

Sinclair continues, "I know that we began in a competitive world, and I have no quarrel with the past. I am looking toward the future; and I say that when men compete with one another for wealth, they produce poverty for themselves."

There is a distinct rumbling in the audience now, a murmur of discontent. Some parents cover their children's ears. The wrestlers, hopped-up sons of unemployed machinists, begin to tremble with an ill-defined sense of rage. They sweat copiously beneath their blue caps and gowns. Veins bulge in their foreheads and their thick necks. Their pupils are pinpricks.

Someone yells out, "Commie!"

"They duplicate plants, they overproduce, they adulterate goods."

"Godless!"

"They lie about their products, they spy upon one another, they buy special favors from government officials."

"Russia!"

"They subsidize lobbyists and politicians."

A woman with a large hat begins to sing "America the Beautiful." The others do not immediately join in.

"They build up political machines, and ultimately undermine the practice of—"

The shot is deafening in the cavernous gym. It is not a sound you ever get used to. Sinclair spins and crumples, clutching his shoulder. On the floor of the plywood stage, he manages to crawl inside the hollow podium. He has miscalculated. They were not quite ready. There is a carved message inside the podium and Sinclair squints to make it out: JJ LOVES PUZZY. He has trouble with his breathing. The blood, when it comes, is thick and slow like sap.

There is Upton Sinclair, once again, wounded and hiding inside a leaning, splintery podium constructed by students who wanted to use hammers. In closing, Einstein writes, "In economic affairs the logic of facts will work itself out somewhat slowly." He writes, and this is the muckraker's favorite part, "You have contributed more than any other person." Sinclair peeks out to the edges of the warped stage, but his secretary has fled. He can hear the chanting and the stomping of the crowd, and beneath it all a hum that is either light or pain. Then the awful blue rush of the wrestlers.

The Logic of Facts,
Working Itself Out Somewhat Slowly

Item Number: 11251968
Item Title: Miracle Bullet
Item Location: Miami, FL
Starting Bid: $7,500
Time Left: 6 days, 14 hours
History: 96 bids
Shipping: Ships anywhere in U.S. Buyer assumes all postage or shipping costs. Seller strongly recommends insurance.

Description: THIS IS *THE BULLET* THAT KILLED SOCIALIST WRITER UPTON SINCLAIR IN WISCONSIN IN OCTOBER 1986. FROM THE GUN OF JOE GERALD HUNTLEY, 55 YARDS AWAY AT GROUND LEVEL IN THE FOG. THE FAMOUS "MADISON MIRACLE." THIS IS THE GENUINE MIRACLE BULLET! COMPARE TO AUTOPSY PHOTOS AT BEWARETHEIDES.COM!! DO NOT BE FOOLED BY IMITATIONS AND COUNTERFEITS!!

Mount Rushmore

Imagine that he wins in '34
And they carve his smiling face on Mount Rushmore
Imagine those ten-foot eyes
Staring down from the mountainside
Imagine that he wins in '34

Imagine California is the place
That starts a revolution in the States
Governor Sinclair says
Take a message for the Prez
Imagine California is the place

Imagine all those bonfires burning bright
And the people celebrating through the night
No more rich and poor
Because he wins in '34
Imagine all those bonfires burning bright

Imagine that you love me like before
Young in love and we didn't need much more
Now the workers can't unite

When you work days and I work nights
Imagine that you love me like before

Imagine that he wins in '34
And they carve his Roman nose on Mount Rushmore
Right beside Honest Abe
Oh baby I wish you'd stay
Imagine that he wins in '34

Let's please pretend tonight
That Upton won that crooked fight
Let's pretend that he won in '34

A Complicated World,
So Very Hard to Be Good In!

He wakes in the night with the white glow of the full moon in the room. There is a woman beside him, bare-shouldered beneath the thin covers. Her wavy hair spreads out across the pillow like the thick roots of an oak.

Upton says, "I am a soldier."

The woman laughs. She says, "I know you are." She shifts onto her side. The mattress is soft and Upton feels himself falling toward her, into her, into a hole. His toe brushes her shin in the dark world beneath the sheets. She is tall, broad-shouldered, with a gravity and thick, wavy hair. She is probably naked.

Upton thinks of bedbugs. As a child he slept on a sofa and the bedbugs crawled over him in the night. He would turn on a gaslight and try to smash them before they scurried away. Bedbugs made him a Socialist. Bedbugs and Shelley.

"How did you get in here?"

"Isn't the light strange? It feels like we're underwater."

"I've been killed by women too."

But she says she won't kill him.

Upton wants to look beneath the covers. He wants to write. He wants the woman to leave. He wants her to leave slowly. He wants to

28

watch her leave slowly in the strange moonlight. He wants to watch her hips. He wants to get just a glimpse of her pubic hair. The dark, terrible thatch. Maybe a nipple as she puts on her robe and then leaves. Then he wants to lock the door and write. Pamphlets, chapters, and letters. As a young man, he averaged eight thousand words a day, every day, Sundays included. He was a virgin until he was married. He was terrified of disease and pregnancy and women and tainted meat. Sublimation made him famous. He was crazy for women, the hell under their skirts. He worked fourteen hours a day. He loved Shelley and tennis, and he hated capitalism. He had constipation and headaches. An entire novel might spring, fully formed, from the sight of her pubic hair. He glances at the table beside the bed for his pen and notebook. And glasses. He says, "I must get my rest." He wrote seventeen books between 1934 and 1940.

The woman moves closer to Upton beneath the sheet. He stares straight ahead, at the wall, at the four long wooden shelves that sag beneath the weight of books about injustice.

Upton says, "That sound outside. Is it crickets?"

"Frogs."

"What a racket."

The woman gently folds back the sheet, exposing both of their bodies. He pulls the sheet back up. He says, "I should be sleeping, young lady. I don't even know your name."

"I'm not that young," she says. She pulls the sheet back down and holds it tightly while surveying the muckraker's devastated body. When it comes down to it, she's stronger than Upton, she can have her way. She makes a noise in her throat, deep and reverential.

"Dear God."

"Well," Upton says. "It isn't pretty."

She doesn't look away. She says, "But it is, in a way. It's beautiful. It's what principles would look like if we could see them."

This is a full decade before Treadway's infamous nudes of Sinclair, but already Upton's frail, ravaged figure is a poignant image, a graphic history of the Left. He lies still. He knows what's coming and he won't refuse her.

The woman runs her finger lightly across a long, rubbery abdominal gash that traverses the horizontal wrinkles in the loose skin of his belly. Upton shivers and she removes her hand quickly.

"I'm sorry."

"No. It's fine."

She returns her hand, presses harder along the wound. "Doesn't hurt?"

"Not anymore."

"Chicago, 1984."

Upton nods.

She moves her finger up to a small, clean puncture wound right beneath his sternum, where his ribs separate. "Wilmington, North Carolina, '91."

Upton smiles. His eyes are shut and he can feel her big perfect egalitarian breast against his shoulder. He is worried about gonorrhea. He is considering bringing Lanny Budd back. He says, "A student of the struggle, I see."

The woman moves her soft palm over a large, ragged crater just above the jut of Upton's right hipbone. "Amarillo, '78."

Upton coughs and says, "I have never been popular in Texas. Some sort of *harpoon*. Very unpleasant."

With two fingers she follows the long, narrow slash across Upton's throat. "Florida Keys, 1974."

"Seventy-three, I believe."

"Seventy-four."

"Oh, yes, yes," he says. "It was January '74. You're right, dear. I lose track." She rolls him gingerly on his side, inspects three knife wounds in his left kidney, where she knows they will be. A flap of dark leathery skin covers the fourth. "Wyoming, '88."

Upton says, "Seems like yesterday."

The woman rolls him back. Upton wonders how frogs can make so much noise. There are things to tell his son. Things to warn him about and things to explain. Dietary and sexual matters. He must write a letter. He has not been a great father, he knows. There are petitions, plays, editorials.

"Right here"—his shoulder—"Virginia, spring of '87."

"Graduation. Such angry young people."

The woman gently traces a small circle around an open bullet hole in Upton's chest, just above his heart. The hole is black against the curly white hair. She expands to a figure eight pattern around an adjacent hole, slightly larger, just as black. In the near dark it looks like Upton's chest has eyes.

She bites her lower lip. "This one," she says, pointing to the smaller hole, "is Huntley's miracle shot. Eighty-six, Madison."

"Of all places."

"Then this one must be D.C., '95."

"Mr. Huntley again. And this, dear?" Upton turns his head and points to the dark round pit at his temple.

"March 15, 1973. New York. Huntley."

"I've never even met the man."

"He'll do five more years, at least."

"In other countries they like me. My books are still in print."

The woman says, "Oh, Upton."

They lie together for a time. There is the steady drone of discussion, strategy, from somewhere in the house. Upton says, "I should get my sleep."

"Do you want your glasses? Do you want to look at me?"

"Yes."

She reaches over him for his glasses. Her smooth armpit grazes his dry lips, her breast touches his cheek. The world is unjust but it is wonderful. This big naked woman and the moon. She puts his glasses on his face. "I want to show you something," she says. "Can you see this? Is it too dark?" She sits up, gathers her long hair in a ponytail above her head, and turns the back of her lovely neck toward Upton. "Can you see it?"

Upton does not need to see to know what it is, but he sits up with a grunt and inspects the simple, neat tattoo of a small red shovel at the nape. The smell of her hair! Herbs! Coconut! He despises the market system, but he must admit that the crucible of competition has yielded extraordinary hair products. There was nothing like this in the first life. It makes him want to write. Something epic. Something in multiple volumes. There was a period in Japan in the '20s and '30s known as *Sinkuru Jidai* (the Sinclair era). Upton eases himself back down to the soft mattress. "That is lovely."

"I'm not going to kill you."

"You should let me sleep."

The woman returns beneath the covers and then straddles the old man, her knees clamping his narrow hips. She hovers above him, holding the sheet and blanket over her shoulders. Upton feels shame and the warmth across his pelvis. He wants her to leave with the light on.

She says, "Does it get any easier?"

The blood that remains in Upton's body begins a long, slow, viscous journey to his midsection. He does not take off his glasses. He says, "What do you mean?"

She says, *"Dying."* Her voice is soft now, nearly a whisper. "Does it get any easier each time?"

Upton would like to tell her yes, but he does not want to lie to this beautiful, naked leftist sympathizer, even if the lie would make her feel better. He shakes his head. "No, dear," he says. "It's bad every time."

She says, "Do you get scared?"

Fear lives in his body like an extra organ, a biological system. It lives below knowing, below thought. Fear carries on like breathing, like the pumping of his heart. He shakes his head. "Fear is not productive."

The frogs overthrow the night. The woman gathers her hair up again and holds it back with one hand. She leans down over Upton and she kisses his chest and smells the root-cellar smell of him and she puts her tongue into the black hole above his beating heart. Upton wants the woman to leave, but slowly. He wants to write a letter to his son. Tomorrow he might be dead again.

Letter to Albert

December 3, 1997

Dear Albert,

I regret to say that I will not be able to meet you at the end of the month, as we had planned. My work with the Friends of the Library here in T—— is taking longer than I expected. There is stiff and organized resistance. The people here do not stop at banning books; they must burn them, as well. They've burned a good deal of the children's books that have to do with sharing and cooperation. They've burned Twain because the next town over burned Twain. They've burned *Robin Hood*, of course. They'll not be content until they've reduced the library to a shelf of Rand and Alger. But the FOL is digging in for a long fight. I expect that we'll prevail, but in any case, we'll be at it a good while. Perhaps we can meet in the summer.

I receive your postcards from the road, but it's tiresome to read your awful handwriting. My secretary can't read it. I can usually catch the drift of your message, but it's hardly worth the strain on my old eyes.

I do hope you are being careful and heeding my warnings about alcohol and women. There are great dangers and temptations in the life you have chosen; you must always remain the master of your urges.

I have not had time to sit and listen to the music you sent, though

I have read two short reviews that crossed my desk. One reviewer was fairly positive and the other called your art "detestable." I hope that he is wrong, but at any rate, you know how I feel about such reviews, Albert. Every knock is a boost, as we used to say. I encourage you to adopt this philosophy.

Enclosed you will find my latest novel and a few newspaper articles. Belated wishes for a happy birthday.

Best regards,
Your father

This Sort of Thing Happens
(From *The Journals of Upton Sinclair*)

5/22/91—Back in jail. Writing in the dark. I fear my arm is broken. Sharing a cell with a barbarian. This fellow has one of those beards that covers his entire face. Hair on his cheeks. He did push-ups all day and glared at me through his beard. He is covered with tattoos that communicate a certain life philosophy and a profligate moral code. I fear he has hepatitis. All day he said nothing to me. I tried to read his mind, but found it to be a seething black cloud. The guard brought me a pen and a few sheets of paper. My cellmate ate his dinner with his fingers. I gave him my dinner and he ate that too. After lights out, I heard him breathing deeply in the bunk below me and I thought he was asleep. But then he said, "*Main Street* I didn't much care for, but *Babbitt* was very good."

There Are Problems
with the Demo, Lyle

GAME ON! Inc.

TO: Lyle Petry, Designer
FROM: T. R. Maynard, VP, Product Line
DATE: September 4, 2000
RE: "Glorious Phantoms!"

Dear Lyle:

We ran the focus group on "Glorious Phantoms!" last weekend. I like to be positive so let me start with what works. First, the graphics are awesome. I don't know if we have another game that can match its look. Frankly, I was a little worried about a game that takes place exclusively at night, or as you say on the demo box, "under the cover of darkness." But the game is visually stunning. Great work with shadows, flashlights, and headlights. I love how the moon moves in the sky and how it waxes and wanes (that was Daniels, right? What a moon freak!). The kids in our focus group didn't seem to notice the moon or the stars, but those are the kinds of touches that real gamers appreciate (and that's what wins awards). The graves and the corpses are also very good (creepy!). What can I say? I would not want to play this game at home alone all by myself.

The members of our focus group were also impressed with the audio components of the game, in particular the gunshots and the digging noises. Lyle, I can report that everybody in the room jumped the first time that shovel hit the casket. They were also "satisfied" or "very satisfied" with the character motion, action, and response. Furthermore, they generally seemed to like the shifts in scale, though there was some initial bewilderment. One of our players thought his character had magically become a giant. This is probably not a problem with the game. (Some members of our focus group smelled strongly of marijuana.)

Just to sum up, everybody involved in our testing loved the look and sound of "Glorious Phantoms!" You and your team should be proud of those aspects. It's a great-looking game with a distinct style. I think it has big potential, but I also think it has some serious problems that need to be addressed before we go to market.

The main problem, Lyle, is conceptual. In your rationale statement attached to the demo, you cited the Hart-Bowie Demographic Report: "The adolescent male gamer identifies strongly with an underdog." This is generally true, and hell, I'm glad you've looked at the HBDR. We spent a bundle on that thing and half our designers never even took it out of the plastic. But Lyle, these kids don't want to be sneaking around under the cover of darkness trying to dig up Malcolm X, Sinclair Lewis, Emma Goldman, Eugene Debs, Mother Jones, Shelley, Old Joe Hill, and all the other people buried in the game that these kids have never even heard of. Hell, I haven't heard of half of them. Let me be real clear about something: When those black-clad sharpshooters came down from the hills and started firing at the grave robbers and the recently resurrected leftists, our gamers grew sullen and despondent. (Some of them even acted out.) Not because they were being fired at, Lyle, but because *they wanted to be the ones shooting.* Here are just a few of our written responses from the exit interview.

"The dead people looked cool but I wanted to kill them also."

"The hag I dug up wasn't even hot and then I got shot which sucked."

"A shuvel is good for wopping but the sassins to far in tree. NEED GUN."

These comments are representative of the general response to the game. And frankly, I didn't need to run the focus group to find this out. Lyle, our demographic might identify with the underdog, but they identify even more strongly with the assassins, hitmen, bounty hunters, gangsters, snipers, bail bondsmen, outlaws, and vigilantes who fire guns at underdogs. If you haven't gotten to the section on violence in the Hart-Bowie, just keep reading. It's a real eye-opener.

Lyle, the kids who play our games don't want to make the world a better place. They don't want to, as you put it, "illumine our tempestuous day." They are unconcerned about the distribution of wealth and access to the means of producing. They want to shoot things. This may be sad, but it's true. Listen, I'm on your side here, politically speaking. I had the Marx and Ingels Reader on my shelf in college. I recycle. I intend to vote for Gore. But we're running a business here, and we've got to run it wisely or we're going to be out on the street following around what's his name. We just can't let our politics mix with our business practices, and certainly not with our games. Frankly, I couldn't take this thing to market even if the kids were crazy about it. You know that the parent groups have been breathing down our necks about the content of our games. The last thing we could do right now is bring out a game that seems to promote universal health care and the sharing of resources. We'd have an easier time with "Red Light District 3" or "Skull Dinner."

I think this game can still work if you make a few adjustments. Make the joystick a gun. Make the main character one of those loners in black who slinks down from the hills (but not Huntley—I think he

may be washed up). You will have to be careful with those radicals.
You can't make them look too old or frail or saintly. They can't look
like someone's grandparents. If we're shooting at them, we can't feel
sorry for them. So make them look kind of like monsters. Like zombies
or vampires. Give them special powers. Give them weapons and flaming motorcycles or something. You're the designer, I know you'll think
of something great. Now get back to work.

  Give my best to Lizzy and the kids.

Sincerely,
T. R.

The Secret of Joke Writing

*I believe that it is safer to go through life
without fear.
You may get killed suddenly, but meantime it is
easier on your nerves.*

    —THE AUTOBIOGRAPHY
    OF UPTON SINCLAIR

There are people who will ask, when you call them collect from a pay phone in the middle of the night to say that you are in *a little trouble*, "What kind of trouble?" In all fairness, these people are better than the ones who do not accept charges at all or the ones who accept them only to ask you if you have *any* idea what time it is. Still, these people—the ones who coolly inquire into the trouble, the ones whose response is conditional, tentative, based on some if-then ethical matrix and an over-riding respect for authority—these are not the people you ever want to tell that you are in a little trouble, if you can help it. Do not assume, of course, that lovers, brothers, mothers, or best friends will not ask, their voices suddenly distant and nearly unrecognizable as the trucks rumble by and the cold wind stings your face, just what kind of trouble you are in. The trick is to find an acquaintance—perhaps a distant relative or a shy coworker—for whom the species of trouble is unimportant, irrelevant, those who without hesitation offer up some dark room or piece of furniture as if they have been planning all along for this contingency. The old basement isn't much but it's yours like an airplane seat is a flotation device. Hope you don't mind dogs.

"Trouble," Uncle Ray repeated after sleepily accepting the charges. I thought I heard his television in the background. I pictured him rubbing his eyes and his forehead, the brim of his baseball hat pushed high up on his bald head. He probably wasn't wearing a hat at this hour. Did he even still wear hats? He said, "I've got the cabin here. It's getting kind of run-down. It's not like some hotel, but you're welcome to it. It's not like some kind of Holiday Inn deal."

I touched the tender knot on the back of my head and I felt dizzy. I told Ray that the cabin would be perfect.

"The electricity is out. I got a little generator. We could rig something up."

"It will work fine."

He said, "You used to play out there when you were a kid. You remember that? All by yourself."

I said, "I had my imaginary friends, Uncle Ray."

"Yeah, who, Murray?"

"Manuel. It was Manuel, Eleanor, and Dr. Hong Kong."

"Yeah, geez, shit, what a weird kid. And Eleanor was a nun, right? Sister Eleanor?"

"Ray," I said. "I've got someone with me."

There was a pause. Maybe he was looking out at the lake, the way the moonlight makes a white path across the water to wherever you are. Where I was there was no moon and it was cold for August. Bright promises skittered across the parking lot. Inside the convenience store, the cashier stocked cigarettes and kept an eye on me. I thought I heard a woman's voice, a woman talking to Ray. He said, "Real or imaginary?"

"Flesh and blood."

"Well bring her with you."

I looked out at the old man in the car. He was reading with the dome light on, an easy target. I had passed beyond something, into something. I watched everyone's hands. The cashier's, the weary motorists'. The gas pump looked like a pistol. So did the cell phone. So did the station wagon, so did the cheese snacks and the packages of cigarettes. The universe was shaped like a gun. I hadn't slept well in a week. My hands were shaking and my left eyelid was fluttering and twitching. I said, "Not that kind of trouble."

"Just come on up," he said. Again I heard the woman's voice in the background.

"Are you sure it's not a problem, Ray?"

"Do you remember how to get out here?"

I had never driven to Ray's. I remembered the dirt roads and the deer, the birch trees with bark that flaked like sunburned skin. The smell of black coffee in a thermos from the front seat. My stepfather driving with his knees while he blew his nose. My stepfather farting and blaming it on the wildlife. My stepfather telling my mother to put a goddamn sock in it.

I said, "I'll call when I get closer. I'm far away."

Ray said, "How long has it been?"

I hadn't seen Ray since my aunt's funeral. I said, "It's been a long time."

It took us four days to get there. The car broke down in Montana and we spent two nights in the sort of dumpy motel whose name is a euphemism for death. Journey's End or Dun Rovin or End of the Road. There were cigarette burns in the comforters and an old dangerous space heater that popped and kept me on edge. I watched soap operas with the sound turned down. I washed the dried blood out of my hair and kept ice on the swelling. He wrote ceaselessly and talked about the old days, writing alone in rented cabins in the Adirondacks, bears at the door. Mississippi tents with mosquitoes in your ear. The relentless ocean winds at

Coronado. Book after book, each one designed to get him out of debt or, at the very least, to save the world. Apparently, it had been worse than this. I drank from a bottle of bottom-shelf whiskey and didn't try to hide it. The sound of his pen accelerating across cheap notebook paper drove me insane. I had given up, and I admit that I wanted to see him give up too. I felt mean and raw. I could not remember the last time I had eaten a fruit or a vegetable. "Poetry makes nothing happen," I said, over and over, like a petulant child. When I finally shut up, he said, "Poets are the unacknowledged legislators of the world." He was fond of that quote from a million years ago, back before satellite television and automatic weapons. "Yes," I said, "and I am the unacknowledged shortstop for the Yankees."

The mechanic called our hotel room at night to say that the car was ready. It was not a long walk from the hotel to the garage, and I said we'd come early in the morning to pick it up. There was a pause before he said no, he was bringing the car to us that night. We had three credit cards and I worried that they were all maxed out. "Tonight?"

"Yes," he said quietly. "Half hour."

It was not at all difficult to imagine this motel room as the scene of a grisly crime. Limbs bent weird, dark blood in the carpet, on the walls. I said, "We'll just come by in the morning."

"Half hour," he said, and hung up.

How did he know where we were staying? Had I told him? I told the old man the mechanic was on his way over. His face was a window; I could see right inside him to his discomfort. Whatever he is, he is not mysterious. On one hand, he wanted to believe the mechanic was a virtuous laborer, putting in extra hours to help his fellow man. But on the other hand, he did not want to get shot to death by another lunatic in greasy coveralls. He stood completely still, paralyzed. I knew that, to him, hiding in the filthy bathroom was tantamount to forsaking the cause, turning away from the future. I watched, let him struggle. It was the guy's occupation that got to him. *Mechanic* had a romantic, Socialist appeal on par with *farmer* and *seamstress*. Wrenches, jacks, dirty fingernails.

There's a story I had heard many times: After the publication of *The Flivver King*, many Ford automotive workers kept the green paperback in their back pockets while at work as a sign of defiance and solidarity. The story, the image, is moving, I admit it. Finally I rescued him. "You should hide," I said.

He looked relieved. "That's probably a good idea," he said.

When the mechanic arrived with our car, I talked to him through the closed door of the motel room. He said, "Let me in." I'll not try to convince you that there was something in his voice I trusted. I let him in. He was small and neat, clean-shaven, with patches of gray in his short black hair. His eyes were of the sort that impatient writers like the old man might describe, if they described them at all, as *piercing*. He wore dark blue work pants and a black jacket and a look of intense concentration that may or may not have been pathological. In the mirror I saw no green paperback tucked into his back pocket in defiance or solidarity. Once inside he said, "Where's your friend?"

"Oh," I said. "He's not here."

My friend chose that moment to shuffle out of the bathroom. He said, "California is one thousand forty-six kilometers from north to south, much too big for one state." I had no idea what he was talking about. The mechanic stared at him, then at me.

"Here he is, after all."

The mechanic said, "You need to get out of here."

"First thing in the morning."

"When it was clear that we had lost in '34," the old man said, "Mary Craig, bless her soul, fell onto the floor weeping and saying, 'Thank God, thank God.'"

The mechanic said, "No. Leave tonight. Get out of here now."

The old man began obediently gathering his things. I said, "What was wrong with the car?"

"Fuel filter." I wasn't sure if he was going to kill me too.

I said, "Do you take credit cards? It's all we've got."

The old man said, "Here's that pen I was looking for."

The mechanic looked at everything and everyone as if he were trying to start a fire or levitate heavy objects. He said, "No charge." Then he turned toward the old man and reached inside his black coat. There are places in rivers that don't move. There are places that swirl, there are even places that flow backward. You may not see the current in the water, but you can watch a leaf on the surface. Time is like that. History. This night was an eddy; we were all swirling leaves. Another dingy motel room, another strange-eyed visitor, another unregistered handgun. It was bigger than all of us and I felt myself surrender. But the mechanic pulled from his jacket not a gun but a book, and he held it toward the old man. He said, "Would you sign this before you go?"

I was not so gone that I didn't look at the book. It was *Mental Radio*, 1930, the one he and his wife, Mary Craig, had written about telepathy. Their own telepathy, proved through a series of home experiments! There's a short and cautious preface by Einstein, vouching not so much for the experimental design, data, and conclusions as for the author's integrity. He signed the book and the mechanic said, "This book has meant a great deal to me." I could see he wanted to say more but was having a difficult time. "It makes me feel less alone. It's a comfort."

The old man smiled and shook the mechanic's hand. The mechanic repeated his warning about leaving immediately and then he left, yes, then he *slipped through the door and was gone.*

I sat down on the edge of a bed while the old man continued packing. There I was, breathing. "Can you read my mind right now?"

"You think this mechanic was a crackpot."

"Very good. You've still got it. Weren't you supposed to be hiding?"

"It's nice to meet an admirer. Feels like the old days."

"Yes," I said, "your old books are still connecting with the fruitcakes to this day. That must be gratifying. Do you know that when he called, the first thing I thought of was my credit cards? Instead of dying?"

"That just goes to show—"

"I know just what it just goes to show. That guy, you know, that guy was probably not even a leftist. He just helped us because he believes in voodoo, just like you."

"You never know which truth will set you free."

"I hope he fixed the fuel filter with his hands and not his mind."

The phone rang then. I picked it up and a voice said, "Do not let the sun set on your communist ass."

I told the caller that the sun had set about forty-five minutes ago. There was a pause. Apparently, I had flustered the gun collector. I motioned for the old man to hurry up and finish packing. The caller said, "Well then, I guess you'd better watch out."

I hung up, grabbed my backpack, and we hurried across the parking lot. The old man still moved pretty good. His tennis partners had called him the human rabbit seventy-five or eighty years ago for the way he covered the court. When I put the key in the ignition, the car did not explode, as I feared it might, in cinematic bloom.

From there we drove straight through. That is, I drove straight through, biting my lip to stay awake, while the old man scribbled notes, napped, and kept us both alive with his stories, like the one about the time in Butte that he and Mary Craig had stayed in a hotel amid a convention of riflemen, one of whom shot a hole in their hotel door so that he could peek in. Must have been '35, right after EPIC. I had heard it before but I didn't care. He told stories about Jack London, Sinclair Lewis, Sherwood Anderson, Theodore Dreiser, and Ernest Hemingway. H. L. Mencken, Eugene O'Neill, and Dylan Thomas. The stories were linked by motifs of booze and turpitude. On straight, flat highways I dozed for seconds at a time, waking with a jolt to find myself still driving and my passenger still talking. He said it suited him to be on the move. He had never stayed in one place very long. He asked me to guess how many entries were in the index of his 1962 autobiography under the heading "Sinclair, Upton, residences of."

I held my eyelids up with my fingers. "I don't know. Twenty."

"More."

"Thirty."

"More."

"Forty."

"Sixty-one!"

"Damn," I said.

He asked if I knew any jokes and I told a dirty one about a horny octopus trying to get the pajamas off a bagpipe. He didn't care for that much. He told me what I already knew, that at seventeen he supported himself and his mother by writing jokes for the comic papers. "I will tell you the secret of joke writing," he said. "Jokes are made up hind end forward, so to speak. You don't think of the joke, but of what it is to be about. There are tramp jokes, mother-in-law jokes, plumber jokes, Irishman jokes, and so on. So you decide to write tramp jokes today. Well, there are many things about tramps that are jokeable. They do not like to work, they do not like to bathe, they do not like bulldogs, and so on. You decide to write about tramps not liking to bathe. Very well, you think of all the words and phrases having to do with water, soaps, tubs, streams, rain, and so on, and of puns or quirks by which these words can be applied to tramps."

I said, "Nobody knows what a tramp is."

He said, "OK, so there's this tramp and he sees a sign above a shop that says, 'Cleaning and Dyeing,' and he says to himself, 'I always knew those two things went together.' Like that."

I laughed because it was pretty funny. I could not tell if we were being followed or not. Every car behind us looked like an assassin's make and model. The workers were never going to own the factories, were they? Wasn't it just best to admit that and go on?

He said, "Here's an old joke from aught three. This is a doozy. I didn't write this one. Ready?"

I said that I was.

"Mrs. Jones goes into her grocer's and asks for a dozen boxes of matches. Says the grocer: 'Why, Mrs. Jones, you had a dozen boxes of matches yesterday!' Says Mrs. Jones: 'Oh, yes, but you see, my husband is deaf and dumb, and he talks in his sleep.'"

I waited for more. "Is that all?"

"Yes!"

"I don't get it."

He said, "It's sort of tricky. It's not like the tramp joke. It's a little mind puzzle." He was smiling. Charlie Chaplin once said Sinclair always spoke through a smile, and it's true.

I said, "You stumped me."

"Just think about it for a while."

"I don't want to think about it. Just tell me."

"Just think about it. We'll tell it to Richard. See if he gets it."

I said, "Who's Richard?"

He said, "Your uncle."

"It's Ray. Fucking tell me what the joke means." I was awake now, awake and pissed.

"You don't really want me to tell you."

"Yes, believe me, I do."

"No you don't."

"It doesn't mean anything, does it? It's nonsense. That's the joke, right? It's on me."

"No, it has an answer. But most people can't figure it out."

"Well, you got me."

"You haven't even tried."

I said, "Tell me."

He said, "No."

When we got close to Ray's, the asphalt ran out along with the town maintenance. We drove the last six miles on a gravel road with deep potholes and ridges. It took us forty-five minutes. The road was in worse shape, but nothing else had changed since the last time I had visited. Acres of birch and pine, obliterating perspective and reference and time. The old man removed his dentures. He asked if my uncle was my father's brother or mother's brother. I said he was neither. He had been married to my mother's sister, who had died very young. He asked if my uncle liked to fish and I said that as far as I could remember that's about the only thing he liked to do. He nodded. He said, "I like to fish. I have not fished in many lives." I thought the road might break his bones. I apologized several times, but he said he was accustomed to discomfort. At least I think that's what he said.

Ray limped up from his dock to meet us in the driveway. His leg had been torn up by a land mine in Vietnam. He was wearing a baseball cap, a flannel shirt, and shorts. The marbled, hairless scar tissue had frightened me when I was a kid. He looked older, of course, but he seemed to be in pretty good shape. Beneath his beer gut, his legs were thin and tan and muscular. I introduced the old man as Louis. Ray shook his hand and looked at him carefully, but if he knew anything, he didn't let on. He took off his cap to scratch his head. He was balder now, and the top of his head was a lighter shade than his face. He shook my hand, his head tilted slightly back in appraisal. He said, "Geez, you're grown up." I nodded, shrugged. He said, "You look like shit."

He showed us to the cabin, about fifty yards from his house along the lakeshore. It was how I remembered it—one room, a bed, a table, a tiny kitchen with built-in shelves full of dusty blue plates and coffee cups. The pine floor slanted left to right. The old man seemed delighted with these accommodations. He inspected the construction, studied the walls and the ceiling, knocked on the floorboards with his knuckles, opened and closed the cabinet beneath the sink. Ray said, "Here's a couple flashlights. You'll need them. There's no electricity and my generator is busted. No hot water. You can shower over at the house or just bathe in the lake. But the water's getting cold."

I said, "Thanks, Ray."

Ray said, "Louis, do you like to fish?"

The old man was now staring out the window at the lake. He didn't respond. I said, *"Louis."*

He turned. "Oh yes, very much. But we must eat what we catch."

Ray said, "Good. We'll get out on the lake then. I've got a new boat I can show you."

I began making a bed on the floor. Ray asked if there was anything else we needed. "No," I said. "Just sleep."

I slept, outside of time. The planet spun around the sun. Outside it got light, then dark, then light again. Loons called on the lake. Fish jumped for bugs. Corporations merged. The old man shuffled across the room, coughed, scratched on paper with pen. In my blankets I rolled across the cabin, down the slanted floor, against the wall. Trucks pulling boats bounced across the corduroy county road. Boats buzzed on the water. The wake from their engines sent small waves against the shore and turned my dreams aquatic.

I got up and took a cold shower. The crickets watched me shave. It felt like afternoon. One of Ray's neighbors sat in his paddleboat, fishing for sunnies in the lily pads. I walked along the lakeshore to Ray's house and went in through the side door, off the deck. A girl in long braids sat on the carpeted floor of the living room, cutting pictures out of magazines. She looked up and said, "Hi."

"Hi," I said, and my voice sounded strange to me. The mounted deer heads and fish were gone, replaced with tasteful nature prints. A nice watercolor. Bold decorating for the Northwoods. There was new furniture in pleasing colors and fabrics. When my aunt Beth died, I had spent hours in this room, sitting on a ripped couch, playing cards with relatives beneath the dusty bucks and walleyes.

The girl kept cutting from the magazine. She said, "I'm Myra." She was at an age when your name explained everything. I introduced myself. I said, "Do you know where Ray is?"

Myra said, "He's out fishing with the old guy."

I sat on the floor next to her. I said, "Do you live here?"

She nodded. She flipped through magazines, considering. Spread out on the floor around her were pictures of a car, a shoe, a dog, lipstick, ice cream, a setting sun, a tree, an apple. I couldn't see the rationale or the pattern. She said, "That guy must be a *hundred*." She started cutting out a picture of an umbrella.

I said, "How do all of these things go together?"

She said, "What do you mean?"

"Well, how does the umbrella go with the ice cream and the dog and the shoe?"

"Colors."

"Oh," I said. And then it was clear.

She said, "Are we related?"

I said, "Sort of."

I stood up and went to the window. I couldn't see Ray's boat on the lake, but it was a big lake with a lot of coves. I hoped they weren't talking politics. The front door opened and closed, and a woman walked in through the kitchen. Myra said, "Hi, Mom." The woman had a pleasant face and a firm handshake. Her name was Ruth. She smiled at me but her eyes were intense and searching. She no doubt came from a long line of people whose livelihood depended on careful watching from deer stands and icehouses. Squinting through the sight of a rifle, squinting through blowing snow and frozen water. She was stylish, but I knew she was tough. She said, "I was starting to think you were an imaginary nephew."

I wasn't sure if she was talking about how long I slept or how long I'd been away. I said, "You and Ray ... ?"

"He didn't say anything?"

I shook my head. "Or maybe he did. I was pretty out of it." I didn't want to get Ray in trouble.

"We live together," she said. "We all live here. Ray's my *boyfriend*." She laughed.

Myra said, "Ray's *our* boyfriend."

I said, "How long?"

Ruth said, "Do you want coffee?"

I said, "Please."

She thought for a moment. "I guess almost five years."

This should not have been hard to believe. After all, it had been more than ten years since I had seen Ray, and yet the last time I had seen him, he was wrecked. We went fishing together one morning before anyone else had gotten up or come over with their casseroles and sweet fruit salads. We made a secret plan to go. He said he knew a great spot. He took me there and I threw down a small anchor, but we never put a line in the water. We just sat in the boat. There was mist on the water, pink light and stars in the sky. We passed a thermos of coffee and ate rolls with raspberry jam. I was seventeen and had already run away from home a couple of times. Something was happening, but I didn't know what. The water was completely calm. Ray looked like he hadn't slept in days. He hunched with his hands in the pockets of his sweat-shirt and stared across the lake. He cried some and wiped his nose on his sleeve while I sat quietly at the other end of the boat. People walked to the ends of their docks and stretched. Dogs barked. After some time, Ray said, "We should probably get back." I pulled up the anchor and Ray started the old 50-horsepower motor. When we had tied the boat to Ray's dock, he gave me a hand out of the boat. I tried to think of something to say to him, but there was nothing to say. Then Ray said, "Look, if you ever need anything, you let me know." I nodded, surprised. "Whatever you need, I want you to know that you got your uncle Ray, OK?" I nodded again, sure, OK. The man with the dead wife comforting me.

Ruth handed me a cup of coffee. Her stare made me uncomfortable, so I looked around us, at the furniture and the art. "The house looks great," I said.

She said, "What we have is good."

Assurance and warning, both. I went down to the dock to wait for Ray and the muckraker.

They came back two hours later with seven nice northerns. Ray brought his new boat in easy, and I caught it and tied it to the dock. The boat was pristine and gleaming, with a big powerful engine, four padded seats, a live well, a depth finder, a GPS, and a locker for the rods and tackle. Louis was smiling and wearing a mesh baseball cap that said, FISH TREMBLE AT THE MENTION OF MY NAME. I helped him out of the boat.

Ray said, "You're alive. Welcome back."

I said, "Nice rig."

"Yeah, what do you think?"

"Real nice."

Ray said, "Yeah, nice, huh? I finally treated myself to a decent boat. Except, get this, we get out there on the lake and Louis wouldn't let me use the GPS or the depth finder."

"That doesn't surprise me."

"I tried to tell him that fishing has changed. It's a science now. It's technological."

Louis said, "Not every advance is progress. When I saw that the depth finder shows you where the fish are, I insisted he turn it off. It's not sporting. We did fine without that nonsense."

Ray said, "He had us feeling our way around the lake. Geez, like Indians. I thought we might have to break out the cane poles and worms."

Both men were enjoying this sportsmen's banter. Louis said, "I caught four and your uncle caught three. It was a grand time. Thank you, Ray."

Ray said, "We'll do it again."

We walked slowly back up to the house. Myra met us halfway up the path and hugged Ray. He gave the fish to me so that he could hold Myra's hand.

Ray cleaned the fish and Ruth breaded and fried them. They talked quietly in the kitchen, and declined my offers to help. Louis and Myra sat on the couch together. Myra held a deck of cards. One by one she took a card from the deck and asked Louis to guess which card it was. I sat in a chair with an outdoorsman's magazine in my lap. I skimmed a couple articles. The writing was better than I thought it would be.

"Guess."

"Jack of diamonds."

"Wrong. Guess."

Louis concentrated. I couldn't tell if he was playing or being serious. "Four of clubs."

"Close. Five of clubs. Guess."

Outside, the lake was beginning to grow dark. I'm hardly the first person to note how ominous and spooky that is, a body of water at night. The room grew chilly and I pulled on a sweatshirt, flipped through the magazine.

Louis said, "Nine of spades."

Myra said, "Awesome."

There was a gunshot, a deep blast that echoed and lingered on the water and in the trees. I flinched and Louis, the human rabbit, was off the couch and behind it before the sound had died away. Myra giggled. She said, "Jumpy, jumpy." She crawled around the couch to find him. "They're not shooting at *you*."

From the kitchen Ray said, "Just some yahoo shooting at a chipmunk."

We all waited for the next shot. The anxiety was a form of desire. I wanted it, but it never came.

Louis emerged and sat back down on the couch.

Myra said, "Poor chipmunk."

Louis looked at Myra. I looked at Louis. Ray looked at Ruth. Ruth looked at me.

The lake was pink glass and then it disappeared. We ate the fish on white rolls with tartar sauce.

Louis wrote for a while in bed with two flashlights. I lay on the floor, tired but awake. I could hear him breathing loudly through his mouth and I could hear the relentless scrawl of conviction, the vigorous dots of his exclamation points. I could hear his flat characters being victimized, then converted. Another novel, constructed hind end forward, like a joke about tramps. This one would turn his hostile critics; this one would initiate radical but peaceful reform; this one would generate the kind of fame he had known, once, nearly a century ago. There was a story about Louis and his wife in a small shop in Bermuda. Louis saw a high shelf full of cans of Armour meat and he asked the shopkeeper about it. The shopkeeper replied that some fellow had written a book and now he couldn't sell a can of the stuff. The knot on my head was still tender, but the swelling had gone down.

He turned off the flashlight and said, "Are you asleep?"

I thought about whether or not to answer. "No."

He said, "I just want to know what our plan is."

I laughed, mean and fake. "Our plan?"

"Yes," he said.

"Well, OK. First, we wear out our welcome here in paradise. We pull out all the big fish from the lake and eat them with lemon. Then, let's see, then we send out our résumés to the Man. We lie about the spread-sheet programs with which we are familiar."

He said, "Are you finished?"

I said, "We get in at the ground floor and we work our way up. At night we watch television and eat frozen pizzas. We grudgingly accept the distribution of wealth. We come to believe that wealth and wisdom are connected. Wealth and character. We shred documents. We throw quarters in cups and guitar cases. We don't provoke the police."

He began to object, but I interrupted him.

"We have no political conviction and thus no guilt. And thus no responsibility. We try not to imagine that the lives of others are fully as large as our own. We play video games with incredible graphics. We determine the number of deductions. Nobody—not one person—fires a weapon at us."

He said, "You know I don't think that is funny."

"There's no *plan*," I said. "Let me tell you a little story. In 1907 a young American writer, not yet thirty years old, published a novel that predicted the USA would be a fully Socialist country by the year 1913. With *Hearst* as our Socialist president. Good God. How about that for a plan? So *fish*. Just fish, goddammit."

Louis said, "I misjudged Hearst."

I said, "You misjudged everything. That's what you are, a misjudger. An epic American misjudger with a bad ear for dialogue and an exclamation point problem. You've misjudged an entire century." I was yelling at an old man. I was trying to assassinate him. "Your record is spotless. You've not gotten one thing right. You were a Prohibitionist for God's sake. Socialism, telepathy, fasting, the metric system. Your books don't make your wishes come true."

Louis said, "My writing has made a difference. That is one thing I know. Through my efforts I got an exercise courtyard in the state prison of Delaware. When Mary Craig and I were in Bermuda, we stopped—"

"No," I said. "The books don't matter. I'm sorry. Not *The Jungle*, not *The Octopus*. Not *The Grapes of Wrath*. Have you noticed? The poor are still with us. We still have tainted meat. We still have layoffs. We still have an economic system that eats people to get stronger. Nobody reads. We have hundreds of TV channels. Nobody gives a shit. This has not been a century of progress."

He said, "It will still happen. I am convinced. The alternative is too horrible."

I said, "That's sound logic. Me, I'm betting on the horrible alternative. All my money is on the horrible alternative. The horrible alternative is undefeated. What is history if not a long dynasty of the horrible alternative?"

He didn't say anything and I listened for his breathing. He of course had heard much worse through the years, even from friends. Mencken once told him that he was always right, except in matters of politics, sociology, religion, finance, economics, literature, and science. Wharton and Anderson upbraided him. Sir Arthur Conan Doyle worked him over. The communists hated him. The wealthy detested him, obviously. He hounded Rockefeller and ended up in jail. Roosevelt once asked him to stop trying to run the damn country. And of course he inspired Ezra Pound to new heights of deranged invective.

"That's a peculiar argument for giving up," he said.

I lay on the floor in a cold cabin. My limbs were heavy. I was a citizen in a democracy. I said, "What?"

"We seem to agree on everything except the practical implications. We agree on what is, but not on what ought to be done."

"Fish," I said. "All the modern philosophers agree: *Fish*."

He said, "Now I don't mind being up here for a time. I can get good work done and I do enjoy being on the lake. But I have pledged my support to several causes and I intend to honor my promises. I'll need to find a new secretary."

I said, "Seeing as how your former one is looking at a lengthy hospital stay."

"That is regrettable," he said. "But my secretaries are fully aware of the risks."

"Just call the next one on the list."

He was quiet for a time. I could hear the pine branches brushing the roof. Then he said, "I was hoping you might be interested."

"In what?"

"I thought you might be my new secretary."

"No," I said. "No way. Are you kidding? That's not going to happen. You've got a waiting list of fifty or sixty. Some bright-eyed revolutionary is out there tonight with his bags packed, waiting for the call."

"I hope you'll consider it."

"I'm out," I said. "I'm through."

"You've changed."

"What can I say? I'm a quick learner."

"Just give it some thought."

"No more thinking."

"Let me tell you a story about the second Roosevelt."

"No," I said. "Don't. I've heard it." I considered turning over on my side. It seemed like a big decision. I felt old and tired. In every way except our actual years, I was older than Louis. I lay there with my aches, my complaints, thinking of Mrs. Jones, her husband, all those damn matches.

One morning, Ray knocked on the cabin door early, while I was sleeping and Louis was writing at the table. He said, "Let's go, gentlemen. There is a place I want you to see."

The three of us sat in the front seat of Ray's pickup. Ray drove, I sat against the passenger door, and Louis bounced between us. The morning was cool and sunny, and the leaves glittered like gold coins in the trees. I stared out the window, happy not to be driving, not to be checking the mirrors. None of us talked. We pointed to the deer and counted them.

It was an hour drive to the Chippewa National Forest. I had heard about the Lost Forty, but I had never seen it. We pulled into an empty gravel parking lot and Ray said, "Here we are." When we got out of the truck, Louis read the big sign, his face inches away from the words, his head moving left to right, left to right. He took out his notebook and pen and made a few notes. The government land survey of 1882 accidentally mapped this land as part of Coddington Lake. It was a rainy-day mistake and because of this error, loggers didn't touch the red and white pine when they cut everything else and sent it down the Mississippi at the turn of the century. The Lost Forty is actually 144 acres of virgin pine. Some of the trees are over 350 years old, four feet in diameter.

Ray got a soft cooler out of the back of the truck and we walked into the forest on a well-marked trail. Louis was excited and he walked ahead of us, gazing up occasionally at the tops of trees that were older than our failed republic. I stayed behind with Ray, whose pace was slowed by the limp. Ray winked at me and called ahead to Louis. "It's about a mile to the picnic tables, Louis. You think you can make it?"

Louis turned around and said, "I once rode a hundred miles on my bicycle. I'll be just fine. I'll meet you fellows there."

Ray said to me, "Is that true about the bike?"

It's a story I had heard many times. "He rode to a friend's house," I said. "It was an all-day trip on bad roads or no roads at all. When he got there, his friend congratulated him on an amazing ninety-six-mile ride. So Louis got back on his bike and rode four more miles in the dark to make it one hundred."

I offered to carry the cooler, but Ray kept it. The forest floor was cool and damp, untouched by the sun. I said, "I'm glad to get to see this place."

"A big mistake," he said. "That's what my father said. He took me here when I was a kid and told me that most bad things in life were carefully planned and most good things were mistakes."

I remembered Ray's father, a foulmouthed, red-eyed chain-smoker who drove way too fast. I had enjoyed him thoroughly. He once took me and all of my imaginary friends to the county dump to see the bears.

I said, "Is he still alive?"

Ray shook his head. "He died seven or eight years ago."

I told him that I liked Ruth and Myra.

Ray said, "Those girls saved my life."

I stumbled over roots along the path, but the war veteran was sure-footed, and Louis was barely visible up ahead.

"Look," Ray said. "I need to tell you. We watch television. We saw it. We saw you. Not you, but him, *Louis,* and the big protest. The whole mess out there."

"I figured." Somewhere high above us a woodpecker hammered away at an ancient tree. It seemed wrong.

Ray said, "I stay out of this stuff. If I had to pick a side, hell, I'd probably pick his. But I don't have to pick a side and I don't want to. I live on a lake with a woman I love. It's my right. I got blown up, I lost a wife, I worked for the state for twenty-five years. I just want to live by a lake."

"I guess I can't argue with that."

"Do you know what I'm saying?"

"It's pretty clear, Ray."

He said, "I know he wants to save the world. And he's convinced some young folks to join him. I'll watch TV and root for him. I hope he shakes things up. But I don't want to get involved. I don't want to make it my..."

We stopped walking. I turned toward him, but he kept facing down the path. "Problem? You don't want to make it your problem?"

"Don't be a shit," he said. "Don't be a know-it-all shit." He turned and stared at me. "Don't get self-righteous. He's a fool. An old fool too, which makes it worse."

"Maybe."

"I sit in my boat and I hit golf balls around my yard with a wedge. I'm not the boss. I'm not the bad guy, so don't— Just don't."

I started walking again. The whole idea of this forest was absurd. Come celebrate this beautiful wilderness that we accidentally preserved! I said, "Where's the McDonald's?"

Ray worked hard to keep up with me. "If it were just me, maybe I'd say stick around, we'd dig in, make it interesting. A few years back I would have done that. But it's not just me. Ruth swears she's been hearing things in the night. She stays up with a shotgun in her lap."

"You've got to be kidding."

"It's no good."

"So you want us to leave?"

"I want him to leave. You can stay. We're happy for you to stay as long as you want to."

I bent down and picked up an empty plastic water bottle by the side of the trail. "Has Louis told you the joke about Mr. and Mrs. Jones?"

"Yeah, and the matches? That's tricky. Took me a while."

When we got to the picnic tables, Louis wasn't there. We sat down and Ray unpacked the cooler. There were turkey and cheese sandwiches with mayonnaise for me and Ray, and a bowl of rice for Louis. Ray said, "Myra made sure that we packed rice. She said it over and over. 'Pack rice for Louis. He likes rice.'"

We waited a few minutes, but Louis still didn't show up. I walked up the trail another quarter mile, calling his name, even his real name, in a hushed, furtive voice. I moved with caution and stealth, as if I were trying to keep a secret, as if the old flannelled loggers were camped nearby, ready to realize their error, ready to rush in with their axes and saws, their songs from many lands. The woodpeckers kept at it, damaging the antiques. Squirrels and chipmunks made the ground shift and rustle, and birds called from the tops of trees, a world away. Only a few small patches of blue sky were visible through the canopy above. I turned around on the trail and I was on my way back to the picnic area when I saw his black canvas sneakers, toes pointed upward. His body was behind an enormous white pine, well off the path. I stopped at the edge of the trail and I saw it all, as if from above: carrying him out of this accidental forest, loading him into the bed of Ray's truck, wrapping the frail corpse in an old tarp. Returning him to the dirt in another cheap coffin, with another thin prayer. All my sorrow and guilt. But I couldn't see anything after that. Beyond his grave I had no vision, only a feeling—of weightlessness, terrible freedom. The woods got black and I dropped to one knee until I felt the dampness of the dirt and leaves soak through my jeans. Then I stood and walked slowly toward his body, already feeling its weight in my arms, so light, even lighter now. And when I came up on him, I saw that he wasn't dead at all. He was alive. He was leaning against the trunk of the white pine, writing furiously in a small notebook. He didn't even look up. "Sometimes it will come to me," he said, still writing. "A whole book. It just comes. It just floats down fully formed. You struggle for years and years, and once in a while you get a gift."

"It's time for lunch," I said. I turned back to the trail and didn't wait for him.

When we pulled into the long driveway at Ray's house, Myra and Ruth were out in the yard pulling weeds from a small flower bed. They both stood and smiled and waved. Ruth walked over and kissed Ray on the lips. He looked embarrassed.

Ruth said, "Did you boys have fun?"

Ray said, "We had a nice little trip."

"Where's your boat?"

"What do you mean?"

"I thought you took the guys fishing somewhere," Ruth said. "I thought you had the boat on the trailer."

"No, I took them up to the Lost Forty."

Ruth said, "Oh."

Myra said, "The Lost Forty is actually 140 acres."

Louis said, "One forty-four, I believe."

Myra grabbed Louis's hand. She said, "Guess what I'm thinking right now. Guess." She closed her eyes tightly in concentration.

Louis said, "Oh, let me see here." He knelt down beside her, still holding her hand. His pants were muddy and wet from the woods. He put his other hand on top of her head and Myra giggled.

Ruth said, "So then where is your boat?"

Ray lifted the cooler out of the back of the truck. "What are you talking about?"

"*Cake,*" Louis said. "You're thinking about cake."

Myra opened her eyes wide. "How did you know? How did you know? You guessed. Wait, what kind of cake?" She closed her eyes again.

Ruth lowered her voice. "Your boat isn't down by the dock."

Ray said, "Well where is it? Did you take it out?"

Ruth shook her head.

"Chocolate," Louis said.

"No," Myra said. "Pineapple!"

Ray turned to me. I said, "We didn't take it out, Ray." But I knew that's not why he was looking at me.

He started walking toward the dock, dragging his bad leg, and we all followed behind. Ruth said, "Maybe it just drifted off a little ways."

The lake that Ray lives on is one of the clearest lakes in the state. The wildlife department conducts periodic tests on the water clarity. Also, the lake is only six or eight feet deep at the end of the dock, so when we reached the dock it was not difficult to see Ray's new boat on the lake floor. There were several large circular holes in the bottom of the boat. The vinyl seats were ripped and the engine was dented and bashed. The steering wheel had been pulled out. The depth finder was crushed and shimmering. When we dragged the boat around to the shore, we found all of Ray's fishing rods had been destroyed, sawed off in pieces. The reels had been hammered. His tackle boxes had been abused and his tackle was strewn about the boat and the lake. Myra in bare feet carefully collected lures, sinkers, and bobbers. She made a small colorful pile on the dock.

After packing everything, I stood in the dark, next to Upton's bed. The lake outside was silent. I listened closely for his deep breathing and thought I heard it. He was an excellent and untroubled sleeper. He went about his sleeping as he went about everything else, with a sense of purpose and conviction. He slept for the revolution. I turned on a flashlight and watched him. He lay on his side, with the covers pulled up to his jaw. I could see the small dark hole in his temple that he tried to cover, during the day, with thin strands of white hair. His face looked both determined and content, and his body made a small, efficient lump beneath the quilts. In 1934, after he lost the election in California, he learned from a friend about a businessman who, having made his will and purchased a revolver, had planned, if Upton had won, to shoot him during his victory speech. I gently touched his shoulder. He didn't move, but he opened his cloudy eyes. "Don't kill me," he said.

I handed him his glasses. "It's me. Come on. We're going."

He sat up. He wore navy cotton pajamas with white piping. "Couldn't we wait?"

I took his folded clothes from a chair and handed them to him. His black canvas sneakers were lined up neatly on the floor at the foot of the bed. "No," I said. "We have to go."

"I actually wouldn't mind staying a while and working on this new book."

"I've packed your things."

"Did you pack my notebooks?"

"Yes."

"What about fishing?"

"You can fish when you retire."

He got up, but it wasn't easy. He groaned and grunted and breathed loudly while he took off his pajamas and got dressed. I bent down to tie the laces of his shoes.

When we left the cabin, I turned off the flashlight. I took Upton's hand and led him down to the lake. He whispered, "What about the car?"

I said, "Don't talk."

It was cold and we didn't have jackets. We walked along the lakeshore, away from Ray's house. Upton said, "Where are we going?"

"Don't talk," I said.

We came to the spot where the narrow beach ended. Thick brush and long grass extended right up to the water. I took off my shoes and socks, rolled up my pants, and helped Upton do the same. The water was a shock. I heard him draw a sharp breath when he stepped in, but he kept a firm grip on my hand and he kept walking. Small shells and rocks cut into my feet, but the water was so cold that I didn't feel much pain. We made our way to Ray's neighbor's dock. I climbed up on it, went to the end, and untied the rope of the paddleboat. Then I pulled the boat over to the shore and helped Upton get in. I loaded my backpack and his duffle bag behind the seats. He whispered, "Stealing?"

"Well," I said. "Yes. Don't talk."

I climbed back onto the dock and pulled the boat into deeper water. Upton slid far down in his seat to put his bare feet on the pedals. He was shivering and I felt like a bad parent. The boat drifted away from the dock, but I held the rope in the dark. He looked up at me and said, "Aren't you coming?"

And that's when it came to me, floated down like a gift. Or if not at that moment on the dock, then later, as we paddled across the deep lake or as we rode in the back of a stranger's truck with an arthritic German shepherd or as I waited in a phone booth for someone, anyone, to accept the charges. *Mrs. Jones*: She lit matches through the night to watch her husband's sign language. It's a tricky one. I pulled a leach off my ankle.

With the rope, I tugged the boat toward me and then got in beside Upton. He said, "Well, good. I'm glad."

We started pedaling. It was a long way across the dark lake. We heard a single loud bang that might have been the sound of an old wooden screen door slamming shut. Upton didn't die yet and we pedaled harder.

Quietly I said, "You once rode one hundred miles on your bicycle."

He was breathing heavy already. "I know."

I said, "Back in those days you had to use your foot on the front tire. As a brake. The sole of your shoe got so hot you had to cool it in a stream."

"Yes," he said. "It's true."

"You saw Cascade Lake at sunset and thought of Whitman."

"Tennyson."

There were gigantic fish beneath us in the black water, fish with teeth and whiskers. There were people who wanted to kill us. I guess I've never been that scared.

Upton said, "What are we going to do when we get to the other side?"

I told him to leave that to me.

He Had Enemies, for Instance, in the Steel Trust

ENGLISH 684!
Advanced Fiction Writing
(Or, Literature as a Class Weapon)
Fall 1999

UPTON SINCLAIR, Visiting Professor
Office: Watson 621
Phone: x6894
Hours: T Th 2:00-3:30 (or by appt.!)

COURSE OBJECTIVES
In this course students will use journalistic techniques and sexual repression to write socially engaged, morally outraged fiction with unambiguous endings. Students will also grow their own food on the narrow but fertile strip of land that runs between the Junior Faculty Parking Lot and the Graduate Student Parking Lot. On Wednesdays we will fast.

REQUIREMENTS
Each student will research, write, and self-publish four novels—three will be submitted to the entire class during the semester and the last

one will be submitted to me at the end of the term in lieu of a final exam. Students are responsible for completing the assigned reading on time and for securing sufficient funds for publication. Class will be run as a cooperative, democratic experiment in communal living, much like my utopian project Helicon Hall, overlooking Englewood, New Jersey, where I spent four wonderful months in the winter of 1906–07, living harmoniously (and platonically) with dozens of others until the house burned down and I barely escaped from the top floor! Frequent visitors to Helicon Hall included John Dewey and a young Sinclair Lewis (before John Barleycorn got him). I have always suspected arson. We will use the workshop method.

POLICIES AND GUIDELINES
- No firearms allowed in class.
- I will not accept late novels.
- Students will abide by the Honor Code. While I expect you to share your ideas, criticism, crops, and love of social justice, your novels should be your own work and not something you found on the Inter-web.
- Drafts of your novels should be typed on a manual or electric type-writer. I will not accept handwritten novels.
- Dress appropriately for workshop. Ladies, please, no "tube" tops!
- If I am assassinated at some point during the semester, carry on with the assigned work. I will rejoin you, if at all possible.
- Please double space and use one-inch margins.
- No alcohol and no sex during the semester.
- I find that a tablespoon of sand helps with constipation!
- No romance novels. No fantasy novels. No coming-of-age novels. No father-son hunting trips. No literal vampires (metaphorical blood-sucking is fine). No beach houses. No divorces or affairs. No suburban malaise. No point-of-view stunts. No fragmentation. No gentle fading of the light. No ice cubes rattling in cocktail glasses. No

coitus against walls. No ambiguous narrative stances. No subtle shifts. No celebrations of chaos. No rhythmic evocations. No irrelevant beauty.

SCHEDULE OF READINGS

- Week 1: Norris, *The Octopus*, and Sinclair, *Oil!*
- Week 2: Howells, *A Hazard of New Fortunes*
- Week 3: Chopin, *The Awakening*
- Week 4: Bellamy, *Looking Backward*, and Donnelly, *Caesar's Column* **(Novel #1 due)**
- Week 5: Dreiser, *An American Tragedy*, and Sinclair, *Boston*
- Week 6: London, *Iron Heel*
- Week 7: Dos Passos, *U.S.A.* Trilogy
- Week 8: Gold, *Jews Without Money* **(Novel #2 due)**
- Week 9: Dahlberg, *Bottom Dogs*
- Week 10: Vorse, *Strike!* **(Note:** Class will meet at Labor Finders on 14th St.)
- Week 11: Roth, *Call It Sleep*, and Sinclair, *Dragon's Teeth*
- Week 12: Wright, *Native Son* **(Novel #3 due)**
- Week 13: Conroy, *The Disinherited*, and Sinclair, *The Jungle*
- Week 14: Steinbeck, *The Grapes of Wrath*
- Week 15: West, *A Cool Million* **(Novel #4 due)**

GRADING!

Grades are the filthy lucre of the American education system. They are a part of the system of rewards (for a *job* well done, for good *work*) that pits students against one another in a ruthless battle for limited resources, that helps sort the winners from the losers, and that ultimately prepares students to take their slots as interchangeable cogs in the capitalist machine. You will not receive a grade for this course unless the dean makes me give you one, in which case a B+ is satisfactory, an A– is good, and an A is exceptional.

U.S. Dreams
(From *The Journals of Upton Sinclair*)

Chased by men with guns. Hobbled into a cave to hide. Discovered that the cave was the barrel of a very big gun. (11/4/73)

Making love to a beautiful woman with a tattoo of someone's face on *her* face. Felt something strange. A bad rubbing. Looked down and saw that her vagina was the barrel of a gun. Tattoo face started laughing and counting slowly to three. (8/24/75)

Shot in a black car. (2/15/76)

Hands without arms, without bodies. Flying like bats. Swooping down and taking my hat, pulling my ear, punching my face. Flying in intricate formations, doing aerial stunts. Hands riding guns through the night like magic carpets. (9/4/80)

With Albert in a cemetery. A nice walk. Rows and rows of simple headstones, each says my name. We come to one that has his name. I get on the ground and try to scrape his name off with the edge of a dime. I ask him if he has anything to write with, but he doesn't. It starts snowing. I can't find anything to write with because of the snow. Then can't find his headstone. Terrible. (11/22/83)

Shot without pants. (Jan. 84)

Swimming in a cold lake. [Illegible] Water somehow became a gun. (9/19/89)

Wake up after surgery. Doctor is looking down at me and holding a silver tray with a gun on it. The gun is covered with wet leaves and dirt. The doctor is a very young man. He tells me that I've been shot so many times there was a gun inside me. He says, "It was a complicated procedure because your small intestine was coiled around the engine." I ask him if he has had any medical training. (5/9/91)

Shot while taking a high school exam for which I hadn't studied. (3/20/92)

Lying in an open grave on a hilltop. Sun coming down and warming my face and hands. Even though I was in a hole, I could see down from the hilltop into the valley. Looked like a painting of agrarian America, with rolling green hills and farms. Muscular farmers and oxen somehow out of scale. Beautiful. (4/8/94)

Giving a speech on the lip of a huge iron cauldron full of people. The people were squirming and writhing and trying to get air. My teeth crumbled and I spit the shards into my hand. Then I sprinkled my teeth into the people. Weird! (2/16/97)

Last night I dreamed that Albert was struck by lightning. I must write him. (8/27/98)

Shot while falling. (1/2/00)

Shameful dream about Carrie Fisher. (7/6/01)

Won the Pulitzer Prize. First writer ever to win it in two different lifetimes. The book had seed packets in it and pieces of dried fruit that readers could eat. Shot while giving my acceptance speech. (10/30/01)

A novel written on my body. When people looked at me, they read the novel. They spun me around. They lifted the folds and wrinkles of my flesh to finish a chapter. I could feel the words on my face. They held me down and shaved my head to read my scalp. I asked for a sandwich and they got agitated. Suppose it all means something, but I've grown weary of the symbolism. (3/11/02)

Watching JGH's parole hearing at home. He shoots me through the TV. (5/2/02)

Elected governor and president. Take a fishing trip with Albert. His guitar falls in the water with snakes. (7/23/02)

Dreamed I was dead and lying in a casket. The casket was a big book that I had not finished. I could hear people talking. I could hear Jack [London] calling my name. I tried to open my eyes, but I couldn't. I tried to move my hands and fingers, but I was completely dead. B. said I shouted and sat up. (4/14/03)

Yours for Socialism As Fast As Possible, But No Faster

Letter to President Ronald Reagan

April 16, 1987

Dear President Reagan:

Enclosed please find a copy of my most recent novel, *Arms for Hostages!* Please forgive the length of the book; you of all people know how very complex this topic is, and I could not find a way to treat it adequately in fewer than 600 pages. My hope is that you will take time out of your busy schedule to read it.

As I am sure you know, I have had the ear of presidents throughout this bloody century. I met with Theodore Roosevelt on several occasions, and while we did not perhaps agree on a vision for the future of this country—and while he took a bit too much credit for the reforms that resulted from my work—I do believe that we had some fruitful dialogues and we certainly cleaned up the meat on American tables (or at the very least, we made it less tainted and rancid than it had been previously!). I met with Franklin and Eleanor Roosevelt, as well, and we worked together to figure out how to pull America out of the Great Depression. It was, of course, FDR's rescinded promise to support my gubernatorial campaign in '34 that cost us the election, thereby thwarting

73

a peaceful revolution and setting back the cause of social justice who knows how many years, but I feel confident that we still accomplished a great deal. The point is, these powerful men read my work and took it seriously, and that is all that I could ask of my president. You may be interested to know that Teddy once told me how uncomplimentary it was that critics had compared me to Zola, Tolstoy, and Gorki. Zola, he said, was evil. Tolstoy had a diseased moral nature. And Gorki's leadership, he said, would lead nowhere save the "Serbonian bog." It is not for me, of course, to judge my own standing in international letters. I will graciously leave that to you.

Please know that I would be honored to visit the White House once again to discuss the matters that concern us both as American citizens (as well as former Californians!). May is pretty much wide open for me.

With the best wishes of,
Upton Sinclair

Letter to California governor
Arnold Schwarzenegger (a fragment)

"Take down this letter, Charles. Ready? Dear Governor Schwarzenegger comma. Congratulations on your recent victory period. As you certainly know comma, I nearly won the same office in '34 comma, but I was done in by the GOP and its corporate stooges period. Perhaps I should have developed a massive chest like yours exclamation point!"

"What?"

"Scratch that, Charles. I trust you have read my EPIC platform period. It is still a relevant document after these many years period. I urge you to consider turning over the idle land and the idle factories of California to the workers comma, and to increase taxes on privately owned property period. Let's see. I don't much care for your movies comma which are violent comma, immoral comma, and occasionally difficult to follow period. I'm getting sleepy, Charles. Enclosed please find a book period. I wrote it period. Idle farms. Idle farms. The gentle winds at Coronado. Looking forward to meeting you comma. Tennis period. Oh."

"Mr. Sinclair?"

"Production for use."

"What?"

"Scratch that."

"Would you like to take your nap now?"

"Hm."

"Do you want to finish the letter?"

"To whom?"

"To Governor Schwarzenegger."

"Oh, you're a clever one, Charles."

"How about a nap?"

"Bugs."

"Nap? Mr. Sinclair?"

Letter to National Football League Commissioner Paul Tagliabue

December 10, 1998

Dear Commissioner Tagliabue,

You have, since assuming your position nearly a decade ago, received my repeated communications about the excessive violence in your league, the ungentlemanly celebrations (by both Negroid and Caucasoid players), the horror of artificial turf, the skimpy uniforms and tawdry routines of the cheerleaders, and your hopelessly outdated yardage system. Though I have never had the honor of a reply, I know from your secretary that you have received the letters, and I trust that you give them the respect and consideration they deserve. In all honesty, commissioner, I must say that ten years ago I had hoped and expected that by this date we would see an NFL in which rough tackling was out-lawed and "high fives" were stiffly penalized. An NFL, moreover, played on ninety-one-meter fields of grass. An NFL, in short, that re-flected our true and best national ideals. But I of all people realize that reform is often painfully slow, and the world does not move unless we put our shoulders to it and push.

I will not trouble you presently with the aforementioned issues. My current letter concerns the issue of fair play. To put it bluntly, commis-sioner, your league is unjust. Entertaining, perhaps, and certainly lucrative, but tainted! One might say, borrowing an analogy from my previous work as a reformer, that there is a finger in the sausage of your football league. My hope, as ever, is that this letter will open up a dialogue and lead to meaningful change.

Last weekend, I had a rare opportunity to sit down and watch the fi-nal period of an exciting American Football Conference clash between the gridders from Gotham and the Seattle eleven. Perhaps you saw it! Nearing the end of the contest, the New York squad trailed its North-west foe 31 points to 26, but they were driving the ball down the field. The Gotham quarterback, a tall and remarkable Italian named Vinny Testaverde, led his team to within roughly five meters of a score with precious little time remaining. But it was fourth down! Instead of at-tempting a forward pass, the clever immigrant sought to carry the foot-ball into the touchdown zone. A sneak! Ah, but members of the Seattle defensive unit responded quickly and knocked him (rather too violently, I thought) to the ersatz turf, almost a full meter from the touchdown zone. The New York gridders had performed valiantly, but they had ap-parently lost the match. Imagine my surprise, then, when one of the ref-erees of the contest, a Mr. Earnie Frantz, raised both of his arms in the air to signify a touchdown for Testaverde and his cohorts in green! The Italian had clearly been stopped short of the line, and yet the Seattle eleven, so richly deserving of victory, fell in defeat 32 points to 31.

It is certainly not my intention to defame Mr. Frantz, who is probably a very competent, judicious, and clear-sighted referee. Mr. Frantz later said he mistook the quarterback's helmet for the ball, which is understandable, even if the Italian's helmet was white and the ball was brown. My complaint here is not about Frantz or human error! No, commissioner, my complaint is about the lack of systemic measures to correct human error. On my television I watched as the network rebroadcast the brutal, fateful play over and over again, from multiple angles and with the movements of the players slowed dramatically. I and every other television viewer could plainly see that Mr. Frantz had erred, that the football had not crossed the touchdown line. The outcome of the game was clearly unfair.

Commissioner, my proposal is quite simple! Allow the officials, who, after all, are human beings and who thus have human limitations, foibles, and prejudices, to utilize the available technology to create a more just sport. Used judiciously, technology can make your league more equitable. Why not allow Mr. Frantz to view the same slow-action rebroadcast that millions of viewers viewed in their homes? Why not allow him to correct his error? I can imagine an NFL in which officials view the rebroadcast after each and every play to make certain that they made fair and correct calls, and to confirm that each player on the field competed with decorum. The games might last a bit longer, but you would be assured of a fair outcome.

Mr. Tagliabue, allow me to use an analogy from your sport. For you it is fourth down and centimeters to go! You must make a tough call. I trust that you will do the right thing by instituting a rebroadcast rule. The very integrity of your league is at stake.

Sincerely,
Upton Sinclair

P.S. Please help an old man understand why the New York Jets play their matches in New Jersey at a venue called Giants Stadium.

Much of the Story of My Life Is a Story of the Books I Wrote

Customer Reviews of Selected Upton Sinclair Books

Dragon's Teeth
Be the first to review this book!

Wide Is the Gate
Be the first to review this book!

Bedbugs!
Be the first to review this book!

The Brass Check
Be the first to review this book!

Presidential Mission
Be the first to review this book!

Gridiron Justice: How I Reformed the NFL
Be the first to review this book!

One Clear Call
Be the first to review this book!

The Journal of Arthur Stirling
Be the first to review this book!

O Shepherd, Speak!
Be the first to review this book!

Return of Lanny Budd
Be the first to review this book!

Bombs Away!
Be the first to review this book!

A World to Win
Be the first to review this book!

The Cup of Fury
Be the first to review this book!

The Profits of Religion
Be the first to review this book!

Telepathy for Beginners
Be the first to review this book!

O Grenada!
Be the first to review this book!

A Captain of Industry
Be the first to review this book!

More Oil!
Be the first to review this book!

The Unvanquishable!
Be the first to review this book!

King Midas
Be the first to review this book!

The Whole Nine Meters: America and the Metric Revolution
Be the first to review this book!

Rice Notions: 100 Easy Recipes
Be the first to review this book!

Wheezing Nation!
Be the first to review this book!

The Goslings: A Study of the American Schools
Be the first to review this book!

Manassas: A Novel of the Civil War
Be the first to review this book!

Safe Drinking Water! A Novel
Be the first to review this book!

Money Writes!
Be the first to review this book!

My Lifetime in Letters
Be the first to review this book!

Arms for Hostages!
Be the first to review this book!

Springtime and Harvest
Be the first to review this book!

The Overman
Be the first to review this book!

The Metropolis
Average Customer Rating: * (Based on 1 review)

* Completely Gross!
Reviewer: Gina from Salem, VA

Sinclare came to my school last year and he was so old and gross. He had some fingers gone and blood in his hair. The janitor had to sweep the floor when he left. Some boys tried to get him. Mr. Wesley got fired from his job and we had a sub for like two months.

Spy
Be the first to review this book!

King Technology
Be the first to review this book!

American Outpost: A Book of Reminiscences
Be the first to review this book!

The Industrial Republic
Be the first to review this book!

Steroids!
Be the first to review this book!

Up from the Grave!: Collected Essays (1970–1986)
Average Customer Rating: ***** (Based on 1 review)

***** Over at the Royal Sudz
Reviewer: LFS, USA

I saw him at the laundromat
with holes in his head and his socks
but it could have been a sleight of hand
it could have been a hoax
if it was him he had wicked static cling
and not nearly enough quarters
but it's probably best to assume
that what I saw was a weather balloon
or a mirage in the shimmering heat of the dryers
might have been hallucination
based on drugs and sleep deprivation
and the deepest wish of my bleeding heart

Pharmaceutical!
Be the first to review this book!

Plays of Protest
Be the first to review this book!

Mr. Universe
Be the first to review this book!

The Devil's Ears!
Average Customer Rating *** (Based on 2 reviews)

* Unfair Report
Reviewer: GMCGA from Washington, DC

While *The Devil's Ears* is ostensibly a work of the imagination, we believe that
Mr. Sinclair has a responsibility to present the facts about genetically modified
corn. We also believe he has failed prodigiously to meet this responsibility.
There are more than four hundred corn-related factual errors or

exaggerations in Mr. Sinclair's novel. We would like to take this opportunity to address and rebut the ten most egregious, libelous, and potentially damaging claims.

1. **LIE**: Industry thugs have threatened and harassed small-time farmers of unmodified corn, and in many cases have destroyed their crops. **TRUTH**: The industry is shocked and saddened by the senseless destruction of primitive corn farms by *non*-industry thugs.

2. **LIE**: Working conditions on genetically modified corn farms are abominable. **TRUTH**: Working conditions on genetically modified corn farms are at industry standard.

3. **LIE**: Each ear of genetically modified corn contains as much sugar as a candy bar. **TRUTH**: This depends on the type and size of candy bar that we're talking about. An ear of genetically modified corn has far less sugar, for example, than the theater-size Kit Kat.

4. **LIE**: Genetically modified corn has less nutritional value than unmodified corn. **TRUTH**: Not if you eat several ears, which you will because The Taste Is 'Ear Heaven!™

5. **LIE**: Genetically modified corn is programmed to last only one growing season, thus ensuring that the grower must buy more expensive seeds the following year. **TRUTH**: Genetically modified corn is programmed to last only one growing season, thus ensuring the purity and high standards of each year's yield.

6. **LIE**: Genetically modified corn has "cloven" tassels. **TRUTH**: Genetically modified corn has *cleft* tassels.

7. **LIE**: Genetically modified corn glows in the dark. **TRUTH**: Genetically modified corn is Goldenlicious.™

8. **LIE**: Genetically modified corn may cause skin rashes, headaches, nausea, double vision, vomiting, or feelings of euphoria. **TRUTH**: There is a *big* difference between laboratory mice and human beings.

9. **LIE**: Genetically modified corn is another "suckered tentacle of the monster that is global capitalism." **TRUTH**: Genetically modified corn brings families together at dinnertime.

10. **LIE**: Genetically modified corn has a strange aftertaste. **TRUTH**: No it doesn't.

Mr. Sinclair is up to his old mud-raking tricks again. The trouble is, he rakes up only lies and deception (as well as swift and devastating legal action). We hope that the corn consumers of America will seek a more balanced and truthful view of genetically modified corn. We also hope that you will try an ear today and find out for yourself why it's The Stalk of the Town.™

Michael Lanier,
External Relations,
Genetically Modified Corn Growers Association

✶✶✶✶✶ Wondrous
Reviewer: Donald from Bozeman, MT

Best corn I've ever had. You could eat it for dessert. The kernels are bright and perfect like my ex-wife's teeth. Don't drive for about an hour after you eat it. The best corn I've ever had.

The Coal War
Be the first to review this book!

America Is Hard to See

We are all Upton Sinclairs.
                              —DONALD BARTHELME

TREADWAY (1959–). Born Samuel Milton Treadway, 1959, Sacramento, CA. Painter, collagist, and conceptual/performance artist. Important works include *The Sunset Exhibition* (1989), *State Capitals* (1992), *Arroyo Olympics* (1995), *Canon (w/Hi-Speed Modem)* (1997), *The Sinclair Centerfolds* (1999), and *Mock Turtle* (2001). Treadway's work has been described as playful, darkly comic, irreverent, sentimental, and apocalyptic.

In *The Sunset Exhibition*, Treadway created a "museum" in the backyard of Frank and Dolores Shaffer's one-story brick rambler in Erie, PA. Each evening of the exhibition, Treadway, calling himself a "curator of the dusk," led museum visitors into the Shaffers' fenced backyard to view the sunset. Given that the backyard faced northeast—and further, that the horizon in the west was blocked by houses, neighborhood trees, and air pollution—the sunset was never directly visible during the one hundred days of the exhibition. Museum patrons wore headphones playing a tape that provided facts and descriptions of the sunsets of the eastern United States. The Shaffers' dog, Sparky, barked incessantly at the visitors and created a surprising amount of waste in the backyard, patches of which he had worn to dirt in his manic sprints. One critic called *The Sunset Exhibition* "a poignant recognition of hope irrepressible." Interestingly, another called it a "nasty, tragic joke."

In *Canon (w/Hi-Speed Modem)*, Treadway took eighty-two canonical Western paintings and digitally inserted, somewhere in the frame, a PC or laptop equipped with a high-speed modem. The result, according to one critic, was a "hilarious and disquieting use of anachronism." Another observer, less impressed, called it "juvenile and suburban." According to a 1999 survey, Treadway's "The Luncheon of the Boating Party (w/Hi-Speed Modem)" is the thirteenth most popular screen saver among American office workers.

Treadway is perhaps most well known for the controversial and disturbing *The Sinclair Centerfolds*, a series of three portraits ("Mr. January," "Mr. April," "Mr. December") of novelist and propagandist Upton Sinclair. The portraits, high gloss and hyperrealistic, portray a nude Sinclair in various poses, his body devastated by weapons and time, his eyes looking directly and intensely at the painter/viewer. Two horizontal creases across the canvas are further suggestive of a centerfold. The portraits, which were supported by a public grant of five hundred dollars, received significant attention (mostly opprobrious) from media, government officials, and critics. One prominent review stated: "[W]ith *The Sinclair Centerfolds*, Treadway crossed a line. Not of decorum or decency, as the stuffy politicians bellow. Rather, an aesthetic line. He crossed out of Art." Ironically, *The Sinclair Centerfolds*, which were almost certainly intended to be a sympathetic portrayal of the leftist, actually damaged Sinclair's cause and image by depicting him as weak, frail, and feminine. The novelist E. L. Doctorow wrote, "If the Left wasn't already dead (and I suspect it was), then the Sinclair Centerfolds killed it."

Two of the portraits in the series, "Mr. January" and "Mr. April," have been destroyed. "Mr. December" is in a private collection.

(See also White, Sharon, *Treadway: American Weirdo;* Recker, Vincent, *Confounding the Uncles: Treadway's Difficult Art.*)

•

TAPEWORM.COM: Why did you decide to paint Sinclair as a centerfold?

TREADWAY: Why did I . . . Do you mean, "Why did *I* decide to paint Sinclair as a centerfold? Or do you mean, "Why did I decide to *paint* Sinclair as a centerfold?"

TAPEWORM.COM: I guess—

TREADWAY: Or do you mean, "Why did I decide to paint *Sinclair* as a centerfold?" Or do you mean, "Why did I decide to paint Sinclair as a *centerfold?*"

TAPEWORM.COM: Well.

TREADWAY: Those are all different questions with different answers. Artist, medium, subject, form. What is required is an interrogative precision.

TAPEWORM.COM: Well, OK, what is it about Sinclair that interested you?

TREADWAY: His courage, his conviction. His just-around-the-corner optimism. His stubborn ignorance and desperate need for attention. He's very American.

TAPEWORM.COM: Do you like Sinclair? Or do you respect him?

TREADWAY: I have no idea how to answer that.

TAPEWORM.COM: The painting—I'm talking of "Mr. December," but it goes for all three, I suppose—looks precisely like a photograph. Many first-time viewers think that it *is* a photograph.

TREADWAY: It's not.

TAPEWORM.COM: No, I realize that. So to be blunt, then, why not just photograph Sinclair as a centerfold? Rather than paint? Why use an obsolete mode of representation?

TREADWAY: Because it's an obsolete mode of representation.

TAPEWORM.COM: Could you elaborate?

TREADWAY: No.

TAPEWORM.COM: I'd like to talk about your process. Is it true that you painted Sinclair, then photographed the paintings, and then painted the final portraits from the photographs of the paintings?

TREADWAY: *[Laughs]* Wherever did you hear that?

TAPEWORM.COM: That's what you told Landfill.com.

TREADWAY: Despite rigorous maintenance and fact-checking, the Internet will occasionally disseminate error and falsehood.

TAPEWORM.COM: Depicting Sinclair's ravaged body in the form of the centerfold seems to comment ironically on notions of desire or titillation.

TREADWAY:

TAPEWORM.COM: Others see an earnest representation of conviction, suffering, even martyrdom. Still others argue that the piece is about Sinclair's unseemly need to expose and to be regarded—

TREADWAY: That's not a question.

TAPEWORM.COM: Well, OK then, can you talk about your intentions, your notion of the tone of the work?

TREADWAY: No.

TAPEWORM.COM:

TREADWAY:

TAPEWORM.COM: Your previous work is generally abstract or conceptual.

TREADWAY: Still not a question.

TAPEWORM.COM: I'm coming to it. Why the shift to realism and representation?

TREADWAY: All my work is representational. You can't not be representational.

TAPEWORM.COM: Why the shift to a more overt political subject or mode?

TREADWAY: Political? All of my work has been political.

TAPEWORM.COM: Perhaps, but not—

TREADWAY: Next question.

TAPEWORM.COM: What?

TREADWAY: Next question.

TAPEWORM.COM: What is your response to the many people who were surprised that you could paint so . . . well?

TREADWAY:

TAPEWORM.COM: By *well* I of course just mean accurately. Realistically.

TREADWAY: My response is, first, that I have always been accurate. All my work is accurate. I have always aimed for accuracy in representation. My response is, second, that I have never been accurate. Not even close. Nothing is accurate. Have you noticed? Has anyone noticed? The centerfold portraits look nothing like Mr. Sinclair. Nothing whatsoever. For instance, in real life, Mr. Sinclair exists three-dimensionally. He has depth. In my portraits, he is two-dimensional, length and width. In real life he moves about quite a bit. In the portrait he just sits there. And so on.

TAPEWORM.COM: Yes, but he *looks* three-dimensional.

TREADWAY: Shading and shadow. Beginning Drawing. Mail-order art degree. Are we through?

TAPEWORM.COM: Sinclair did in fact sit for you?

TREADWAY:

TAPEWORM.COM: And did he in fact disrobe?

TREADWAY: Do you mean—

TAPEWORM.COM: You know what I mean! I mean did he take his clothes off. You've suggested previously that—

TREADWAY: It bears on the work how? Does it make the work more or less remarkable if his clothes were off?

TAPEWORM.COM: Well, it might be argued that if he was not nude and you painted him nude, the focus of the work shifts away from the subject and toward the artist, toward composition. The imagination.

TREADWAY: That's dumb and it's not a question.

TAPEWORM.COM: It was an answer to your question.

TREADWAY: Are we through?

TAPEWORM.COM: Your depiction of the body wounds is accurate, according to multiple autopsy photographs. The question—

TREADWAY: Photographs from the Internet?

TAPEWORM.COM: The *question* would then become, how did you get an old prude like Upton Sinclair to pose naked? Was it voluntary?

TREADWAY: Are we through?

TAPEWORM.COM: If you had to do it over again, would you depict Sinclair as stronger or more vital? Less vulnerable?

TREADWAY: What, like a tattoo? An ammo belt?

TAPEWORM.COM: Well—

TREADWAY: A raised fist? How about a big, swinging cock?

TAPEWORM.COM: That isn't—

TREADWAY: I don't answer to the workers of the world.

TAPEWORM.COM: OK then, to whom do you answer? Or to what?

TREADWAY: That's your first good question.

TAPEWORM.COM: You're not going to answer it, are you?

TREADWAY: No.

•

From *Confounding the Uncles*:

We have plenty of evidence to suggest that Treadway and Sinclair did indeed meet in the winter of 1996. Beyond this simple and solid fact, however, we know little. To make further statements is to wander into the marshlands of rumor, speculation, and fantasy. Treadway's driver and Sinclair's secretary offer vague and conflicting reports. Sinclair is reticent and embarrassed about the matter. Treadway is oblique and obstinate. We are not likely ever to know what, if anything remarkable at all, happened in that cabin on that cold, snowy January day. The "truth," like Treadway's Pennsylvania sunset, is invisible, unavailable. Ultimately, all we are left with is the truth of his art. (113)

My Last Leftist

That's my last leftist nailed up on the wall,
Looking like a naked corpse and for all
I know he is—note Treadway's use of red—
He stripped the old man and painted him dead.
Why don't you pipe down and hear what I say?
No, I'll play neither "Freebird" nor "Stairway"—
Well fuck you, too, pal—Not that you would ask
But I will tell you how he got that gash
Across his throat and those holes in his chest—
His books proclaim that this is not the best
Of all possible worlds—that's all it takes
To get assassinated in the States.
Those are nice ones, ma'am, be careful up there—
(Was Sinclair so easy?) With a nice pair
Of eyes you can see that his face is flushed red—
It's the heat of the woodstove or instead
Modesty—perhaps Treadway chanced to say,
"Let's see . . . Could you put your glasses away?"
Or, from behind his easel, "But I feel
Your cardigan—though nice—will just conceal
Your convictions"—Somehow the painter got—

With a gun, candy, or just the right mot—
Sinclair as naked as seventy-eight—
(Eighteen Seventy-eight, that is—the date
Of his first birth)—There is December, bare
As belief in his books—Look how he wears
One of them like a fig leaf—And I thought
That novel was meant to expose and not
Conceal—But maybe Treadway simply said,
"Your flesh is manifesto to be read
By the American people"—He had
A heart—how shall I say?—easily flat-
tered by praise—Still does—wasn't alcohol
That brought Sinclair into the 'fold—Last call!
Find your shirt, miss—I see what Treadway meant
But without pecs and abs the art got bent
To the right—His portraits were all undone—
Painter's brush was just as good as a gun.
There he stands as if dead and you don't care,
But he'll be back tomorrow, preaching fair-
ness Cuz that bird you cannot change
Lord knows he won't change.

Love Is Obviously a Big Risk

Do you recognize any of these men?

Let me see. Yes. That one. He was in here this morning. He was a strange, sad old man. Weird. He actually kind of looked like *that* one too.

These are all the same man. These are his disguises.

Oh. You never think of old people as having disguises.

The elderly are a heavily disguised segment. But they generally have to disguise themselves as other old people. They're sort of hemmed in in this regard.

Do you want coffee or pie or anything?

Decaf, pecan. We've seen disguised babies, disguised grandmothers, disguised pets. Anyone can be in disguise. Statistically speaking, half the people in this diner are in disguise. Not being in disguise can be a form of disguise. Do you know who this is, ma'am?

No.

It's Upton Sinclair.

The guy who wrote *Alice in Wonderland*?

Thank you. No, that was Lewis Carroll.

Oh. Well this guy was writing.

Yes. Upton Sinclair is a writer.

Why are you looking for him?

Can you tell us what you remember about him?

Yes. I remember him very well. He was at one of my booths. Number eleven.

Was he with anyone?

No, he was alone. He was writing on a napkin.

Did you get a look at what he was writing?

No. That's none of my business. Plus his handwriting was just terrible and I couldn't read it. Looked like my little boy's. There's something so sad about old people's handwriting. Like birthday cards from grandparents?

Was he wearing this dark suit?

Yes. It seemed too big for him. There were ink stains all over his clothes and hands. His skin was

Wrinkled?

Yes, but also

Mottled?

That's it.

What else do you remember?

I remember him very well because I poured him some coffee and then right away he spilled the whole cup in his lap.

Ouch.

I didn't do it. Lord knows I've done it before, but I didn't do it this time. He did it himself.

What happened then?

It was very hot. Just like the sign says out front. We're not kidding around. There was steam coming up from his legs, but he didn't move. He didn't react. He just sat there. He took off his glasses and started rubbing his eyes.

Were they these glasses? Or these?

Um. Those.

Hat?

Sort of like that one.

Then what?

I offered to help him. To get him more napkins or a cold towel. He was really in rough shape.

You would be too.

How old is he?

Depends. What happened then?

He started talking. He still hadn't wiped up the coffee. It had to hurt. The sun was bright, I remember. He was all lit up. He said, Do you have any idea, young lady, how much coffee I have spilled on myself? I kind of laughed because I thought he was making a little joke of it. But he was real serious. He said, You're young. How old are you? Twenty? He said that, twenty. That was flattering, even if it came from an old man. I said, Close.

Says here you're thirty-eight.

Detective, I *know* how old I am. I'm just telling you what he said.

Please continue.

He said, It's my one vice. My only. I don't smoke. I don't touch John Barleycorn.

John Barleycorn. Wow.

I eat rice and fruit, and I fast regularly. It's my one vice and it punishes me. I end up wearing it like Hester Prynne. He said the coffee bean industry is awful. I didn't know that. I mean, I suppose I could have guessed it.

Hester Prynne. Go on.

He said, You've no doubt spilled some coffee on yourself. I said, You have no idea. Just look at this scar right here. He said, But you're at an age when it still feels like an accident, some freak occurrence that will never happen again. But see, I know. I know that scalding coffee on my clothes and on my flesh is in the very nature of things. It's predictable. I never know exactly when it will happen, but I can depend on it happening. The burn is familiar now. I won't say comforting, but familiar. The rising steam off my crotch or my wrist. It's part of the fabric of existence.

He said that, fabric of existence?

Yes. The spill really got to him. He seemed

Insane?

No.

Dangerous?

No. Tired and sad.

OK.

He said, I started drinking coffee in 1892. That's what he said, 1892. He said, I had to sneak it. My mother wouldn't allow it in our house because it's a stimulant. I suppose it was a form of rebellion. I got hooked. You figure I've spilled a 240-millileter cup on myself once every two months or so since then. That's a conservative estimate, both in terms of frequency and quantity. That's not even counting little drips and splashes that must surely add up. Take off a few years for being dead if you like. He tried to figure out how many presidential administrations he had spilled coffee on himself in, but he gave up. Sweet, senile old man. Why in the world are you looking for him?

We just want to have a talk with him.

About what?

Tell us everything you remember.

He said, It's liters and liters of coffee. Think if we could see all that coffee right now in a big glass tank, sloshing around and steaming. So much coffee. It's a reckoning. A human life. I've come to see it as built-in. Not really random or accidental. There is an amount of coffee you will spill on yourself in a life. There are a number of stairs you will trip up and fall down. There are a number of splinters way up under the skin.

Hold it. OK.

There is a quantity of blood you will leave on handkerchiefs and toilet paper. Maybe within a certain range. But the point is, when you're twenty, you think it's an accident. You're surprised by the splinter, by that black patch of ice. You don't think of it happening again. You don't think of it as part of a long, inglorious pattern of life. Burst ink pens. Melted lip balm. Crumbling teeth, cracked glasses, stubbed toes, paper cuts. The wind takes away your trash cans and their lids. Maybe you find a lid later, three blocks away, under a car that's leaking oil. But maybe you never find it at all.

What did you say to him?

What could I say? I had other tables to get to, but I didn't just want to leave him. I asked if he wanted more coffee. I said surely it won't happen twice in a row.

What did he say?

He looked out that window right there. He still had his glasses off. His eyes were all cloudy and wet. He apologized to me. He said he was sorry for all that gloomy talk. He stared out that window. I started to leave. He said, I just miss Mary Craig.

That's what he said? I just miss Mary Craig?

Yes.

And that's all?

He said, It's not the same without her.

Killer Line

REPORTER: Is there anything you want to say?

HUNTLEY:

REPORTER: Now's your chance.

HUNTLEY: My lawyer has advised me not to speak on the matter.

REPORTER: We've got fifteen million curious viewers tuned in right now. You don't have anything to say to them?

HUNTLEY: Well. I'll say this. I aimed for Sinclair's heart, and by accident I hit him in the head.

At One Point Upton
Was Huge in Japan

(From www.hiecoup.com)

Dew shines in meadow
Flying birds unzip the sky
Upton shot in neck

Richest one per cent
Owns Earth, Incorporated
Get out the shovels

Quoth Wilde: "No artist
Desires to prove anything"
Upton's remaindered

What's the difference
Between bullets, bad reviews?
Bullet wounds will heal

Like dripping daggers
The icicles hang from eaves
Sinclair dies again

Lefty in a ditch
And between his teeth they find
Modified tassels

Lives in king-size silk—
Keeps the wealthy up all night—
Upton the bedbug!

That tapping you hear
Amidst the gunfire chatter?
Upton's typewriter

Interviewer: Why?
Sinclair: Well, capitalist—
Interviewer: Thanks.

Saw him at Starbucks
Wearing a white foam moustache
Might have been Dreiser

Muckraker in debt
Needs cash to fight the power
PICTURE YOUR AD HERE

Dear Sinclair, You are
A puny, weak-brained crackpot
Best wishes, Ezra

The days grow longer
Melting snow fills the rivers
Upton's car blows up!

U.S. holiday:
Hot dogs, apple pie, fireworks—
Those burning novels

Professional Messiah

It is always easy to understand what I am
trying to say.

—U.S.

The failure arises from diction.

—E. L. DOCTOROW

Flags flew everywhere. The American flag had become a symbol of a symbol. The real was no longer accessible or manageable. Of course at this time in our history the public relations firms determined what could be thought. The Pentagon hired public relations firms to handle the wars, to give them good names. Statues of foreign leaders were torn down and dragged through dusty streets by American military vehicles. The footage was replayed on television every half hour, along with scores from professional sporting events. Cameras showed people celebrating with rifles in the air. Apparently nobody was dying in this war except journalists. There were large contracts to rebuild countries that American bombs had destroyed. There were conflicts of interest. There were leaked memos. American reservists from poor families died every day in a war that had a good name and was over. We had won. The public relations firms said the U.S. Army was a great way to receive an education and to learn skills that employers value. Not everyone was grateful to the USA. One million people in London marched against American aggression. Three hundred thousand marched in Berlin. Four hundred thousand marched in Paris. Public relations firms told Americans to hate the French and to love war. Restaurants changed their menus to offer Freedom Fries. A popular bumper sticker on very large automobiles read, GIVE WAR A CHANCE. This was a perverse allusion to a song by a folksinger who had been shot on a city street more than twenty years earlier. Folksingers were being hunted into extinction. Two hundred thousand people marched in Dublin, among them a young American coaching basketball in Ireland. When he returned to the United States, he found that things had not changed. Upton Sinclair had been killed twice and was rumored to be alive again. Everyone was middle class. The basketball coach brushed his wife's hair and told her the news of the world. He made the hair shine. Wind blew sand beneath the door. Kids drank beer and danced to Latin music on the banks of the Rio Grande. The water was down, revealing the trash in the riverbed. Mexico sued the United States over water rights. The basketball coach told his wife his team had played hard but had finished with a 6–20 record. The unemployment rate was high. His wife was a poet. She said, Kiss me on the mouth. She said, It's no good when you go. The FBI watched them both.

At this time in our history the writer E. L. Doctorow was still writing his novels. Years earlier he had made his name as a serious writer who wrote about American politics. He had written about radicals. He had claimed that radicals were an important part of the national family. He had written about the Rosenbergs. He had written about Emma Goldman. His books sold well and made money. Nobody who thought about this could understand it. One of his novels, perhaps his most famous novel, used real historical figures and rewrote turn-of-the-century American history as a history of suffering, oppression, and accident. He stole part of the plot as well as the novel's prose style from a German writer named von Kleist. The narrative distance allowed equally for nostalgia, sentiment, reportage, and irony. This sort of larceny was very much in fashion. The book sold millions of copies and was made into a musical. Many readers today do not know if Emma Goldman was a real person or a fictional character. When asked if the events and chance encounters in the novel really happened, Doctorow answered coyly, They have now. This answer upset those on the left and the right. It seemed decadent. On the occasion of a significant award or honor, an interviewer came to Doctorow's house to discuss his life in letters. The conversation of course soon turned to art and politics. Doctorow had not wanted to grant this interview and yet he felt obligated. He was a private and retiring man with a nagging sense of middle-class guilt. He opened his mouth and words came out. Doctorow said American fiction had gotten small. He said American writers used their incredibly developed technique to write about what happens in the kitchen, what happens in the bedroom. The interviewer kept asking him about politics because there was nobody else in the country to ask. Doctorow did not want to talk about politics. He said writers had pulled the shades down in the bedroom and there were riots in the street. He said novelists of the 1930s and '40s began as journalists and thus were predisposed to engage with the world. The phone rang in another room. The interviewer and Doctorow switched from coffee to beer. The interviewer's beer foamed onto the antique oak table and onto the tape recorder. You can hear the men laugh. Doctorow said Americans like political fiction as long as it's from another country. He said, We've all become novelists for the Republican Party. He said a political writer has to be careful. He quoted Auden: A writer's politics are more dangerous to him than his cupidity. He said, Political sentimentality is as bad as any other kind. You have to acknowledge ambiguity, complexity. There is a kind of death that creeps into your prose when you're trying to illustrate a principle, no matter how worthy. The interviewer flipped the tape over. Doctorow didn't want to be talking about art and politics. He said that a national emergency calls for a poetics of engagement. The interviewer made him say it again in case the tape hadn't started. The interviewer asked Doctorow what his politics were. Doctorow would never state his politics in an interview. He said, My politics are simpleminded, elemental. Don't steal. Don't kill. And justice must be universal. It must exist for all. Plato defined justice as the fulfillment of a person's truest self. That's good for starters. The interview was published in a doomed literary journal with a small circulation.

Coincidentally, the unanswered phone call during the interview was from muckraker and political novelist Upton Sinclair. This was the time in our history when Sinclair was being resurrected and assassinated. Ours was a nation of shovels and guns. The published diary of a famous Sinclair assassin was a best seller. Teenage boys in the suburbs locked their doors and cleaned their firearms and read the diary. There was a reading-group guide in the back. Sinclair was all over the Internet. Over his long lifetime and his many afterlives Sinclair had written countless books. Perhaps one hundred or more. He was a symbol but he was also an old man and he had called to invite Doctorow to dinner. When he heard Doctorow's voice on the answering machine, he thought he was speaking to Doctorow. He said the place and time and he waited for Doctorow to say something. He fiddled with his hearing aids. There was no response. He hung up, confused and angry.

Doctorow had wanted to stay at home that night and watch baseball on television, but he felt obligated to have dinner with Sinclair. He respected the old man's tireless pursuit of social justice and his ridiculous optimism. He was astonished by Sinclair's literary career, his Fordian productivity. He had grown up hearing stories of Sinclair's 1934 gubernatorial campaign in California. Frank Merriam's deep pockets and dirty tricks. The writing had not held up, it was true. The writing was bad. The death had crept into the prose. The end of *The Jungle* was a disaster. But the passion and the scope were laudable. A poetics of engagement would necessarily begin with the novelist's refusal to cede the world to politicians and comedians and cable news networks. Doctorow was worried that he would get shot or asked to provide a blurb. He limped slightly from a tennis injury. He took a train into the city and met Sinclair at a tiny Chinese restaurant. Sinclair believed rice was the key to longevity and health. He was wearing a ridiculous disguise that only drew attention to himself. There was poorly applied makeup covering his fatal wounds. The men shook hands and sat in a booth with ripped vinyl. Sinclair said, You are Jewish. Doctorow nodded. Sinclair said, I like Jews. Half my friends and half my readers have been Jews. I sum up my impression of them in the verse about the little girl who had a little curl right in the middle of her forehead, and when she was good, she was very, very good, and when she was bad, she was horrid. Doctorow stared at the Chinese zodiac. He always forgot what animal he was and had to look again each time he was in a Chinese restaurant. He was the Ram. People born in the Year of the Ram are elegant and highly accomplished in the arts. They are often shy, pessimistic, and puzzled about life. Sinclair studied the chart, as well. The year of his first birth, 1878, was not listed and the math proved difficult. He said, Oh well, I am everything. I am rat, horse, monkey, ox, dragon, rooster. I am every one! Doctorow looked at Sinclair's face and laughed only when the other man did. Sinclair said, Mr. Doctorow, do you believe in ESP? Doctorow shook his head. Sinclair said, My materialistic friends make fun of me. They know these things are a priori impossible whereas I assert that nothing is a priori impossible. It is a question of evidence, and I am willing to hear the evidence about anything whatever. I should very much like to speak with you about ghosts, ESP, reincarnation, and other paranormal phenomena. But now is not the time. The menus arrived and both men ordered. Sinclair drank hot tea and his cup trembled at his lips. The only other people in the restaurant were FBI agents. Sinclair said, You write beautifully, Mr. Doctorow. I wish I could write sentences like yours. It is not my gift. I am a writer but not a poet. My gifts lie elsewhere. Doctorow thanked Sinclair. Sinclair said, I read your sentences and I sigh. But you squander your gifts, Mr. Doctorow! You are too much the artist. Your character Tateh, let us talk about this character. He gives up his

Socialist ideals and he becomes wealthy and important. This is Alger. How is this different than Alger? The egg rolls arrived. At this time in our history Americans thought nothing of the Chinese, either good or bad. For a moment Doctorow could not remember the character Tateh. He had not thought about Tateh in many years. He recalled the man gradually and fondly, like a distant relative. Sinclair said, And this history of yours is a madman's history. Why do you on the one hand tell a true history. I was living then, Mr. Doctorow. I can tell you it is a true history. And yet on the other hand you say all history is just a story. You say we make it up, we create it. You give and you take away. Sinclair had both hands in the air, gesticulating forcefully. There was a finger missing on one hand.

Doctorow ate an egg roll with his fingers and drank a Chinese beer brewed in Texas. He did not know if Sinclair was referring slyly to the contrasting hands of a ragtime player, the steady beat of the left hand, the syncopated rhythms of the right. Sinclair might have been turning his metaphor against him. Or perhaps it was just an unwitting idiom. This was the question, of course. Sinclair was an extraordinary man, but it was not clear to Doctorow if he was a man of extraordinary intelligence and wit. He said, I think it's a bit more complicated than that. Sinclair said, No, it is not, young man. Doctorow looked amused. He was at this time over seventy. Sinclair said, Facts are important. Lynchings are important. Child labor is important. You did not make this up. You made Ford a Jew-hater. I was there at this time, Mr. Doctorow. I met Ford when he lived in Altadena, just a few miles from my house. Ford and Gillette sat by my fireplace, discussing politics and culture. The Flivver King and the Razor King. Neither listened to the other. They were like billiard balls colliding. I read Ford's newspaper, the *Dearborn Independent*. He did in fact hate Jews. He gave money to the Nazis. You see, you would not make up such a fact about a man. It is one thing to have Goldman giving Nesbit a massage—I should say I very much disliked that scene for reasons quite apart from its fabrication—but it is another matter to say a man hates Jews. Such a fact is not created by the historian. The dinners arrived with chopsticks and perfect mounds of steamed rice. Doctorow stared down at his shoes. The shoes, brown lace-ups, he had bought from the catalog of L. L. Bean. They were good comfortable shoes. But Mr. Sinclair, Doctorow said, a Nazi history would treat Ford's anti-Semitism as quite a different sort of fact than we treat it. Rice rained from Sinclair's quivering chopsticks. That is sophistry, young man. Sophistry! That Nazi history would be as flawed as the nostalgic history you corrected in your novel. Doctorow wanted another beer but feared a rebuke from the puritanical Sinclair. He said, Perhaps the Sophists were onto something. He wasn't sure if Sinclair had heard him. He said, One might suggest that a history cannot be flawed. It can only be narrated in a more or less convincing fashion. Sinclair seemed tired and defeated. He leaned back in the booth. Only his head and shoulders were visible above the table. Quietly he said, One might say it, but would you say it, Mr. Doctorow? Would you go that far? Doctorow wiped his mouth with his napkin and shrugged. Sinclair said, This is what I come back to. I die and I return to this idea. The World Trade Center is gone and so is truth and so is history. And so is the Left. I do not think you believe what you claim to believe, young man. Doctorow had heard enough. He said, Mr. Sinclair, you have a Jesus complex. Sinclair's eyes sparkled and the old man laughed himself into a gruesome coughing fit. When he recovered, he said, My old friend Mencken once called me a professional messiah. But you see, Sinclair told Doctorow, the way I see it, the world needs a Jesus more than it needs anything else, and volunteers should be called for daily. Sinclair's fortune said, Those at the top of the mountain did not fall there. His lucky numbers were 6 16 23 8 39 31.

The check arrived. Sinclair took the opportunity to ask Doctorow for a few words of support for his next novel and Doctorow promised to consider it. Sinclair underpaid his meal and overpaid his tip. The men shook hands and parted.

Thus did a friendship begin between the two leftist writers. Through the years they met occasionally for dinner at inconspicuous ethnic restaurants. Incidentally, Sinclair was never able to convince Doctorow about telepathy.

We Were Sort of a Family

Upton washed and I dried. The water in the sink was so hot that his glasses steamed up. He looked up at me and smiled, his vision fogged over, his hands in the soapy, scalding water. "I can't see a thing."

"Here," I said. "I'll help." I took the glasses off his face and wiped them with my dish towel. Then I put them back on his face. He wrinkled his nose to adjust the glasses. An old radio on the windowsill above the sink played classical music. Upton scrubbed a dinner plate, top and bottom, with a sponge. He held it up to the light, squinting, then handed it to me. I rinsed it in cold water and dried it. He said, "When I was nineteen, I bought a violin for seventy-five dollars. That was a lot of money."

A dog trotted into the kitchen, its tags jingling. It sniffed along the pine floor for crumbs, didn't find anything, left happily. Upton said, "Well hello there, fella. I always moved around so much that I couldn't have a dog. But I like dogs."

"Did you learn to play?"

"The violin?"

"Yes."

"I took lessons," he said. "I read music. I felt that music could save me. I was full of so many feelings. Strong feelings. I had to let them out somehow. I went into the hills with my violin and my book of music."

I removed Upton's glasses again and wiped them clear. He stood still, his dripping hands raised in front of him. He lifted his head to allow me to put the glasses back on. I pointed into the soapy water. "Be careful," I said. "I think there are some sharp knives in there."

He said, "I would see families coming out on picnics. They would stare up at me, the parents and their children. I remember little girls staring and pointing up at me on the top of the hill. A skinny young man playing his violin poorly and crying."

"You were sensitive."

"That I was! If your towel gets too wet, get another one. You don't want to wipe streaks into those plates."

The days were short and cold. It got dark out so early that every night it felt much later than it actually was. It wasn't that late. The window behind the sink had steamed up like Upton's glasses.

He said, "In my class there was a lad named Martin Birnbaum, who played beautifully. I watched and listened. I practiced every day. My fingers bled. But I could never play with much grace. Each of us, I suppose, wants to do what he cannot." He handed me a tall glass. I dried the outside and then stuffed the dishtowel inside the glass where my hand would not fit. He said, "Do you play an instrument?"

"No," I said.

"Is that it for the plates?"

"I think so. Watch out for those knives. You might want to drain the water."

He pushed up the sleeves of his flannel shirt and groped in the murky water with the four fingers of his right hand. He pulled out a ladle and scrubbed it with the sponge. He brought up a fork, a couple spoons.

"My dad bought me a saxophone," I said. "We had just moved to a new town. He thought it would help me make friends, be popular. I don't know where he came up with the money. He certainly didn't have it. It was beautiful and shiny, and it had this nice case with red velvet on the inside."

Upton said, "Yes."

"But I couldn't play it. I was terrible. I'd adjust the neck strap and tap the keys and get my mouth ready, just like the good players. But then I'd play and it was just ugly sounds. There is nothing uglier than a saxophone played poorly. So I quit. I stopped trying to play. I failed band. I went to study hall and drew pictures on my desk. I didn't say anything to my dad. I never said anything. I just put the saxophone in my closet. It was like a corpse there in the closet, hidden away. But I knew it was there. And then one day I was in my closet looking for something else and I noticed that it was gone. He must have took it and sold it back or something. He never said anything, ever. Neither of us did."

I took a dry towel from a drawer beneath the counter and I dried the silverware that Upton passed to me. The water in the sink had cooled off and the window was clear and dark. It rattled and ticked in the wind. Upton pulled the stopper in the sink and the gray water drained slowly. The signal on the radio got faint, the stations overlapped. I could hear a man's voice over the music, selling something, and I turned the radio off. The bottom of the sink was covered with wet crumbs, soap bubbles, and flecks of yellow sponge. Also, there were two knives, silver with black handles.

Upton stared into the sink. He said, "Those are sharp ones. I could have hurt myself." I heard footsteps upstairs. He picked up a knife and scrubbed it cautiously beneath the running water. He said, "That is a terrible story about the saxophone."

The Medium Is the Medium

Culture Safari

Q: I love the band Ezra Pound Postcard. Can you tell me how they got their name?

Cindy Redmon
Ames, Iowa

CS: Cindy, this answer is for you and for the hundreds of others who have sent in this same question in the last few weeks.

Unless you've been living under a rock for the last year, you know about Ezra Pound Postcard. (Actually, the thumping bass and the blazing guitars would probably still reach you under your rock.) The quintet from Portland, Oregon, has released two critically acclaimed CDs on its own label (Brutal Music) and has built up a strong fan base through steady touring. The band is (in)famous for the intensity and the staggering volume of its live shows. No fewer than three lawsuits have been brought against the band by fans who claim their hearing was permanently damaged at an EPP concert. (All three cases were thrown out.)

Says Fenn Reese, EPP singer and one of its three guitarists, "When we started, we set out to be loud. That was our thing. That was our way of getting your attention. There are so many messages coming at people constantly. We just figured, 'OK, let's just be louder than every other message.' Let's be impossible to ignore. At our shows, we didn't want people to be able to talk or order drinks or sing along or anything. We just sort of wanted to overwhelm people, to stun them, put them back on their heels."

The band's name is connected to its philosophy. Reese said he came up with the band name after watching a television documentary on the assassinations of radical writer Upton Sinclair. After Joe Gerald Huntley fatally shot Sinclair the third time (in 1995), the dying Sinclair allegedly clutched his chest and said, "That felt like an Ezra Pound postcard."

Says University of Michigan history professor Dr. Rinehart Mays, "First off, the story is probably apocryphal. It's unlikely that Sinclair said *anything*, much less this memorable line, after being shot in the chest by Huntley at close range. But it's a good story. The reference, of course, is to the modernist poet and Mussolini sympathizer Ezra Pound, who sent Sinclair a series of vitriolic postcards during and after Sinclair's 1934 gubernatorial campaign in California."

According to Dr. Lisa Hecht-Reynolds, a literature professor at Washington and Lee University, Pound's postcards were "wild and unhinged rants." Says Hecht-Reynolds, "He used capital letters and strange abbreviations and profanity. He was really abusive. Just merciless. He called Sinclair an egomaniac and a fool and a coward. In one postcard, he wrote, 'R/S/V/P givin me the date yr and the hour in which you finally decided that you knew EVERY g[**] d[***] thing there wuz and iz to be known.' In another, 'You are too puny to admit the existence of ideas you haven't elaborated in yr own kitchen. Put yr ego out to grass for a week.'"

Despite the origins of the name, Reese says the band is not interested in making political statements, left or right. "We're not a political band," he says. "We're a loud band. We all liked the name because it gets at the sense of force or impact that we're after. The aggressiveness. Someone once told me that the band's live show was like bad weather. Like it was difficult to sit there and endure it. I liked that. That was a compliment."

Letter to Albert

November 24, 1999

Dear Albert,

This letter is long overdue. I regret that I didn't meet you in B——
in September. I was injured quite seriously and could not travel. I had
no way of contacting you before our arranged meeting date. I hope you
were not overly inconvenienced. I realize that you were hoping I might
come see you perform, but I must tell you, even if I had made it, I
would not have spent a late evening at a smoky saloon with loud music, drunk motorcycle riders, and lascivious women. Even in my youth
I did not go in for this kind of evening. You mustn't expect me to now.

I received the music you sent. You of all people know that I don't
have spare time in my days to sit idly and enjoy music, but I have gone
through the tape once. There are nice moments, Albert. I feel that you
are good when you set out to be. But too often you ruin a perfectly good
song with profanity and irony. Your songs about me are snide and absurd. The tone undercuts any positive message that you might have.
Heaven knows I get enough trouble from my enemies. I hardly need it
from you. Keep in mind, Albert, that the proletarian artist is an artist
with a *purpose*. He thinks no more of art for art's sake than a man on a
sinking ship thinks of painting a beautiful picture in his cabin. He

thinks only of getting ashore. When we get ashore, then there will be time for your clever art.

Also, I am no musician, but it seems to me your songs are rather sloppy and ill-formed. There is a lack of symmetry and structure. I fear this is a direct consequence of the dissolute life of the musician. I can only hope that you are showing good sense in matters of personal health and hygiene.

Regards,
Your Father

P.S. I confess that I exaggerated, in the opening of my letter, the extent of the injury I sustained last fall. The truth is, I have been healthy and energetic. (I find that rice and fruit are all a man needs to remain trim and mentally sharp.) You will be glad to know that I feel like I am seventy-five again, and I am deep into a novel that just might turn the tide. I don't know why I should have seen the need to lie to you. I tell you now, it is simply that I am, as always, extraordinarily busy with my teaching, writing, and agitating. It is not easy for me to travel. I dedicate long days to the cause, and I don't see why I should have felt any shame about that. We will meet soon, Albert.

P.S.S. Perhaps it will please you to know that my secretary, Lawrence, is a fan of your work, though he is, I must say, something of a libertine.

Midnight at the Grand

*Perhaps by the time I am a real old man
the social revolution will be over and I will
have some leisure.*

—LETTER TO WILLIAM ELLERY
LEONARD, DEC. 10, 1931

We drive an hour. We drive two hours. We drive four hours, in the cold
clear night, the heater vents slanted in and up toward our hands and our
faces. We see deer by the side of the road, we see waddling possums.
There is a rattle in the right front tire and we wonder how long to stick
with this old car, knowing that we'll guess wrong. We will pay for one
major repair too many. We follow crude directions scrawled on en-
velopes and take lefts on state roads. We watch out because the turn
comes up fast. We take rights on Main. Our children are at home in their
used beds, asleep wearing headphones. The box springs on their beds
are tattered and shot. They say it's fine, no big deal, but it's what we
think about in the night, those bad beds. They were doing OK in school
and then *bam*, all of a sudden. We have to work tomorrow, early, and we
hate the jobs that we're lucky to have. We have seen our coworkers, in

their finals days on the job, pack up their equipment so it can be shipped to the new plant, the new country, and we have not looked them in the eyes. What we have is guilt, relief, and rage. We can't tell if that's ice or water on the dark road. Are we driving on ice? We steer with both hands, reaching occasionally for the flask, the thermos. The price of gas is outrageous.

We cut our headlights as we reach the dark and deserted center of town. The hardware store with the Scandinavian name is having a going-out-of-business sale, everything 50 percent off. Inside, the shelves are cluttered and almost empty. There are red bows on lamp-posts, wreaths behind barred windows, strings of lights swaying wildly in the wind. We drive slowly past the old theater and read the marquee for another movie in which Christmas is threatened and then Christmas is saved. By children who brutalize greedy, sneering adults with crooked teeth. We park on small side streets, five or six blocks away from the theater, and we walk, hats pulled down and scarves pulled up against the blunt wind. We don't think of ourselves as radicals. The lining of our coat pockets is ripped, and our gloved hands float deep inside us. Trash cans are chained to posts, parking meters line the walk like sentries. We look behind us to make sure we're not being followed, then we look again; there is a thrill to the danger. We go through the alley beside the theater and the wind comes harder here, blowing trash at eye level. We look for the narrow black exit door and find it, propped open an inch. We say the password through the dark crack, our mouths so cold that the words come out slurred and heavy. "Dragon's Teeth," we say, and we are admitted. None of us will be turned away.

We enter the darkness on a sticky and slanted floor. The theater is cold and drafty inside, but we feel the human warmth of each other. We smell the wood fires and kerosene, mixed with the smell of old popcorn. There is a small, weak light across the room, a flashlight, and we move toward it, slowly, trying not to run into seats or other people.

When we get there and find two tables set up with large coffeemakers, our hearts fill with gladness. We take off our gloves and whisper, *Please, go ahead. After you.* Maybe we think we see a coworker, but we don't use names, we don't speak or nod. We pass around the flasks and splash whiskey into the black coffee, laughing because we can't see how much we are adding. The hot liquid splashes onto our fingers and the backs of our hands, and it burns and we lick it off. We hold the Styrofoam cups with both hands as the room fills. We are violating fire codes. Everyone who comes will be admitted. We try to find a seat, carrying our coffee in one hand, close to the chest, and holding our other arm out in front to protect it. We don't spill our coffee! We find a seat in the middle of a row. We scoot past others already seated and others scoot past us once we are seated. We whisper, *Excuse me, sorry. No problem.* We say, *Is anyone sitting here?* We say, *There's an empty one over here.* Our boots crunch the unpopped kernels of popcorn. We sink way down into the old cushions and feel the springs pressing through, into our butts and legs, into our backs. We remember theaters like this. Above us there is only darkness, but we know from memory the balcony, the flaking and faded mural, the elaborate gilding and molding. We know the sconces and the heavy velvet curtains, the dusty chandelier that hangs in the dark directly above our heads. We keep our coats on and we are comfortable. The exit door closes quietly and the flashlight turns off, making the darkness complete. We begin to warm up as we sit in black, drink black, breathe black. We don't have a theory of the revolution. We're hunters, a lot of us are. Maybe we read *The Jungle* in high school and maybe we didn't. Some of us tried to go see Upton Sinclair give a speech two years ago. We waited and waited for him in a hot and crowded community center, while a police car loitered in the parking lot. Most of the force was across town, providing security escort for a KKK rally. Sinclair never showed up because he was dead. We got the word after midnight and we all went home. We don't imagine, not now, this same dark theater in one hundred other towns tonight. We don't think of ourselves as part of a movement. Here is our politics: We do not want to be lied to anymore by shithead liars. Also: We're so goddamn tired. We wait in the dark theater and we are not impatient. We go through our lives worrying, creating private spaces in our heads. What could we sell? What could we do without? Where would we stay? Who would take all of us in? Our knees hurt and we take a passing interest in the lives of television stars.

And what can we say of the love, the once-burning love? When we started out, nobody told us we might come to begrudge the soul mate for having a second glass of milk with dinner. We understand our parents much better now, but our parents are dead or they are dying or they don't recognize us anymore.

There is rustling in the projection booth. We do not know quite what to expect here tonight. The new guy at work, the young guy, told us about this theater, this secret midnight showing, during a lunch break last week. He wouldn't say much about it. It's a documentary, he said, made by Preston Geronimo. Had we heard of him? No. Cut your lights when you get to town, he said. Park a few blocks away from the theater and make sure that nobody follows you in. He gave us directions and the password, which changes at every showing. We asked how much it costs and he said it's free. He kept looking around the cafeteria to make sure nobody was listening. He said it's worth our time. We acted uninterested, skeptical, and here we all are.

The film begins without previews, advertisements, or credits. First we hear loud talking and the clinking of bottles and then we see the small dark club, nearly full of people standing by the bar or sitting in booths and at small round tables. Through the smoke we see the young musician in the far corner. There is no stage. This is all filmed with a jittery handheld camera. The sound is garbled and the picture is grainy. Judging by the hairstyles, clothes, and the slogans on beer posters, we guess that the movie is ten or fifteen years old. The jittery

camera is a problem. We put our feet flat on the floor and close our eyes
tightly to fight the dizziness and nausea. We open our eyes and tilt our
heads to see around the heads in front of us. The musician has a guitar
around his neck and the guitar has something written on it, but we
can't make it out because it's too dark and smoky. The musician says,
"OK, then. Let's try this." He's very young and he sings without playing his guitar.

> *I dreamed I saw Sinclair last night*
> *Alive as you or me*
> *Says I, "Sinclair, you're ten times dead"*
> *"I'm back again," says he*
> *"I'm back again," says he*

> *"In Illinois," says I to him*
> *Him looking lean and worn*
> *"They shot you from a catapult"*
> *Says he, "But I'm reborn"*
> *Says he, "But I'm reborn"*

> *"The Sunday critics trash your work*
> *They call you dinosaur*
> *For mixing art with politics"*
> *Says he, "But what's art for?"*
> *Says he, "But what's art for?"*

Nobody in the bar is watching the musician and nobody is listening
to him, but we watch and listen. Is this a folk song? We're pretty sure
that this is a folk song. It is a horrible thing, his nakedness, his principles. His eyes are closed.

> *And as he stood beside my bed*
> *In the middle of the night*

> *Says he, "What they don't realize*
> *You can't kill wrong and right*
> *You can't kill wrong and right"*

Someone in the bar actually shouts "Free Bird!" The people in the bar laugh, but we don't. We slouch and squirm in our seats.

> *"You're not asleep," says he to me*
> *"And I am not your dream*
> *Let's take this country at its word*
> *And see what freedom means*
> *And see what freedom means"*

> *"From San Diego up to Maine,*
> *We'll prove the workers' will*
> *And show the world equality*
> *A beacon on the hill*
> *A beacon on the hill"*

We are stirred and embarrassed. There is solidarity and there is scorn. Our affiliations and sympathies shift and jitter like the camera. We jump from audience to audience, dark theater to dark bar. We want the musician to please stop singing now and we want him to finish courageously. He is admirable and ridiculous.

> *I dreamed I saw Sinclair last night*
> *Alive as you or me*
> *Says I, "But friend, the movement's dead"*
> *"It's back again," says he*
> *"It's back again," says he*

The camera jerks and scans to find the one person clapping, the old bartender. The voice of the person holding the camera says, "Bill, what time is it?" We assume that this is the voice of Preston Geronimo. What kind of name is that, anyway? We wonder if the film's poor quality is by choice or necessity.

A voice beside him, Bill's, says, "Twenty till."

Preston says, "We should go."

They leave, still filming. They walk through a door and up a narrow flight of stairs. The walls are covered with homemade posters for bands and drink specials. Preston trips going up the stairs and nearly falls. The camera records the wild stumble and recovery. Preston says, *"Fuck."* Up ahead Bill turns around. We can only see his shoes and hear him laughing. His shoes are no longer fashionable but they probably will be again. "You OK?" The musician begins another song back in the bar. Preston is breathing heavy. "We can cut that part out," he says.

They walk through the parking lot. We can see Bill's breath in the cold. The camera is driving us crazy. We admit that we expected something more professional. As they approach an old sedan parked at the far edge of the lot, Preston says, "Hey Bill, do you want to introduce yourself?"

Bill turns away from the car, toward the camera. He smiles and puts his finger over his lips. He whispers, "I'm the Socialist's *chauffeur.*"

Preston says, "You have nothing to lose but your license."

Bill gets in the driver's seat and Preston gets in the backseat. Bill starts the car. There is someone in the front passenger seat. Some of us cough. It's a little bug we've not been able to shake. Preston films the space between the two front seats, framed by the head of Bill on the left and the head of muckraker Upton Sinclair on the right. At least we think that's Sinclair. Yes, it is Sinclair, alive as all of us, looking both ancient and much younger than in recent photographs on television and in the newspaper.

Preston says, "Flip on the dome light, Bill."

Sinclair says, "You were gone quite some time."

Bill says, "Sorry."

"I think I nodded off. This is much too late for me."

Bill says something that we can't make out.

"Was he in there?"

"Yes."

"Were there many people there to see him?"

"There were quite a few people there."

"Did you speak to him?"

"No, we were across the bar. And he was playing."

"How did he perform?"

"He was fine. He—"

"Was he clean?"

"Clean?"

"Was he terribly thin? Was he drunk?"

"Mr. Sinclair, he seemed fine to me. Didn't he seem OK to you, Preston?"

"He seemed fine. Completely healthy. Very sincere. We can show it to you later."

"I couldn't bear to watch."

"He seemed fine. He seemed good."

"Not too pale or thin?"

Bill shakes his head.

"No sores on him?"

"I couldn't see any sores, Mr. Sinclair. He looked good to me."

"I take it there was alcohol being served."

"Um. Yes."

"Were there loose women around?"

"I didn't see any loose women. Did you, Preston?"

"Not too many."

"He's just a boy. He's really still just a boy. He seems to think that this is a career."

"He seemed fine. Really."

"Do you think he won the people over to our side?"

"Hard to say."

"Was his hair down in his eyes?"

"Well. It was pretty shaggy, yes."

Sinclair stares at Bill, leaning over into the space between them. Bill puts the car in gear and looks straight ahead while Sinclair turns his head around and stares directly into the camera. His wrecked face fills our big screen like a moon, a planet. We have never seen him like this. We have never seen someone so alive. He is a beautiful old man. Others have said this before, and it is true, we see it now. He stares into the camera, into the theater. His eyes are large and sharp, his nose is big, his top lip is longer than his bottom lip. He is so old and beautiful and we have trouble looking directly at him. On his cheek we cannot be sure if it is the old movie screen or his flesh that is torn. We do not want him to die in this documentary. That seems suddenly like a possibility. The coils in our old seats push through the torn padding and stained fabric, into our legs and backs. Sinclair turns back around and says, "I just hope he wasn't trying to play that harmonica."

Bill turns off the dome light and drives out of the parking lot. Sinclair says. "Is it far from here?"

"Maybe ten minutes."

"We mustn't be late."

"We've got time. We'll take the scenic route."

"Mr. Sinclair," Preston says, "maybe you could say something about your current project."

We are suffering from nausea. The camera is jittery and it is in motion, filming the dark town through the windshield and the windows. This art is making us ill.

"I'm here tonight doing research for a novel," Sinclair says. "And I think that's all I had better say about that."

We can make out boarded-up storefronts covered in graffiti, bundled bodies on the sidewalks, living or dead. At a stoplight, Preston films a prostitute in a fake fur coat, her legs long and bare. She is saying something to the car, but we can't hear it.

"I think she's talking to you, Mr. Sinclair."

Sinclair locks his door.

"Bill grew up here."

"Was it like this?"

Bill says, "It was fine for a while because we got several plants to come in here and there were jobs. But now. Well, you can see. Now we mark time by the gang initiation rituals."

This was a well-known line, years ago, from the stand-up routine of an edgy black comedian who now wears pleated slacks in a sitcom. We remember it and we knew the truth of it. This was our town too. There was the Year of the Severed Pinkies. The Year of the Skull Tattoo. The Year of the Necktie. We never knew quite what was true and what was not. Our local news station made us terrified of young black teens. For instance, *whose* pinkie—the initiate's or a bum's or some poor guy in the Laundromat's? We never knew. We stared at hands that year, trying to know. During the Year of the Necktie, the gang initiates used sharp knives to cut the neckties from the throats of businessman, then they wore the ties around their heads, the checked and striped headbands. Paisley and plaid headbands. They strutted past with golfing headbands, boating headbands. Ties became less popular that year. But then someone said maybe these thugs just bought or stole cheap ties from T.J. Maxx. Did you ever think of that? Nobody actually knew a businessman who had been victimized. Nobody actually knew a businessman. They didn't live in our neighborhoods. We each owned one church tie. An intrepid reporter from the local news station had a weekly piece called "Streetwatch." It was mostly fashion and fluff, but one week he did a little on-air demo—he cut off his own tie beneath the knot and he showed that the cut-off piece wouldn't make a good headband. It actually made two short pieces, neither of which was long enough to fit around the head with enough left over to dangle menacingly down the back of your neck. Urban myth, he concluded, gripping the two short pieces of tie and shaking them at the camera. It was good TV. But then he disappeared shortly after his segment.

Preston says, "Are we still in Honk and Shoot?"

Bill says, "I think so."

Sinclair says, "Is that a gang over there?"

"No, that's just three guys smoking."

Sinclair says, "What is Honk and Shoot?"

"Honk and Shoot is when the gang initiate drives a car up to a red light and when the light turns green, he doesn't go. He just sits there. Then, when someone behind him honks—it only takes a second or two—he gets out of the car and shoots the honker."

Sinclair says, "With a gun?"

"Yes."

"He does this to be accepted into a gang?"

"Yes."

This happened, we remember. Our newspaper had reported two instances and we were all a little anxious, you can imagine. A cab driver without health insurance was in critical condition for months. We sat patiently at green lights, fidgeting with the radios and the vents. When the jobs were gone, we were scared of black people again. There were stories in the paper about their brains and their genes. The new lady on "Streetwatch" did a little segment about how some folks were disconnecting their horns because they didn't trust themselves not to honk when the light turned green.

Sinclair says, "It's so cold to be outside." He scribbles notes in a small notebook.

We see, in beds of glittering glass, newspaper blankets and newspaper shoes. We really feel sick.

Sinclair says, "Why do the Negroes spray-paint everything?"

Bill says, "Mr. Sinclair, do you mind if I smoke?"

Sinclair says, "Very much."

Preston says, "Mr. Sinclair, Bill is a writer too."

Sinclair says, "What have you written?"

We close our eyes to keep from vomiting.

Bill says, "Well, I have a science fiction novel about these people—basically humanoid creatures—who live on another planet and their society is basically unfair but it's a lot better than ours."

"Who published it?"

"It's not published."

"Ah, the capitalist presses. That's an old, old story, let me tell you."

"Well, I haven't sent it out anywhere."

Preston says, "But it's really good. Tell him about it."

"Well, so, on this planet, they pretty much make sure that everyone is taken care of and they have these centralized resources that are shared pretty equally among the citizens. But there are still people who make maybe nine or ten times what other people make."

Sinclair says, "That's hardly fair."

"That's what I'm saying. I know. So there are still basically bosses and workers. It still makes a big difference what kind of family you're born into. There are people there who think this is unfair and they protest and speak out against it. But other people, people at the top, say that an egalitarian system is basically impossible and that it is in their very nature—like this species' *biological* nature—to be the way they are. Like they are naturally competitive, they say, and so they have to compete with one another for resources and ultimately their society reflects their biology."

Sinclair says, "Do people *live* in those things?"

We open our eyes for a second and then close them again. There is no way people live in those things. There is really no place to throw up if we have to throw up.

"In those? I'm afraid so. But basically these creatures have constructed a fairly decent society, with all kinds of safety nets designed to help those who are hurt by the system. It's pretty humane, though that's not the word they use because they don't call themselves human. Well, they don't even speak English, of course, though it's written that way. OK, so then these people design a one-man spaceship that can fly to Earth."

Sinclair laughs. "A spaceship!"

"Yes, a one-man pod, though of course they don't call themselves *men*. That's not important. So this humanoid creature flies to Earth and secretly lands in the desert and—"

"Wouldn't we pick him up with our radar or something?"

"Well, in the book I go to great lengths to explain this cloaking technology that this alien culture has developed."

Preston says, "*Great* lengths."

"So this humanoid guy stays on Earth, in the USA, for six months—they use a different calendar than ours, but it's six months of our time—and he observes what to him looks like a pretty horrible society, with tremendous poverty and violence and pollution and basic indifference. And shopping, a lot of shopping. He's pretty horrified and homesick. It makes his society back at home look incredibly fair and decent, even though he's always been one of the people who argues that it could and should be better. And even though he's outspoken in this way, he's still allowed to be a prominent space traveler, which is another indication of the basic openness and decency of his society. And there are some funny bits—it's not all gloomy—there are things he has to figure out on Earth, like how a toilet works. He lives with Native Americans and he works in a retirement community, cleaning the pool. This would make a good movie, I think. This is a 150-page section that I'm skimming over now."

Sinclair says, "Is that a gang?"

Preston says, "Where?"

Bill says, "There? No."

Preston says, "Those are trash collectors."

"What *happened* here?"

"There were riots, fires."

"Recently?"

"No. Like two, three years ago."

We open our eyes to see the scorched buildings and empty lots. What kind of movie makes you sick to watch it?

Bill says, "So he collects a bunch of data and he leaves and returns to his planet. And on the way home—it's a long, *long* trip—he has this idea. He decides to *lie* when he returns and gives his report about Earth. It's this huge deal where once they give him a medical exam he goes to their version of the capital to give a report on his findings. And it's going to be on their version of television, which, I should say, is far less culturally significant and, well, dumb as American television. And he decides to tell a whopper."

Preston says, "Hey, look at that. On your right."

We open our eyes and see the big red shovel spray-painted on the boards of a boarded-up storefront.

The camera shifts to Sinclair, who is craning his neck and squinting to see the graffiti.

"Vandals," he says.

We chuckle quietly. Was that funny? We start to feel better. Still a little queasy, but not bad. We wonder has there been any thought given to cutting or editing any of this material? We can't figure out if this film has been crafted in the least, if the sloppiness is anything more than sloppiness. But we're strangely interested in the basic plot of Bill's utopian novel. We share the sticky armrests with our neighbors.

"And so he goes before the politicians and he gives his report and he tells this huge lie about how Earth people had created an egalitarian society. He bases it on his own blueprint for a fair society, based on years of discussions he's had with friends and what we call professors. He's had a long time to work this out because the trip home from Earth takes, like, six of our Earth years. He developed the plan with incredible specificity and detail, and he reports this plan he's worked out, but he says it's been achieved on Earth. And it's a gigantic lie, right? His friends are onto him, but they don't say anything. He makes the point that the humans on Earth are biologically very similar to his own people, and so there is nothing *naturally* prohibitive about this type of society. And the people—not people, but you know, *creatures*—are just blown away by his report and it creates a huge stir. Their natural competitive urges kick in and they don't want to finish second to this Earth in economic justice. The guy, the clever space traveler, had intentionally included in his plan a few minor things in his blueprint that were inefficient and unfair and poorly planned, so that his people could recognize them and improve upon them and feel good about themselves. Basically, it takes a long time—I'm really skimming a big section here—but basically this society shifts over to the so-called Earth Model, with some significant modifications and improvements arrived at through serious deliberation, and it works. I mean, it takes a lot of fine-tuning and hard work and deliberation, but basically it works and this society achieves—"

Sinclair says, "I rather like that, young man. I always find endings difficult."

"That's not the end."

"Send that to Morris at RSP. I'll tell him to be looking for it. You might need to trim it down."

"Well, but there's quite a bit more to the book. Because after one hundred of our years or so, humans on Earth develop the technology to fly to this planet."

Sinclair says, "Do you know where this meeting takes place?"

Bill says, "Yes."

Preston says, "This is the best part."

Sinclair says, "Are we almost there?"

Bill says, "Almost."

We keep our eyes open now and see the car come to a stop behind another car at a stoplight. Bill shifts to neutral and turns toward Sinclair. "The astronaut from Earth comes and sees this other planet, the one that has developed this incredibly just society based on the bogus Earth Model. And by this time, the space traveler who had traveled to

Earth is dead—their life spans are similar to ours—and he took his secret with him to the grave. Well, they don't really have graves, but you know what I mean. So the planetary lore is that the great, wise, fair people of Earth had inspired the humanoids to create a better society."

Sinclair says, "But that wasn't true at all."

Bill says, "I know, but they don't know that. On this planet, the people of Earth are celebrated and mythologized and held in great esteem. And so the Earth astronaut—who is this bowlegged Texan with a crewcut—receives an incredibly warm welcome and the humanoids line the streets and throw their version of confetti into the air, which is confetti that is biodegradable and doesn't need to be cleaned up by cleanup crews the next day. And it's probably worth mentioning here that the basic custodial work of the society is done by rotating crews of citizens. Kind of like jury duty."

When the light turns green, the car ahead does not move. Sinclair says, "Let's go." He leans over and taps the horn.

Bill shouts, "Oh my God, don't do that!"

Preston says, "Not good. Not good at all."

Sinclair says, "We're going to be late."

Preston says, "Not good." He zooms in on the car ahead, which looks to us like a Ford Fiesta.

The driver's-side door opens and Preston says, "Bill, go back. Go backward. Reverse."

"I can't, there's a car behind us."

The camera swings wildly to the headlights in the back window, and then back to the front.

Bill says, "Oh, God. I love you, Mom. Did you get that, Preston? Mom, I love you!"

Preston says, "Should we make a run for it?"

Bill shouts something that we can't make out. Sinclair appears to be writing in his notebook.

A man gets out of the car ahead, a balding, middle-age white guy in a flannel shirt and padded vest. He waves apologetically and Bill says, "Wait. No. Wait."

The light turns yellow and the car behind waits patiently.

Sinclair whispers, "Is he a gang?"

Bill says, "I don't think so."

The man walks over to Bill's side of the car and Bill cracks the window.

The man says, "Sorry, we're a bit lost. Are you by any chance going to the thing? The meeting?"

Bill says, "No. Sorry."

Sinclair leans over. "Yes," he says. "Yes, we are."

The man peers into the car. The light turns red, we can see the red glow in the night. He says, "Hey, is that *Sinclair*?"

Bill says, "No."

Sinclair says, "Yes, but do not tell anyone. I'm just doing some research, keeping a very low profile. Follow us to the meeting. Quick, we're going to be late."

The man looks excited. "OK, I'll follow you. I'll follow. I'll hurry." He jogs back to his car and gets in.

Bill hits the steering wheel. "That was so stupid. That guy could be a mole. He could be a cop. He could be a *killer*. Jesus."

"He's fine," Sinclair says. "I've got a good sense about these things."

Bill says something that we can't make out.

Sinclair says, "Go. It's green."

The man ahead pulls to the side and lets us by. That's how we feel, sitting in the dark theater, that he's letting *us* by.

Bill says, "*Jesus*. Jesus, that was awful. Do not mess with the horn, Mr. Sinclair. Just keep your hands over there."

"Your mom will be touched, Bill."

"We're cutting this whole part out."

"Finish telling me about the book."

"I don't feel like it now."

Preston says, "Finish. Come on."

Bill says, "That was terrible. That was just—my God, my heart is still racing. That was terrible."

Preston says, "But it was like a Fiesta, I think."

Bill says, "Still. Jesus, do not mess with the horn. I do *not* want to get shot. I need a cigarette."

Sinclair says, "Please finish telling me about the novel."

Preston says, "Yeah, come on."

"God. Where was I?"

"The confetti."

"Do not touch the horn."

"Yes, no, I won't."

"So, whatever, they give this big Texan a grand welcome. And they have banners that say they love Earth, love the USA. They have managed to find out what the American flag looks like and they have mass-produced it—except they included way too many stars, like seventy—but they have these flags and they're waving them around. The Texan can't believe it. He's soaking it up. He feels like he's landed back at home. Except one thing that seems a little strange to him as he makes his way around is that everyone here seems to enjoy a nice standard of living. And the leaders and important people who are showing him around don't seem to have opulent houses or cars. I mean, they're pretty nice, but nothing special. And there aren't many police around, and they don't carry any firearms. And the planet is *clean* and most people use mass transit. The whole thing is really weird to him and kind of creepy. And then it quickly becomes evident that something is wrong. All the people on this planet want to talk to him about how they've modeled this society on the society of the USA on Earth."

"But that's not what happened at all."

"Right. And how one hundred years ago they lived in an unfair, market-driven society in which some people actually made *ten times* more money than others, but after the secret space mission to Earth, they were able to create this really decent planet. Sure, they had some problems, but it was so much better than it used to be. And the Texan finally says, 'Wait, wait, *wait*. Wait just a second. You're right, the USA is the best damn country in the universe, or in any universe, but we ain't communist. You got it all wrong. We don't have this sissy robot society where everybody's equal. People have to work for what they get. You work hard, you can have a decent life. But those at the top aren't dragged down by having to support all the losers at the bottom.'"

Preston says, "There's the warehouse, right there. But let's park a few blocks away. Cut your lights."

Bill cuts the lights and drives slowly past the warehouse. He talks more quietly now. "And the people of this planet are just kind of shocked. They stop waving their flags and throwing the organic, eco-friendly confetti and they go home to their modest houses with shared kitchen and bathroom facilities. So it comes out that their famous space traveler, who was considered to be something like the midwife of egalitarianism, lied about Earth one hundred years ago, and they had modeled their society after a lie, after something that didn't really exist. They find his old journal, some old documents, and the whole lie comes to light. His descendents are embarrassed. And the Texan is miffed and really creeped out by the fairness. He leaves early in his spaceship to return to Earth."

While Bill parks on a dark side street and turns off the car, Preston turns and films the other car as it pulls in behind. "And on his way home—it's a long, long trip, like four years—the U.S. astronaut has an idea, which is fairly unusual for him. He decides, on this long trip back, that he will *lie* about what he has seen on this planet. He does not want any of the few remaining hippies and radicals on Earth to get any big ideas of what is possible." We see the two faces, turned toward each other. "He does not want to fuel any utopian movements back home. They've been pretty much shut down and snuffed out, and he doesn't want to bring them back. Let the sleeping dog lie and all that. He's not exactly smart, but he's smart enough to know that you should never ignore or underestimate the threat of the Left. Best not to give the smelly freaks any traction. He has a long time to construct his story, to rehearse it, down to specifics and details. And when he gets home—after the medical check and the hero's welcome and the parades with American confetti—he gives his report. It's on TV. Well, first he kisses the ground of the runway. It's the photo in all the papers and magazines, this astronaut kissing the ground of the USA. And also he tells the truth to high-ranking military officials, who immediately draw up a policy of surveillance and containment. They're concerned about galactic dominoes. In the report that he gives to Congress and the nation, the astronaut says that he has seen a truly brutal and ruthless society that does not honor freedom and democracy. He says the people live in fear and squalor. He says he barely made it out of there alive. He says we all live in the best nation in the universe, of any universe, God bless us."

"My word," Sinclair says. "That is dark."

Preston says, "There's a little more."

"After he leaves the other planet, the people there are freaked out because their whole way of life has been modeled on a lie. Perhaps justice and decency are not really a part of their nature, after all, and so perhaps it is not possible to live equitably and harmoniously. They've been duped. They get anxious and paranoid, and things start to fall apart. Gradually at first, and then suddenly, when trust and goodwill break down completely. And then people become really weird and fearful, and they start grabbing what they can, and there is violence and chaos, and within five years' time—what we call years—the society has devolved into a brutal and inequitable and inhospitable place that does not value freedom and democracy, with a few families and clans wealthy enough to live well and barricade themselves against the squalid, rioting masses."

Sinclair says, "And that's it? It ends there?"

Bill looks exhausted. "Pretty much, yes."

"That is really something," Sinclair says. He writes quickly in his notebook.

"What's it called?"

Bill says, "It's called *The Lies*."

Preston says, "It's fifteen hundred Earth pages."

We will try to remember to look up this novel to see if Bill ever got it published.

Sinclair says, "Send it to Morris. But if I could make a suggestion, I'd say cut everything after the creation of that fair society."

Bill says something that we can't make out, and he and Preston laugh. They get out of the car. The bald guy in flannel and his friend come along too. Bill lights a cigarette.

The bald guy says, "Mr. Sinclair, I—"

Bill says, "Shhh."

They walk four blocks in the dark cold. They walk quickly, looking back twice to make sure nobody is following. We cannot see much in the dark, but from what we see, it looks like a bomb fell here. We hear distant shouting and laughing and yelling, sirens and songs, the rappers boasting about still being alive. The sirens come from the rap song or the documentary city or our theater town, we're not sure which. The group turns down an alley beside the warehouse and comes to a narrow door that is open an inch. Preston jogs in place to stay warm, which we wish he would not do. Bill whispers something into the dark crack of the door, we cannot hear what, and then the door opens quickly and we all move into the dark and that is the last we see of anything. Preston is still filming, but he's filming the darkness. The theater is as dark as the warehouse and the warehouse is as dark as the theater. We cannot see the cups we drink from. We hear them climb stairs and enter a room. There is a small, dim light in the back of the room, but it is not enough to see by. The room sounds big. The sounds of the footsteps and the scraping of chair legs on the floor seem to echo and carry high into the ceiling. Our hearing improves in the dark. We hear a plane pass overhead and we hear tires screech on the streets below. "Here are some chairs." We think it's Bill talking. "Would you like some coffee, Mr. Sinclair?" Sinclair says, "No, I shouldn't, not at this hour." Then he says, "Yes, actually, I would love some, please. Nothing in it." Bill gets up and walks away. We hear the people entering and sitting, coughing and whispering and slurping their hot coffee. Bill returns. This kind of darkness leads to resignation and then acceptance and then something like trust. It's comforting, even, not the privacy or anonymity of it, but the completeness, the immersion. We're all in it, we're all blind, and we forget for a moment about guns and the long drive home, the Christmas shopping. Eventually a voice says, "Welcome, everyone. Welcome. Thank you for coming. Let's go ahead and get started. I'll moderate tonight." The voice might be old or young, male or female, we'll not say. The other voices grow quiet. "We're accustomed to saying that we are joined in these meetings by the spirit of Upton Sinclair, but tonight, tonight I am told—though I fear this is a joke at my expense—I am told that he joins us in the flesh." All of us in the warehouse and the theater want to applaud, but we fear the noise and we're holding cups of coffee, so we pat our thighs with our open hands, all of us, and the sound is like night rain. The moderator says, "We are a crowd of believers, I see. Mr. Sinclair, if you're here, would you like to say a few words before we begin?" There is complete silence then, a silence to match the blackness, and we hold our breath and wait. The moderator says, "No? Mr. Sinclair? If you're with us?" Again there is a silence, measured out by the beating of our hearts. "No?" The moderator's voice is a summons, soothing and occult. We all wait a surprisingly long time, far beyond the point at which it is clear to everyone that Sinclair will not speak. And then we hear the old man clear his throat, he can't hold back any longer. He says, "Yes, I am here." He waits for our muted applause to die down. "Thank you all for your warm reception. I had wanted my presence here tonight to remain a secret. I am here to do research for a novel, and I do not want my attendance at this meeting to alter or affect what takes place. So I ask that you carry on as you normally would. I am here only to observe, so that I may record your struggle accurately. But I want to congratulate you on your courage and your conviction." There is more slapping of thighs. The moderator's voice says, "Thank you, Mr. Sinclair. It's an honor and a thrill for us that you're here, even as an observer." We hear Sinclair stand from his chair. He says, "Forgive me. I'll be brief. You need to understand that you are part of a proud tradition. I was at a meeting very much like this one in 1936 in Flint, Michigan, where the UAW planned its sit-down strikes at General Motors. We had the big, burly workers set up at the light switches so nobody could sneak up and turn on the lights. If you learn nothing else from me to-night, there's a good tip: Put your big fellows by the light switches." We laugh soundlessly and Sinclair sits down. The moderator says, "Thank you. We should have thought of that a long time ago." Sinclair says, "Please, carry on." The moderator says, "Well, I feel certain that your research will be fruitful tonight. And while we are inspired by your presence, I can assure you that it will in no way affect what—" Sinclair stands again and his chair scrapes the floor. He says, "And then we took the battle to Henry Ford. And my God, what a struggle! But we won." We pat our thighs some more. "But I fear we've lost that ground and we need to win it back." Sinclair's voice is not as loud now. No, it is still as loud, but it is not as close. He is moving away from Preston's camera, making his way down an aisle of workers and toward the front of the room, where the moderator stands. Anyone could grab him in the dark and strangle him, anyone could hit him in the back of the head with a blunt object. He is talking and moving at the same time. How is he moving so nimbly through the dark warehouse? He says, "I will just be a moment. I will just start the meeting, if I may." He is out in front of us now, all of us, and his voice is strong and clear. He asks how many of us have watched our friends lose their jobs without so much as a notice. We slap our thighs. He asks how many of us work more than forty hours per week with no overtime pay. We slap our thighs. He is a religious man, ultimately. He asks how many of us are too tired at the end of the day to spend good time with our families. Our thighs are sore from the beating. And how many of us grow further and further in debt each year, he asks. It is true, yes, all of it. Sinclair has become a character in his fiction and maybe it's bad fiction, like the reviewers say, maybe it's embarrassing. But this isn't fiction. This is our lives and we are moved. He says that they want us to work faster, harder, more efficiently. And they tell us to work hard to get ahead, but in truth we work so hard, he says, just to hang on to what little we have. This strong old voice in the dark. We've got to fight back, he says. We want to cry or shout out. Our eyes ache from trying to make him out in the blackness. But if we cannot see him, surely we cannot shoot him, not this night. He says that he has seen people organize and bring about change. He says it takes courage and it takes imagination. He waits for the scream of the ambulance siren to recede. Sinclair, who has witnessed a century of horror, who has been killed countless times, tells us that for every act of greed, hatred, and violence, for each Ludlow Massacre, he has witnessed one hundred acts of compassion and cooperation. Do not, he says, tell him that we cannot remake our world. Do not! And, he tells us, he knows this is not a union state, but there is a kind of union that they cannot deny us. When the noise dies down, he says he will tell us what needs to be done and we all grow quiet and for an hour he speaks and we listen. We cannot repeat what he says. And then he takes questions from the warehouse workers, many of whom, like us, have to be at work in a few hours. His voice grows hoarse. He stays and talks with them until they must leave. Preston remains in the warehouse, filming the blackness, ultimately pointing the camera at the small, dim light at the end of the big room. He leaves the camera there and yes the symbolism is heavy but we don't care. We stare at the distant light and we sit in the silence. And how long is it before we understand what the light on the screen means? Five minutes, or ten. Not just symbol, but invocation. It means the film is not over. One of us enters it, speaks, one of us volunteers to moderate, and eventually we all join in. It happens here and it happens in other old theaters in other towns, as well, as it has for the last ten or fifteen years. We talk of what must be done and we are filled with a sense of possibility, of creation. We cannot tell what it is we say, you will see soon enough. Some of us are filming. When we are finished talking, when it is getting too late to stay any longer, we leave through the narrow door, back out to the cold alley, the gusty wind. We nod good-bye to one another and we pull our hats down, our scarves up. It is so cold out here and we can see now, we can see sharply, and what we see is another dreary town. Painted bricks and potholes, iron bars over windows and doors, the red bows on lampposts. We lost one of our gloves in the theater. We find our cars, half expecting to see the Fiesta parked behind. Our heaters take forever to blow warm. We make the long drive home, slapping our faces to stay awake, swerving to miss the deer. And once we are alone, we understand that the hardest thing, the hardest thing of all, will be to keep, somehow, the faith.

Chestnuts

I wish there had been more humor,
so that I could lighten up the story.
                    —*I, CANDIDATE FOR GOVERNOR:*
                    AND HOW I GOT LICKED

Upton Sinclair walks into a bar. It's a pretty rough place. Bartender says, "What'll it be, old-timer?"

Sinclair says, "Do you have cranberry juice? I'm parched."

So the bartender shoots him with a gun.

•

It's Upton Sinclair with a black guy, a Jew, a Mexican, a redneck, and an Eskimo. They're in New York City and it's dinnertime and everyone is getting hungry.

So the black guy goes, "Check it out, let's go get some fried chicken."

And the Jew replies, "No, I'd prefer some matzo balls."

And the Mexican says, "Come on, *hombres,* I'm in the mood for some tacos."

And the redneck starts eyeing the squirrels across the street in the park.

And the Eskimo says, "Nook, nook. Good whale joint around corner. Nook, nook."

And Upton says, "Wait, wait, wait. Everyone just hold on. I think I've been shot by Joe Gerald Huntley."

•

How many former Sinclair secretaries does it take to screw in a lightbulb?

How many?

There are no former Sinclair secretaries.

•

So these captains of industry hire a couple goons to find Upton Sinclair, take him out to the desert, and kill him. These thugs find Upton, put him in a black car, and take him out to the desert. It's blazing hot. Middle of the day. Cow skulls, tumbleweeds, cactuses. Buzzards overhead and all that. These guys, instead of killing Upton right away, they make him start digging his own grave. They're those kind of guys. So they're sitting in the air-conditioned car while the old man is digging a hole in the sand with a shovel. Every time he makes a little progress, the wind blows sand back into his hole. Once in a while the goons unroll the windows to say, "Hurry up. We ain't got all day." Sinclair, he's digging, and then all of a sudden his shovel hits something metal. He bends down and uncovers a small golden lamp. Then he—

Wait. This is the one with the genie?

Yes.

I've heard it. Where the genie shoots him?

What? No, no. This is a different one.

Because I already heard the one where he wishes for Socialism and the genie shoots him. That's a good one.

This is a different one.

I've heard that other one.

This is different.

OK.

So Sinclair finds this lamp and he's brushing the sand off it. The goons in the car are eating sandwiches and they don't see Sinclair put down his shovel. He's cleaning off the lamp and then of course this genie comes out and says, "I'm the genie in the lamp. Thank you for finding me out here in the desert. I will grant you three wishes." Sinclair says, "Anything I want?" The genie says, "Anything." It's about this time that the goons notice that Sinclair is talking to a genie and not digging his own grave, so they get out of the car with their big guns. Sinclair says, "Genie, my first wish is to get out of here right now." The genie says, "Smart wish," then he claps his hands and Sinclair suddenly finds himself, along with the genie, in a cozy log house in the middle of a cool green forest. There is a fire in the fireplace. There is a bubbling creek outside the window. All that. Sinclair says, "Hey. Nice." The genie says, "What is your second wish?" Without hesitating, Sinclair says, "My second wish is that our cruel and greedy capitalist nation would transition peacefully into a just and cooperative Socialist state within one year's time." The genie, he goes absolutely nuts. He says, "Are you kidding me? Think about that for one second. Do you know how difficult that would be? People in power don't tend to give up that power very easily, pal. The rich people have the guns and the tanks. The rich people have the media and the corporations and the lobbyists. And just think of all the ideological barriers to this transition—the individualism, the patriotism, the meritocracy. Anti-communism. The American dream. Social Darwinism. Social mobility. The fluid, classless society. Racism. And then there's television and the schools and the Jesus freaks. My God, we couldn't even convince the people who would stand to gain—which is just about everyone—much less the CEOs and tycoons and warlords. How in the world are we going to pull this off peacefully? A novel sure as hell ain't going to do it, I'll tell you that. And Jesus Christ, *one year*? One year? You want to do this in a year? I'm a genie, I'm not fucking Zeus. I'm not fucking Donald Rumsfeld. Give me a break. Skip that one. Tell me what your third wish is." Sinclair, he's pretty bummed out by the genie's reaction. He's spent a century fighting for Socialism, and now here's this genie telling him it's impossible. He sits down by a window and stares out at the bubbling creek. He thinks for a while about a modest third wish. Then he perks up a bit, but he looks sort of sheepish. He says, "Well..." The genie says, "Go ahead." Sinclair says, "I don't know. I was thinking..." The genie says, "Look, there's no need to be embarrassed. You wouldn't believe some of the selfish and lurid things people wish for. I've heard it all. Fire away." Sinclair says, "I just feel bad about wishing this when there are so many people suffering." The genie says, "Is it a bigger dick you want? Just say it. We can do that." Sinclair says, "My God, no. Stop talking like that. My third wish—OK, I'll say it—my third wish is to get just a couple good reviews on my next book." The genie just stands there, considering. He rubs his chin with his hand and he stares into the fire for a long time. The bubbling creek bubbles outside. Finally he says, "Listen, buddy, would you settle for eighteen months on that Socialism deal?"

Fame Is Tiered Like a Stadium or a Well-Landscaped Yard

DODGE: Hello and good evening. For those of you on the East Coast, good morning. Welcome to *Arena*. I'm Paulson Dodge, host of *Arena*. Tonight I think we have a very compelling program for you. We will be talking about the "Men Who Have Killed Upton Sinclair." I have four guests joining me in the *Arena* studio. My first guest requires no introduction. He is on television more than the president. He is the author of four best-selling and award-winning books on three-time Sinclair assassin Joe Gerald Huntley, and he is most recently the editor of a collection of Huntley's letters from prison called *Incarcerated Patriot*. He is currently serving as a lead adviser on an upcoming movie about Huntley, starring, I believe, Nicolas Cage. He has been a guest on *Arena* many times. I'd like to welcome back Lionel T. Pratt. Good evening, Mr. Pratt.

PRATT: Good evening, Paulson. It's nice to be back.

DODGE: I take it that Nick Cage is playing you in the movie.

PRATT: My wife and daughters wish that were true, Paulson.

DODGE: My second guest is George Felton, author of two books about Grady Law Smith, the Sinclair assassin known as the Amarillo Harpooner. Paroled, I believe, two weeks ago. Is that correct?

FELTON: Yes. Two weeks exactly.

DODGE: George Felton also oversees the most popular Sinclair

147

assassination Web site in the U.S. It's called Beware the Ides dot-com and it says here, George, that you get forty thousand hits per day.

FELTON: Actually, it's a bit more than that.

DODGE: Amazing. Mr. Felton has appeared twice on our program. Welcome back to *Arena*, George.

FELTON: Thank you, Paulson. Nice to see you, Lionel.

PRATT: Hello, George.

DODGE: My third guest is Dr. Anthony Estep, assistant professor of history at Hooper College. He is the author of *Cult of Huntley*, and he teaches courses on the third wave of Sinclair assassinations, 1991 to 1997. Welcome to the show, Dr. Estep.

ESTEP: It's my pleasure, Paulson. Good evening, gentlemen.

PRATT: Good evening.

FELTON: Hello.

DODGE: I want to thank my final guest, Rudy Peebles, for filling in on very short notice.

PEEBLES: *M.* Rudy Peebles.

DODGE: My apologies. M. Rudy Peebles. My original guest, Walter Sizemore, curator of the Museum of Upton Sinclair Assassination, fell ill and was forced to cancel, and Rudy agreed to join us. Or M. Rudy, rather. M. Rudy is writing a book called *Fatal Volley: Randy Holiday Swan, the Tennis Court Assassin.* Thanks for coming, M. Rudy.

PEEBLES: It is a great honor to be here, Paulson. I never thought I'd be in the same room with these three gentlemen. And on TV too. What a thrill. Lionel, I can't begin to tell you what your work has meant to me.

PRATT:

PEEBLES: I actually own the bullet from the Madison Miracle.

ESTEP: One out of every three Americans owns the bullet from the Madison Miracle.

DODGE: OK, let's begin. And of course, as always, we must turn to

Lionel Huntley—to Lionel *Pratt*, rather—I beg your pardon, Mr. Pratt—because any discussion of Sinclair assassination must begin with Joe Gerald Huntley.

PRATT: Indeed.

PEEBLES: Indeed. Yes.

DODGE: You have spent a great deal of time with Joe Gerald Huntley. Could you just tell us what he is like in person?

PRATT: There is no denying that Joe Gerald Huntley is pretty rough around the edges. He is a high school dropout. He came from a poor family in a very poor town. He is not what you would call sophisticated. But I will tell you this: You can find Huntley in the prison library a lot more often than in the prison weight room. He is an avid reader and a real student of history and politics. After many hours in his company, I have come to see that he is intelligent and thoughtful. And politically astute. Beneath the anger.

PEEBLES: This is sounding a *lot* like Randy Holiday Swan.

DODGE: Mr. Pratt, do you think Huntley is mellowing with age?

PRATT: No. I wouldn't put it like that.

DODGE: How would you put it then?

PRATT: We all change when we get older. Certainly, Joe is not the hothead he once was. He is not consumed with what he once called righteous rage. But he is still an intense guy. And still a dangerous guy, if your name happens to be Upton Sinclair.

DODGE: And would you please explain, as you've done here before, why Huntley has dedicated his entire adult life to killing Sinclair?

PRATT: Certainly. This is interesting because Huntley, like most of the Sinclair assassins that have followed him, comes from a poor family. His father was a mill worker who got laid off. His mother was chronically ill and died when Huntley was still in his teens. Huntley himself flirted with the Left when he was a young man, but then he was drafted into the army and served two tours of duty in Vietnam, where he witnessed the horrors caused by nondemocratic forms of governance. The diaries are pretty explicit about his hatred of communism and of American peaceniks. Huntley sees Sinclair's politics as a grave threat to the individual and to the world. He is a fierce proponent of competition and free markets. He believes in a thoroughly American ideal of the man who overcomes the limitation of his circumstances to achieve greatness, to transcend his place and time. He believes noncompetitive systems eradicate this ambition and this potential for greatness. He himself was—and is—very ambitious. The ethos of sharing and of the common man, and all of Sinclair's rhetoric about humanity in general—without reference or regard to the individual—does not sit well with Huntley. Not well at all.

DODGE: And so he has assassinated Sinclair.

PRATT: Yes.

PEEBLES: *Nailed* him.

DODGE: Three times, in fact. And he is eligible for parole at what time?

PRATT: Four more years.

DODGE: Is it your feeling that he will attempt to kill Sinclair again, given the opportunity?

PRATT: I have little doubt that he will try. He still believes he has what it takes and he bristles at the suggestion that his career is over. He's not likely to set down his rifle. The kids are going to have to run him off the field. Certainly Huntley is not as young as he once was and the competition has gotten pretty tough. There are a lot of well-trained and well-prepared assassins. When Huntley started out, it was just a bunch of farm boys and hunters with pitchforks and rusty shotguns. It has become professionalized. It's much more of a science now. He created a science, I guess you might say. Things have really changed, and Huntley is the one who changed it.

FELTON: You played no small role yourself, Lionel.

PEEBLES: Yes, Lionel.

PRATT: I'm a reporter. I've simply reported. That is all.

DODGE: And if he strikes again, will you be there to report it?

PRATT: I feel that it's my duty.

DODGE: Much has been written about a potential link between Huntley and the CIA. What is your stance on this issue?

PRATT: The data is inconclusive. I have tried to stick to the facts and stay out of speculation and conspiracy theory.

DODGE: What is your impression of Huntley's reputation among the American public?

PRATT: His approval rating is 65 percent. Not as high as it once was, but still strong. He is by far the most recognized Sinclair assassin internationally. He receives thousands of fan letters every day.

DODGE: And can you talk about when and how you first became interested in Huntley?

PRATT: When Huntley shot Sinclair the first time, in '73—

PEEBLES: March 15th.

PRATT: I was in the middle of my last semester of journalism school. I of course remember exactly where I was when I heard the news.

PEEBLES: Don't we all. I was in second grade. Mrs. Harris told us and then let us have a party.

PRATT: Excuse me.

DODGE: M. Rudy, we'll get to you.

PEEBLES: Sorry.

PRATT: I was in the student center, drinking coffee and studying for an exam and wondering if I really wanted to be in school. Frankly, I was considering dropping out and going into business with my father in Columbus, Ohio. I had lost interest in journalism. But then Huntley shot Sinclair in the head and I saw the footage of him being led away in handcuffs. It's that famous footage—his arrogant line about aiming for Sinclair's heart; the people cheering him on; the cops putting him gingerly in the car; the way he smiled in the backseat. There was just something about him. I wanted to know more. I wanted to become an expert. I wanted to know more about Joe Gerald Huntley than any other person in the world. So I finished school and for the first time felt a passion for what I was doing.

DODGE: You're watching *Arena*. We are talking tonight about the men who have killed Upton Sinclair. Let's turn now to George Felton. George, talk about Grady Law Smith.

FELTON: Well, I should say first off that I feel pretty humbled being here with Lionel. I need to preface my remarks by saying that Grady Law Smith is just not in the same league as Joe Gerald Huntley. No other Sinclair assassin has that kind of hold over the American imagination. Smith has that stutter. He is overweight and slovenly, and he just doesn't have the stature or the mythic persona of Huntley. Huntley has that great hair. Very few people remember exactly where they were when Smith harpooned Sinclair.

ESTEP: He's no Huntley.

PEEBLES: Huntley really does occupy a special—

PRATT: Come on, George, you're being too modest here. Grady Law Smith has an undeniable charisma and flair. The harpoon was unusual and daring. There's the whole Texas ethos. Huntley, of course, was impressed.

DODGE: Was he?

PRATT: Yes, he was in prison at the time. And when he found out, he reportedly said, "Ain't nobody that'll remember me now."

ESTEP: Probably apocryphal. It's the account of a prison guard.

PRATT: I've looked into it and I have reason to believe it is true.

FELTON: I appreciate that, Lionel.

DODGE: So how did you come to write about Smith?

FELTON: In college I had read Lionel's books on Huntley and I was just really blown away. It's something I was interested in doing—heck, everyone was—but it didn't seem like a realistic career goal. It felt more like a childish fantasy. I was covering city hall in Amarillo when Smith killed Sinclair in '78, so I was right there, close to the action. And I called Pratt on the phone. I still can't believe I did that. I didn't know him, had never met him. I just called him up out of the blue and asked him if he was going to cover it. I didn't want to step on his toes. And he said no. He said he had his hands full with Huntley. He told me to go for it. But I of course learned everything I know about assassination writing from Lionel. He taught a generation.

DODGE: Mr. Pratt, do you remember George's phone call?

PRATT: Vaguely.

PEEBLES: Funny thing, I had read about George calling Lionel like that, so when Randy Holiday Swan gunned down Sinclair, I called Mr. Pratt, as well. His wife said he was in the shower.

FELTON: Randy Swan did not *gun down* Sinclair.

PEEBLES: Yes, he did.

FELTON: He shot Sinclair in the thigh and Sinclair died twenty-three days later.

PEEBLES: Twenty-one.

DODGE: Let's turn to Dr. Estep. Can you give us a brief historical perspective?

ESTEP: There's no doubt about it, Huntley's reputation is secure, thanks in no small part to the truly extraordinary work of Mr. Pratt. He's still as popular as ever among students. His diary is in its seventeenth printing. Certainly, there have been other important assassins— Smith, Purdy, McDaniels.

PEEBLES: Randy Hol—

ESTEP: But most, if not all, of these second-tier assassins deliberately emulated Huntley. They studied him, they copied him. They copied his methods and tactics, and even his hairstyle, his clothes. Huntley made them want to kill Sinclair, and he showed them how to do it. There have been a lot of flashes in the pan through the years, but nothing like Huntley. He had a style and a passion that people respond to, especially young people. My senior seminar on Huntley and Pratt is overenrolled, year in and year out. He had that special something.

PRATT: And I can tell you that he still has it.

PEEBLES: You better believe it.

ESTEP: Yes, yes. I don't mean to suggest otherwise.

DODGE: We're almost out of time. M. Rudy, how is the book on Randy Holiday Swan coming?

PEEBLES: *Fatal Volley* is nearing—

ESTEP: Hold on. Did anyone else notice that when Swan first shot Sinclair—

FELTON: In the *thigh*.

PRATT: From close range.

ESTEP: Yes, when Swan first shot Sinclair in the thigh from close range on a sunny, windless day on an almost empty public tennis court, when this was first reported, his name was just Randy Swan. Just Randy Swan. But then at some point during the coverage, he suddenly became Randy *Holiday* Swan. Did anyone else notice this?

FELTON: I did.

PEEBLES: He was always Randy Holiday Swan. From the very beginning, when he fired that shot along the service line that will echo on through history.

ESTEP: He shot Sinclair in the leg and then was beaten unconscious, with a tennis racket, by Sinclair's secretary.

PEEBLES: He set off a historic chain of events, culminating in the painful death of Upton Sinclair.

ESTEP: He made a mockery of Sinclair assassination. He set us back fifteen, twenty years.

PEEBLES: He was always Randy Holiday Swan.

FELTON: He did not kill Sinclair.

PEEBLES: Not immediately. He made him suffer.

ESTEP: Three weeks after the shooting, Sinclair, without a noticeable limp, checks himself into the hospital for walking pneumonia and is poisoned by a hospital orderly named Wayne Dillard Moses.

PEEBLES: Weakened immune system. Infected thigh. Historic chain of events. Randy Holiday Swan was a protégé of Huntley. Huntley took notice.

DODGE: Mr. Pratt, we have time for one last word. Care to comment on Huntley's reaction to the tennis court assassin?

PRATT: Well. Yes. Joe Gerald Huntley did indeed take notice of Swan's botched assassination. He read about it in the newspaper. He read quietly and patiently, and when he was through, he folded the newspaper carefully and placed it on the floor next to his cot. And then he said, "I am no more responsible for Randy Swan than America is responsible for Upton Sinclair."

DODGE: Fine last words. I want to thank all of my guests. Lionel T. Pratt, George Felton, Anthony Estep, and M. Rudy Peebles. You've been watching *Arena*. Tomorrow night: How safe is your child's school?

What We Talk About When We Talk About the Liberal Arts

Note: The staff of The Burgundy *is excited to announce a new series called "The Road Taken." In each issue, beginning this month, we will profile an alum who has an interesting or unique occupation. If you or someone you know has an odd job, please contact us with suggestions for future issues!*

A self-described "nerd" and "bookworm," Tom Pendleton (English '81) is not your typical special agent. He does not have an alias, a disguise, or an array of fake passports. He does not carry a gun or any 007 gadgets, like a wristwatch that shoots blue lasers. Indeed, Pendleton, 37, packs his lunch in brown paper bags and rarely leaves the office during workdays. And yet this bookish bachelor—slight and unassuming, with thin hair and thick glasses—is a vital member of the CIA's Dangerous Persons Task Force.

A senior writing analyst, Pendleton identifies and profiles the bad guys from the safety of his desk. It is well known in intelligence circles that Suspicious Persons (SPs) and Dangerous Persons (DPs) are often prolific writers. According to Miriam Young, author of *The Hurtin' Kind,* "The SP or DP profile is a disgruntled, arrogant loner with a huge ego. He wants to leave his mark. He wants to have a legacy. He wants attention. He often writes letters or manifestos, long and rambling tracts. Just think of Marty Bund, the Holiday Inn Bomber, back in '93–'94. Or last year, Jesse Teller, the so-called Dayton Troll. These guys each wrote and distributed hundreds of pages."

This is where Pendleton comes in. In many cases, field agents are able to acquire a writing sample from an SP. Pendleton and his four-person team of writing analysts scrutinize the written material to determine whether or not the author is a potential DP whom the agency should monitor.

"They say the style makes the man," Pendleton said, while sitting in his immaculate, warmly lit office, a veritable library of trade journals and twentieth-century American fiction, his passion. "We can create a fairly accurate psychological profile from a relatively small sample. Think of a written document as a fingerprint, a unique marker. A personality is encoded in the lines. I'm not talking handwriting analysis here—that's ancient stuff. That's phrenology compared to the new stylistic analysis. We have learned through study that there are clues, warning signs. Habits of punctuation or diction or repetition. There is a syntax of pathology. There is such a thing as dangerous grammar."

Pendleton is not allowed to discuss specific cases, but he says that in the past several years his team has been able to identify "close to one hundred" DPs. In many cases, the writing analysis has led to surveillance, which in turn has prevented violence and casualties. "We've been quite successful," Pendleton said. "I'd like to think we've saved some lives. It's not an exact

> "I'd like to think we've saved some lives."
> —TOM PENDLETON,
> CIA WRITING ANALYST

science, but it is a science. We've got theory and data. We've developed a good bit of cutting-edge software. And you'd be surprised at how accurate the analysis can be."

Some of the most important writing analysis software was developed from Pendleton's painstaking study of the leftist writer (and perpetual

DP) Upton Sinclair. Ten years ago, on a hunch, Pendleton decided to read all of Sinclair's work—nearly one hundred and twenty books at the time. It took him almost two years. "I read every word," he said with a sigh. "That was not fun. Imagine Sinclair as your bedtime partner for twenty-three months. Imagine that voice in your head for all that time. I thought I was either going to commit suicide or go join the Wobblies."

It may not have been fun, but the work was productive. Take hours of intense study, add the spark of a brilliant idea, and a science is born. "With Sinclair," he said, "we're obviously dealing with a pathological, obsessive, maniacal personality. So at some point it struck me that I could just work backwards from personality to style in order to create a scientific logic that would then allow us to move the other way, forward, from style to profile.

"Look at a novel like *Oil!*, 1927. We learned a lot from this book. Let's just focus on punctuation. All right, and within punctuation, let's just focus on the use of exclamation points. There are 1,539 exclamation points in *Oil!*, not counting the one in the title. That's nearly three exclamation points per page. I mean, in a sense, what else do you need to know about this guy? That pretty much says it all. Relentless, dogmatic, maniacal, repressed. And of course just a plain old-fashioned bad writer,

> "*I thought I was either going to commit suicide or go join the Wobblies.*"
> —TOM PENDLETON, ON READING THE COMPLETE WORKS OF UPTON SINCLAIR

although I must say that *Oil!* is actually not a terrible book. I don't have the data for this, but I think it's safe to say that Sinclair has exclaimed more than any other writer in the long history of literature. I like to think of him as a human exclamation point."

From his thorough analysis of *Oil!*[*], Pendleton developed the now widely used unit of measurement called a Sinclair. The Sinclair is a unit of hysteria equal to 2.92 exclamation points per page. According to Pendleton, the threshold for a DP is about 0.7 Sinclairs. "Anything above that," Pendleton said, "sends up the red flag." One recent anti-taxation manifesto came in at 6.6 Sinclairs (or more than 19 exclamations points per page!). "We rang the bell real loud on that one," Pendleton said.

Asked if he wishes the Sinclair were known as the "Pendleton," the bookworm Bond laughed. "I had the opportunity to name it a Pendleton," he said. "Since I developed the data, the agency let me choose what I wanted to call it. But it's basically a unit of unhealthy obsession and misdirected passion. That's not really the legacy I was after." Pendleton can rest assured that he will long be remembered for the Pendleton Report, his 900-page groundbreaking study of Sinclair and the theory of dangerous style.

Those who knew Pendleton in his college days as a long-haired, freethinker with a portable Zola tucked in his back pocket might be surprised to learn he works for the CIA. "I'm sort of surprised myself," he admitted. "I never would have dreamed it. But you know, at some point

---

[*] Sinclair's Crude Craft: Exclamation Points in *Oil!* (1927)
- Number of pages in novel: 527
- Number of exclamation points in novel (not including title): 1,539
- Percentage of pages with at least one exclamation point: 84.6 (446/527)
- Average number of exclamation points per page: 2.92
- Most consecutive pages with at least one exclamation point: 97
- Most consecutive pages *without* an exclamation point: 4
- Number of pages with five or more exclamation points: 114
- Number of pages with ten or more exclamation points: 16
- Most exclamation points on one page: 22 (p. 509)
- Number of exclamation points in final chapter (30 pp.): 162
- Number of exclamation points editor William Maxwell famously and judiciously advised a writer to use in a *career*: 2

(Source: The Pendleton Report)

we all have to grow up and get a haircut and accept the world as it is. I like my job. I get to work with language. And I feel like in small but significant ways I'm making the world a safer and better place.

"It's funny, I studied English simply because I liked to read, but my professors in college were always talking about how you could do so many different things with an English major. I guess I'm proof of that."

Five Short Stories
About Upton Sinclair

• Inflatable Butler™ •

When I went to get Upton for dinner, he was asleep on the couch with the television on. I shook his shoulder gently and he woke up and followed me to the table. We all drank a toast to Upton's new novel, and then another one to the next day's march. None of us drank alcohol, of course, out of respect for our guest. Upton beamed and said we were getting closer every day and then he took all of his pills. Once we had begun passing plates and eating, Upton said: "The television was on and I must have fallen asleep in there. I dreamed I saw an advertisement for this sort of *manservant* that you *blow up* and put in your house. He didn't have legs, really. His bottom half was full of sand, so that he wouldn't tip over. But you inflated the thing. And his arms and hands were held out in front of him so that he could hold jackets or keys or whatever. And you had to make three payments of fifty dollars to buy this. His name was Blevins. People in the advertisement were pointing at it and laughing and saying it would make a wonderful Christmas present for people they knew. I tell you, my mind must be rotting out to dream such a thing." He laughed. He was in very high spirits. We kept our eyes on our rice and kicked each other beneath the table. None of us had the heart to tell him.

• Conversion •

On the wall of the bathroom stall in my office building someone has written, *Where in the world is UPTON SINCLAIR?*

Below it, someone has answered, *He's 1.8288 meters under.*

• Leafleting •

First you hear the martial thrum of the propellers coming in low, beating the thick air of the projects like cake batter. Then the leaflets explode from the choppers like ink from squids, and the sky grows dark and the birds in their brick-hole nests get worried and chirpy. The chopper pilots fly away with a quivering in their bowels, with a final glance back at the settling cloud. The leaflets swirl and spin and shimmer, tumble like tickertape after wars and World Series. There is a child in a top-floor window, his eyes open, his mouth open, his palms open at his sides, as if to receive. It's his first leafleting. Leaflets settle on rooftops and fire escapes, slide between crowded buildings and into narrow alleys. Skim across windshields, nestle into potholes and cracks, blanket the buckled asphalt. One leaflet might flutter against your window, might perch on the ledge, nervous as a sparrow. From inside the window you might be able to see his photograph, might be able to read the warning, might even be able to see the gaudy frames of the comic strip. A nice black bunny lets an old man stay in his cozy hole. Two frames later, the old man has horns and pointed teeth, and he's spit-roasting that X-eyed rabbit over cartoon tongues of fire. The leaflet alights and you go back to your show.

That night there will be rain. The orange ink of fire and the black ink of a toll-free number will seep into the brick and tar, will inoculate these blocks. In the alleys the soggy leaflets will adhere to empty bottles like the labels of a potent summer brew. The boy in his small room will count and recount the seventeen identical leaflets that fell from the sky onto the front steps of his building. He will spread them out around him. On a bare wall he will draw a crude rabbit with the nub of a crayon. He will draw a devil. He will draw five rabbits and three devils. He will smash bugs with his palm. Water will soak the frayed carpet. The boy will stare at his wall, stare at the sliding rain, and he will wonder what he has done.

After midnight, a man with a guitar and a harmonica and an expired license will drive his one-eyed van into the city and he will see, through the steam and rain, the plastered leaflets like tissue on razor cuts. He will see the fresh red graffiti—the crude shovels, the exclamation points, the 34s. He will see black cars creeping slowly through the dark streets, hunched and predatory. And he will know: The old man is back.

• We Were Only Trying to Help •

We took Upton to the mall because he needed new clothes. It comes as a surprise to some people that political radicals and crusaders occasionally need new clothes too. But what happened was we lost him and we were worried sick. We knew he had been in B. Dalton because he had autographed all the Cliffs Notes to *The Jungle* and he had asked a young clerk with acne where the Socialist section was. We knew he had browsed tennis rackets in a sporting goods store. No fewer than seven people had heard him say, "Look, now I don't want some kid's plastic racket. Where are the nice wooden ones?" A woman in a vitamin kiosk said she saw a man matching Upton's description—optimistic, spry, exhumed—and she told us which direction he had passed. In this way we were able to track him through the mall. And when we found him, finally, he was curled on the floor of a dressing room at Old Navy, asleep in cargo pants.

• The Bullet •

The bullet is a vote. The bullet is public opinion, approval rating. The bullet is a report on human social arrangement. The bullet is a theory of economics, a theory of justice. The bullet has an ethical dimension and a history-filled tip. Upon impact, the tip explodes and shards of history fill the body cavity and lacerate the vitals. The bullet is a rhetorical trope, like paralipsis or auxesis, only faster and more persuasive. The bullet is painted so we know who got him, who collects. The green or white or lavender bullet is tweezed from the wrinkled organ and converted into jewelry. The bullet exits the body and becomes lodged in a museum or a folk song. It is auctioned electronically with a minimum bid. We come to find out that Turkish gunpowder blew up the Parthenon! The bullet flies faster than anything, faster than anything. It stings once and then dies, like a bee, like a lover. The bullet finds its way: Click here to see Upton's studded heart.

Conveniently Located at the Intersection of First Amendment and Second Amendment™

Last year, ten million people from all fifty states and eighty-four nations walked through the tip of that bullet. What we have here, I think, is a breathtaking structure that celebrates and honors some very distinctly American tensions. Plus it's just fun.
—WALTER SIZEMORE, CURATOR, MUSEUM OF UPTON SINCLAIR ASSASSINATION

A Key to the MUSA Map

GROUND FLOOR

1. Entrance
2. Sculpture: *At Close Range*
3. Sinclair's Inflammatory Art
4. What Is Socialism?
5. Stalin Kiosk
6. Human Nature Room
7. Stairs
8. Video: *The Timeless Novels of Jane Austen*

9   Bloody Clothing Exhibit
10   The Formation of a Muckraker
11   A Time line of the Afterlives
12   Disguises Exhibit
13   Unfavorable Reviews Room
14   Restrooms
15   Video: *Sinclair Autopsy*
16   Sculpture: *Shovel and Gun*
17   Children's Drawings
18   Stairs/Elevator
19   Gift Shop

TEXACO MEZZANINE
20   Grade A Food Court
21   Restrooms (with Diaper Changing Stations)
22   Video: *Because It Works*

SECOND FLOOR
23   Firearms Exhibit
24   Huntley: The Early Years
25   Huntley: Pioneer Assassin, Acting Alone with No CIA
     Involvement
26   The Diaries
27   The Disciples
28   Assassination Simulator™ (Ages 10 and Up)
29   Stairs
30   Video: *Madison Miracle: The Shot Heard 'Round Wisconsin*
31   The Bullet from the Madison Miracle
32   Scopes and Silencers Kiosk
33   Kids' Shooting Range
34   Close Calls Exhibit
35   Stairs / Elevator
36   Bullets Past and Present

•

Comments Overheard in the MUSA Ticket Line, Which, Excuse Me, Sir, Begins over *There*

"Historically, Socialism has only worked in very cold places."

"Last time, the security guard let Joey touch his gun."

"Huntley wrote you back? Every time I just get the form letter and the signed glossy."

"But this is America."

"No, with communism everyone lives in the same small apartment."

"The building really *is* amazing."

"I didn't realize he wrote books too. I just thought he got shot."

"But that's the great thing about America."

"The thing is, he's not even a politician or an economist. He's a *writer*."

"We've started the Atkins."

No, I think he should be able to *say* it. I *do* think he should be able to say it."

"I'm sorry, I've worked hard for my gas grill."

"I haven't been back since they re-enhanced the bloody clothing."

"So because there is a finger in your sausage that means capitalism is bad? It's capitalism's fault that the hot dog has rat and bleach in it? That's what I don't get."

"Well, see, that's America."

"Honey, can you hear me? Can you? You'll never guess where I am."

"That's not what I said. I'm *not* against shooting him. All I said was I couldn't do it myself."

"Wait, I thought capitalism and democracy were the same thing."

"Tim got laid off."

"But Socialism is only applicable to countries with distinct social classes."

"I know. Half the kids in Logan's class are sucking on inhalers."

"They've added a grilled chicken sandwich."

"They didn't warn him, they didn't give him severance pay. He worked there sixteen years and then one day he goes to work and they tell him it's his last day."

•

Excerpt from an Interview with MUSA Architect Beverly Sinclair (No Relation)

BEWARETHEIDES.COM: The building is incredible.

SINCLAIR: Thank you.

BEWARETHEIDES.COM: Have you always had an interest in Upton Sinclair—

SINCLAIR: No relation.

BEWARETHEIDES.COM: No. No relation. Have you always had an interest in Sinclair and in the assassinations?

SINCLAIR: To tell you the truth, no. I'd see it on television like everyone else. I read *The Jungle* in high school (well, most of it!) and I read Huntley's memoir in a book group, but I didn't really follow the afterlives or the assassinations. I didn't take any special interest in them. And I actually think that helped me in the project. I think you get in trouble as an artist when you have strong feelings about a subject. It can cloud your aesthetic judgment.

BEWARETHEIDES.COM: You've done some work for the city and you've done a fair amount of corporate design. MUSA, though, seems like a different kind of project. Was it difficult to be involved in something that is so politically charged?

SINCLAIR: Honestly, I didn't approach MUSA as a political project. I was commissioned to design a museum, just as I am commissioned to build a research park or a corporate high-rise. My process and my mind-set were the same. I suppose there are politics involved there, but none that really concern me as a working artist. I did my research and I tried to capture and convey a spirit. But this is what I always do.

BEWARETHEIDES.COM: I'm not sure quite how to put this, but the museum seems—architecturally—*tense*. Or anxious. Does that make sense?

SINCLAIR: Yes, it does. That's a good way of putting it, that is certainly part of its spirit. It is fairly dark inside—the windows are high and small. There are a lot of corners and narrow passageways. I wanted to impart an ominous mood, a mood of excitement and impending violence and extremism. That's the reason for the radical shifts in scale, and the use of black and white. Most of all, I wanted people to feel the thrill of the hunt. That's what it's all about. A friend recently sent me an article—someone has done a study and found that people's resting heart rates are higher inside the museum than outside. So...

BEWARETHEIDES.COM: So that's good architecture!

SINCLAIR: Well, in most cases I'd like to *lower* heart rates, but in this case I guess it means I did my job well.

Some Notes on Punctuation

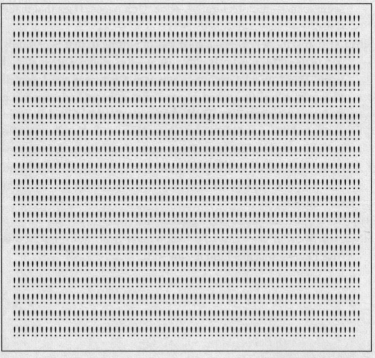

Figure 12—U.S. Armory

•

INTERVIEWER: Did you know there are 1,539 exclamation points in *Oil!*?

SINCLAIR: What?

INTERVIEWER: Were you aware that you used 1,539 exclamation points in your novel *Oil!*?

SINCLAIR: Well? What would you have me say? Evidently I didn't use enough.

(February 20, 2003)

•

Talkin' U.S. Exclamation Point Blues

Well Upton was in his cabin working
On a novel that would never end
The ruthless reign of corporations
Much less that literary trend
Uh-oh, trouble in the kitchen
And the bedroom
Domestic strife!

The book was full of exclamation
Scream and shout, rage and yell
He fired the points off at his readers
Like some pinko William Tell
Not as accurate, maybe
Or efficient
Duck, y'all!

Old man wearing out his keys
All the days spent tap, tap, tappin'

Till the morning that he hit
Shift and 1 and nothing happened!
He was out
Couldn't make his point
It happens when you get old

Well Upton knew just what to do
He took his cane from behind the door
And set out walking for the projects
To harvest passion from the poor
Stick with me now
Switchin' metaphors
Upton the farmer!

He wandered through the crumbling streets
And witnessed every shout and cry
With his canvas sack he gathered
The punctuation from the sky
Big yield
Being poor sucks

His next stop was the factory
To listen to the boss man scream
At the lazy no-good workers
For losing to the Japanese again
One guy's got his finger caught in a machine
Exclamation points rolling off the floor
Like Fords!

Upton had just one more stop
He dragged his sack to College Town
Went upstairs to Intro Writing
And thought that he would surely drown

In exclamations
Alarm clocks going "BEEP!!! BEEP!!!"
Easy does it, kids
Those aren't toys
You're gonna put an eye out!

For Upton it was back to work
The snipers prowled outside his door
He figured he could exclamate
For three more novels, maybe four
Hard to say, though
When people get deaf
You got to shout more

He sat down in his writing chair
With aching back and aching joints
He hunted and pecked, shifted and oned
Pages filled with the people's points
It's recycling
It's a new damn record
Better duck, y'all

The Anniversary of Something

You are a very difficult person to be right about.

          —VAN WYCK BROOKS, LETTER TO U.S.

The car slid back and forth across the steep, icy road. In the backseat Sam leaned against the window and looked out at the blowing snow, the gray monotony of the guardrail. His terrier Sparky sat in his lap, nose pressed placidly against the glass. Up on the canvas of the mountain was some kind of animal, stoic and ungulate. The engine revved as the wheels slipped and spun.

Sam said, "I can't decide if you're a great driver or a terrible driver."

Thomas said, "Me? I'm a great driver. The conditions are terrible. This car is terrible."

"But you probably shouldn't be drinking."

"It actually helps."

"Is it snowing or is the snow just blowing around?"

"From a driving perspective, there's not much difference."

Sam looked at a piece of paper on the seat beside him. "These directions you got are not very good."

"Dude's a convict. He's not some, what's his name, Lewis and Clark."

"I never asked you why you were in prison. I suppose I should have asked. I suppose it should have been part of our interview process."

Thomas downshifted and steered the car around a switchback. "It was one of those wrong place at the wrong time kind of deals."

"Do you have a license?"

"I used to."

"Are you sure we haven't passed it?"

Thomas shrugged. "Is that a *goat*?"

After two more first-gear switchbacks, Thomas passed a leaning mailbox and turned right into deep snow. "This is it. I think this is the driveway. But there's no way we can drive up there."

"How far is it to the cabin?"

"I don't know."

Sam moved Sparky off his lap. He looked down at his shoes and frowned. They were leather clogs, creased and paint-splattered. He wasn't wearing socks. He was surprised that the mailbox was still standing. The angle was thrilling and improbable.

Thomas said, "Do you want me to come or stay here?"

Sam found one glove and a knit cap in the pockets of his army coat. He said, "Stay here for now."

"Dog staying?"

"Yes. If he starts whining, let him out."

The driveway began straight, with a slight incline, but then curved steeply to the left. There were no footprints in the snow in either direction. Sam felt the distinct violation of snow in shoe and he turned philosophical. Most other animals—well, *all* animals—just run around with bare feet, and then there's us with our tender soles! It was nice in the woods. Quiet, though Sam could hear loud, muffled music coming from the car. Squirrels chased each other around a tree, there was a barber pole effect. He couldn't quite say why he was here, why, for the first time in his life, he seemed to be interested in something or someone that a lot of other people were interested in. Even as a child, he didn't want the regular toys and action figures. He wanted old, dead machines from junkyards and salvage lots and landfills. Mysterious systems with rotors and cogs. Buttons, switches, and hatches. His father put red ribbons around junk. Christmas at the Treadway home looked primitive and postapocalyptic. Pine tree sprouting from the wreckage of civilization. Popcorn garlands. He was not here to kill the old muckraker, of that he was certain. He was just curious.

The driveway curved back to the right and remained steep. Sam walked through the clouds of his own breath, noticing now that the snow had almost stopped. The few flakes still falling were thin and light, glittering like metal shavings. He wasn't wearing a watch, but figured it was around one o'clock. There were massive layoffs planned for the next fiscal period. Famous designers had been brought on board to redesign uniforms, to make them more stylish and, in some cases, more sexy. Sam saw the cabin through the bare, snowy trees and he slowed down and then stopped. Certainly he would be interrupting Sinclair's work. He could not say why he was here and his presence suddenly felt like a mistake, an intrusion. When he discovered from his ex-con driver that Sinclair was holed up a couple hours away, he decided to visit him, perhaps (but he didn't know) as one would visit a mythic national landmark, like Disney World or Mount Rushmore or the Liberty Bell. (As a child Sam had taken a class field trip to see the Liberty Bell and had been grossly disappointed to discover how small it is.) Perhaps his interest in Sinclair was similar to his interest in wax museums or enormous balls of tinfoil in the Midwest. He grew nervous as he neared the cabin. Sinclair was ridiculous, it was true. *How many lifetimes does it take Upton Sinclair to screw in a lightbulb?* And he wasn't really much of an artist, either. Sam had tried to get through a couple Sinclair novels, but he found their guileless sincerity embarrassing and anachronistic. Still, Sinclair wasn't a roadside attraction, either. He wasn't, it now occurred to Sam, made of wax. Sam stood still, slouching in his big army coat, with one glove and no socks. His feet were burning cold and his cheeks were rosy and round. The hair beneath his wool cap came down into his eyes. He was afraid that he might look like an assassin, but he didn't need to worry about that. Typically, assassins are neat and meticulous. They are erect and deliberate and stiff-jointed, and the bones of their wrists and knees register subtle meteorological shifts. They paint their faces. Assassins are generally lean, rangy, with pursed lips and gray eyes. Sam considered returning to the car and even took two steps backward in the snow. But then he moved forward again, walking toward the cabin, feeling like an ugly American tourist.

The cabin was small, square, rudimentary. Smoke poured out of a chimney and firewood was cut and stacked neatly against one wall of the house, dry beneath a blue tarp. Sam could only see one small window, and it was covered from the inside by a white curtain. There was one door, short and narrow, like an afterthought. Sam knocked painfully and then heard shouting inside. It was an old man's shouting, slow and deliberate and hoarse. He knocked again and saw the curtain move in the window, then heard bolts and locks opening. The old man was still shouting as the door opened a few inches. It was dark inside the cabin compared to the white glare of the snow. Sam squinted to see a tall young man standing in the opening, taller than the door. His eyes were just beneath the frame. He said, "What do you want?"

"I want to see Sinclair."

"He's not here."

The old man shouted, "What is it?"

Sam said, "I know he's here. I just want to see him. Just for a minute."

Inside the cabin the old man shouted, "It's no use even *trying*. I don't know why I even try."

The tall young man said, "Mr. Sinclair is not seeing anyone right now."

"Come on. Five minutes."

"Who are you?"

"I'm an artist. Mr. Sinclair's work has been important to me."

"Wait," the young man said, leaning out of the door frame and staring hard at Sam. "Are you Treadway?"

Sam said, "Yes."

The young man opened the door wider. "Why didn't you say so? I'm sorry I didn't recognize you."

Sam could make out another figure in the dark cabin. It was Sinclair, pacing back and forth, shouting and gesticulating. He ignored Sam. "It's hopeless. I am hopeless. All that whipped topping. That *whole* container."

The young man said, "Did you walk up the driveway?"

"Yes."

"Your work is amazing."

"Thank you."

"Upton's writing has been important to *you*?"

"Well, not really," Sam said. "But there's something about him."

The tall young man, Sinclair's secretary, was named Derek. He said, "I think I know what you mean." He looked into the cabin and then back at Sam. "He's having an episode right now. Not pretty. But come on in."

Sinclair shouted, "And the taffy. I don't even *like* taffy. I tell you, I am not master of myself!"

Sam walked through the door and set off an alarm. Derek said, "Sorry, sorry," and scrambled to turn off the alarm. "Metal detector. Can you just—sorry—just open your coat there? I have to do it."

Sam unbuttoned his coat and held it open, looking around the room. "There's nothing in here. I don't have anything." Derek pointed sheepishly at an inside pocket. Sam looked down and saw, in the inside pocket, the three cheap paintbrushes with metal bands. He took the brushes from his pocket and studied them. What a surprise! The shades of dry paint on the brushes were not anything Sam could remember using, or even ever wanting to use. What forgotten project was this? What fleeting vision? He tested the stiff bristles on the palm of his hand and then dropped the brushes into an empty coffee can by the door.

Derek said, "Thanks. Would you mind stepping through again?"

"Look—"

"Please. I have to do this." Over his shoulder he said, "It's nothing to worry about, Mr. Sinclair."

Sinclair disappeared behind a curtain, a hanging sheet. He was still shouting hoarsely about the devil, wrestling the devil.

Sam stepped back through the door and set off the alarm again. He patted his pants pockets, removed a ring of keys and a lighter, which he placed in the coffee can with the brushes. He stepped through the door once again, this time without activating the alarm. Derek closed the door behind him, took Sam's coat and hung it on top of other coats on a hook on the back of the door.

The cabin was basically one square room. To Sam's left, just inside the door, a large black woodstove hissed and generated an intense, dry, wavy heat. Sam noticed that Derek was short-sleeved and red-faced. The left wall was crowded and literary: a small homemade bookshelf, packed full and nearly obscured by tall stacks of books on the floor; a large wooden desk with a lamp, a typewriter, and a jar of ink pens; and a smaller desk, probably Derek's, on top of which rested a cardboard box full of mail and two towering manuscripts. On the far wall, a modest kitchen: a sink, a counter, four open cabinets, and a small refrigerator. A half-gallon container of ice cream was overturned in a brown puddle on the floor in front of the sink. A bedsheet hung diagonally across the far right corner of the cabin, concealing, Sam guessed, a bathroom. Bunk beds were built into the right wall and each bed was neatly made up. A wooden ladder led to the top bunk. In the corner to the right of the door Sam saw a floor lamp, a music stand, and a scuffed violin lying in an open case.

The cabin had two windows, both covered by curtains. The lamps cast a dim light. The room was extraordinarily hot.

From behind the curtain, Sinclair shouted, "I'm sick! I'm sick now! I blame this on you, Derek. It's my fault and it's your fault."

Sam whispered, "What's wrong with him?"

"He ate too many sweets again."

"Maybe I should leave. I could come back in a little while."

Derek shook his head. "Mr. Sinclair, you have a visitor."

Sinclair said, "It's not my son, is it?"

"No. You know who it is? It's Treadway."

Sinclair wretched behind the curtain. "Treadway?"

"Yes."

"Treadway the bourgeois artist? The one—the liberals' darling? The great—the great voice of the middle class?"

Sam stared down at his feet. Derek said, "The artist, yes."

Sinclair shouted, "I'm a *drunkard*. I'm no better than my father. I'm a drunkard of sweet stuffs, confections. I can't stand it! It's the story of my father all over again. It will be the end of me. Derek, I blame you too. Why do you buy it? Why do you bring it here?"

Derek rolled his eyes. "Because you told me to, Mr. Sinclair. Because you told me you wouldn't let me back in without it."

Sinclair wretched again. Derek said, "He does this every once in a while. He can't eat just a normal amount."

Sinclair shouted, "Drunkard!"

Sam said, "Is that your mailbox at the end of the driveway?"

Derek laughed and said, "Yes, I know, it's about to fall right over."

Sinclair flushed the toilet. He said, "I shall resolve to master myself. Derek! Bring me paper and pen."

Derek took the paper and pen from a drawer in the small desk and handed them to Sinclair behind the curtain. Sinclair shouted, "Hereby...and...with shame...resolve to resist...the cake and

the ice cream . . . the chocolate candy . . . syrup . . . sweet stuffs . . . cara-
mel   and . . . things . . . *pie* . . . cookies . . . yes . . . Fudgsicle . . . a   resolu-
tion herewith." He parted the curtain and walked briskly to the
kitchen, where he hung the paper on a nail above the sink. He was
short—about 5'7"—and very lean. He wore baggy khakis belted high
on his waist, and a plaid flannel shirt over a white T-shirt. He had yet
to acknowledge the visitor. His breathing was heavy and loud.
"There," he said.

Derek said, "Do you feel better, Mr. Sinclair?"

Sinclair said, "I'm weak of spirit and I'm fat."

Sam laughed nervously and put his hands in the pockets of his
pants. He should have brought a gift for Sinclair, some token. He really
should never have come. He felt large and uncomfortable in the small,
hot cabin. He wanted to leave.

Sinclair began pacing again. "Gandhi used to write me letters from
prison," he said. "I sent him my work and he read it and enjoyed it.
Derek, put some more wood in the stove. You, Mr. Treadway." Sinclair
stopped pacing and approached the other artist. He held out his hand
and Sam shook it. It was sticky.

Sam said, "It's an honor to meet you, Mr. Sinclair."

"I'm a drunkard and I'm irrelevant," Sinclair said. "Please have a
seat. You may have received a letter or two from me over the years. I
don't care much for your stunts."

Sam sat down. "My stunts?"

"Your art, Mr. Treadway." He sat down too, but then immediately
stood back up and began walking the room. He jotted something down
at the large desk. He looked through the curtains. "It's snowing again."

Derek finished loading the stove and said, "Would either of you like
coffee?"

Neither man answered. Sinclair sat down and put his head in his
hands. Derek shrugged apologetically to Sam, then picked up the ice-
cream container and scrubbed the melted mess off the wooden floor
with a wet towel. Sinclair might have been asleep in his chair. The room

was so hot and dry that Sam had trouble breathing. At last he said, "I should probably go."

"Nobody talks about capitalism anymore," Sinclair said. "Nobody even mentions the word. Capitalism has always been killing people and starving people, but at least we used to be able to *name* it. Businessmen and politicians would at least acknowledge its excesses, its cruelties. There wasn't a sense that it was inevitable. Now, you know, it's like fish don't notice the water. You can't fight for an alternative when people don't even recognize the possibility of an alternative."

Sam nodded, though Sinclair still held his head in his hands. He could not believe Sinclair was talking about capitalism. He was like a wind-up doll. "We want every child to get a great education and get a great job. We want every child to have a nice house and a nice family. Everyone can be rich! Everyone can go to Harvard! Everyone can have a corner office! Nobody need be poor or jobless. As if any of this were possible under this system that we are not allowed to speak of!"

Sinclair stood up again and began his pacing. Sam was embarrassed for the old man, his naked righteousness. He had trouble looking directly at him. Sinclair was a cartoon, talking about capitalism and justice to a visitor. Before coming, Sam hadn't given much thought to what they might talk about. Tennis, maybe, or Mencken.

Sinclair said, "Of course, even when you could talk about capitalism, you couldn't *write* about capitalism, you couldn't have your characters talking about capitalism. Not in America. No, the editors and critics wouldn't stand for that. That's not art! That's phony and preachy. That's not what real artists do."

"But you know," Sam said, looking up from a faded rug, "it does sound kind of phony and preachy."

Sinclair bent down to the floor and did three slow, groaning push-ups. Then he clapped his hands and got up slowly. "Maybe so, Mr. Treadway," he said, trying to catch his breath. "But it's all that my characters know how to talk about."

Sinclair sat back down next to Sam and closed his eyes. Sam considered that he could politely leave in five more minutes. "Mr. Sinclair, are you working on another book right now?"

Sinclair sat still with his eyes shut. Quietly he said, "All that ice cream."

Sam looked at Derek, who was sitting on the bottom bunk. Derek held his palms up and shrugged again.

Sinclair said, "Do you know what I want?"

Sam said, "Yes, I think so." Everyone knew what Sinclair wanted.

Sinclair said, "I want a drink."

Derek stood up. "Mr. Sinclair, I don't—"

Treadway said, "Booze?"

Sinclair said, "Yes. I want some booze."

Derek said, "I think it's nap time."

Sinclair said, "Shut up, Derek. Now listen, I've never had a drop of that poison in all my lives and now I want some. I want whiskey. I want Jim Daniels. Mr. Treadway, I imagine that you are a heavy drinker. Do you have any Jim Daniels whiskey?"

Derek glared at Sam and shook his head. "No," Sam said. "I'm sorry, I don't."

Sinclair looked disappointed. "I'm just like my father," he said. "I need it. I feel the need for it. It's inside me. I'm an alcoholic."

Derek said, "Good Lord, you are *not* an alcoholic."

"I can't have just one drink."

"You've never even had one drink."

"Exactly."

Sam said, "I think my driver might have some whiskey, Mr. Sinclair."

Sinclair said, "You have a driver?"

Sam avoided the secretary's stare. "He's waiting in the car at the bottom of the driveway. I think he has some. Do you want me to check?"

"Yes. By all means do."

Sam got his coat from behind the door. Derek sat back down on the bottom bunk and said, "What about your writing, Mr. Sinclair?"

"Today," Sinclair said, "is a research day."

Sam left the cabin and walked down the driveway. The snow had indeed begun again, and it covered the windshield of the car so that Sam couldn't see in. He had the sudden thought that Thomas would not be in the car, that Sparky would be mangled in the backseat and Thomas would be gone. He opened the passenger side door and saw Thomas asleep with the driver's seat reclined all the way. Sam got in the car, Thomas woke up, and Sparky began whining in the back. Thomas said, "Was he there?"

"Yes."

"Did you talk to him?"

"Yes."

Thomas stretched and brought his seat back up. "What's he like?"

"He's about what you'd expect. He's a weird little kid. He loves Socialism. He's shorter than I thought he'd be."

"Are you glad we came?"

"Sort of."

"Ready to go?"

Sam said, "I think so. Can we make it out?"

Thomas started the car, cleared the windshield with a sweep of the wipers. He said, "We can make it." He put the car in reverse and tried to back out, but the tires spun in the ice and snow. He tried again, but the tires just spun deeper. He put on his gloves and said, "I just need to dig us out a little bit. It's not a problem."

Sam said, "Wait, listen, do you have any whiskey?"

"I got two handles in the trunk."

Sam stared up the steep driveway toward the cabin. "Let's not worry about the car right now."

Derek was the first of the men to take off his shirt. Once it was clear that he could not stop Sinclair from drinking whiskey, he gave up trying. He hadn't even commented when Thomas came into the cabin and set off the alarm on the metal detector. He just shut the alarm off and lined up four glasses on a foldout card table. He said, "Here we are, gentlemen."

Sam said, "To the working class."

They all raised their glasses and the three younger men drank while Sinclair hesitated. The glass shook in his hand, and so he held it with both hands. He sniffed the liquor, he stared at it. Then he set the glass back on the table and picked it up again. The other men politely pretended not to notice. Derek refilled the empty glasses.

Sinclair said, "I was a Prohibitionist."

Derek said, "To Prohibition."

"My Prohibition novel, *The Wet Parade,* was made into a movie at MGM starring Myrna Loy, Robert Montgomery, and that other fellow."

The drinkers drank to Myrna Loy. Thomas said, "I sometimes forget that drinking was illegal."

"Mr. Sinclair," Sam said, "you really don't have to drink that."

Sinclair drank quickly and violently, his head thrown back, the whiskey running down his chin and across his cheeks. He squeezed his eyes shut and pulled his lips into his mouth. He dropped his glass on the floor and put both hands across his face. The glass did not break. Sparky sat up, panting.

All the men's faces were flushed with the heat and the drink. Derek took off his shirt and Thomas stared at Derek's smooth, narrow chest, and at the small red shovel tattooed, handle up, above his heart.

Thomas said, "How did that glass not break?"

Sinclair gasped, "Jimmy Durante."

The snow continued outside in big feathery flakes. The poverty line was ridiculously low. Tax breaks were pretty much a constant answer to a question no one asked publicly. The thing to do was to claim a good Internet name and then sell it to the people who wished they had thought of it before you. Here was a warm cabin, interesting company, and spirits. Derek refilled glasses and Sinclair said, "I'll have another, since there is little chance I'll get hooked on that foul stuff."

Sam felt pretty good. The afternoon had taken a turn. He would no doubt be late now for a gallery appearance that night, but that was OK.

Sinclair said, "What's today?"

Derek said, "It's either the twenty-third or the twenty-fourth."

Sinclair said, "It's probably my birthday. It probably marks the anniversary of my death."

"Or the twenty-fifth."

"You live long enough, every day is the anniversary of something."

They drank to Upton Sinclair.

Sam stood and browsed the books on the bookshelf. He pulled Shelley and read dramatically:

> Rise like lions after slumber
> In unvanquishable number—
> Shake your chains to earth like dew
> Which in sleep had fallen on you—
> Ye are many—they are few.

Sinclair, it appeared to the other men, began to cry. He told the story of Shelley's death. When his body was found washed up on shore, it was unrecognizable. They were able to identify the body because they found a waterlogged book of Keats in the jacket pocket. Then they burned Shelley's body on the beach and his heart would not burn.

Thomas said, "What?"

Sinclair said, "His heart would not burn. They pulled it from the flaming pyre."

Sam said, "So the story goes."

Thomas said, "Wait. Who was this?"

Sinclair said, "They pulled his heart out of the flames, unburned." He requested "England in 1819" and Sam read it well.

Thomas took off his shirt, revealing his prison chest. Derek kept his eyes in his glass, right down into his glass and nowhere else.

Sinclair said, "I was twenty-seven years old when *The Jungle* was published. You need to understand. One day I was an unknown hack and the next day I was an international celebrity."

Treadway nodded. Some of his work had shown up on screen savers and mouse pads. He did not receive much mail. He wasn't inclined to feel sorry for Sinclair.

Sinclair said, "I was a hack, then a huge star, and then a hack again. In one lifetime! How can that be? You need to understand. There were a few decades—I was a powerful figure, Mr. Treadway."

Treadway did not know what to say. He struggled to appear sympathetic. He said, "The Roosevelts."

"Ah, yes, but FDR stood me up in California and Teddy left me out of his autobiography!"

Treadway tried to make a surprised look on his face.

"How could he leave me out? I can understand him calling me a pain in the neck. I did not leave the poor man alone. That would have been fine if he had said I was difficult or hardheaded or maniacal. Just fine. But to leave me out?"

Treadway said, "Seems unfair." He noticed that Thomas and Derek had removed themselves from the conversation. Derek was showing Thomas something on his laptop and Thomas was laughing.

Sinclair said, "In 1934, Mr. Treadway, the *Literary Digest* took a poll of American newspapers as to who had been the most outstanding persons in the world during that year. And do you know the results?"

Treadway said, "You were first?"

"What? No."

"Oh. Second?"

"I was fourth, Mr. Treadway. Me, a writer, fourth. I was behind FDR, Hitler, and Mussolini."

The group of men came together and broke apart. Sparky was lethargic in the heat. People had their projects. Derek played the violin poorly. Thomas collected all four glasses and dropped each one, scientifically. Every one of them broke into thick shards and he swept them up with a broom. All four men drank from the bottle. Derek loaded wood into the stove and stripped to his boxers. Thomas said, "Don't cut your feet."

Sam sat with Upton, who under the influence seemed to be thinking more about his career than about social justice. It was understandable, but no less annoying to Sam. "I can give a speech now or go to the mall and nobody really cares. They used to picket. They used to plot my assassination and shoot high-powered rifles at me."

Sam said, "They're still shooting, Mr. Sinclair." It was true. The cold war was long over, but Sinclair remained a vastly unpopular figure and a frequent target of violence. "Give me a break. You're still despised. They're still after you."

"I had to be whisked away in secret tunnels. I had to speed off in cars with blown tires. It was like I mattered. The sound of the gunshots."

Before Sam could object to Sinclair's self-pity, Thomas rejoined the two artists, suddenly and energetically. He said, "Let's see the old soldier! Let's see the battle wounds." He was at this point naked and quite drunk, pointing at Sinclair.

Sinclair laughed. "The chauffeur would have me strip."

Thomas said, "Let's see the warhorse! Old Ironsides!"

Sinclair said, "He wants to see a fat Socialist."

Thomas said, "Take it all off, Chairman!"

Sinclair took another drink and made a terrible face. "Very well," he said.

While most of the events of the day would be hazily and imperfectly remembered by the three other men in the room, each of them would retain a very clear memory of what happened next. Standing in the center of the cabin, Sinclair slowly unbuttoned his flannel shirt, slipped his arms through the sleeves, and dropped the shirt on the floor. He paused, bent down, picked up the shirt, folded it neatly, and placed it back on the floor. At this point Sam still thought Sinclair was joking, that he would stop. He certainly wanted him to stop, but Sinclair lifted his T-shirt over his head, shook it out and folded it, then put it on top of his flannel shirt. This all seemed to take a very long time. He slipped off his black canvas sneakers and lined them up beside his folded shirts. He unfastened his belt and stepped out of his pants, which he also folded and added to his neat stack. Sam and the other men looked on, rapt but deeply uncomfortable. The merriment was now gone from the room. Then Sinclair removed his small white underpants so that he stood in the middle of the cabin wearing nothing but his black socks. To Thomas he said, "This is what you wanted to see?" Thomas made no reply. Sinclair said, "I am not ashamed," but clearly he was. He held his thin, hairless legs close together and pressed his arms to his sides. The other three men stared at Sinclair's wrecked body. They felt that it was overwhelming evidence for something, that it proved something beyond any reasonable doubt, but they were not sure what. Sam experienced some extraordinary mixture of admiration, wonder, and contempt— he was drunk and he felt he might laugh or weep or vomit. Sinclair turned to Sam and held his arms out. "You might ask yourself, Mr. Treadway, if this—*this*—is what you give to your provocative art."

Sam said, "I think we're on the same side, Mr. Sinclair."

Sinclair said, "When they open fire, now that's when you know you're making art that matters." He wobbled as if he might lose his balance and he began to shiver. "I feel a draft," he said. He walked across the room and got into the bottom bunk, beneath the thick covers. He closed his eyes and said, "But leechlike to their fainting country cling." Then he said, "Taffy," and fell asleep.

The room was still and silent for a time. Sparky scratched his ear, rattling his tags. It was Thomas who spoke first. He whispered to Derek, "Let's go chop wood."

Derek said, "There's plenty of cut wood already."

Thomas said, "Let's go."

They stumbled out of the cabin wearing only unbuttoned shirts and unlaced boots. Their butts were good, Sam noticed. They were high, firm, and smooth, like the timeless butts of statues.

Sam had a snack of cheese and crackers in the small kitchen. Unlike the others, he had kept most of his clothes on. He looked at a manuscript on Sinclair's desk and found himself wanting to like it, wanting to be captivated. He read through several pages, looking for a good sentence, an elegant phrase. Mostly, though, people were *plunged into darkness*. Houses were *engulfed in flames*. Children cried, "No, Papa!"

Sam searched Thomas's jacket for the keys to the car and found them in a zipped pocket, along with a small silver pistol. He took the keys and the gun and walked out of the cabin. Sparky came along, happy to take a walk in the snow. It was late afternoon, growing dark. Thomas and Derek were around the side, swinging axes and grunting, their genitals shrunken in the cold. The snow had almost stopped now. The gun was heavy and warm in Sam's pocket.

He walked down the driveway, past the car and across the mountain road to the guardrail, below which was a long steep drop. He threw the gun down the slope, then walked back to the car and swept the thick blanket of snow off of the trunk with his arm. He opened the trunk, unzipped an old duffel bag, and took out a large pad of paper and a charcoal pencil. The snow made the dusk bright and strange. The terrier ate snow and romped like a young dog, though he was at this point seven. Sam closed the trunk, sat up on it, and with a cold hand sketched the mailbox truthfully. He did not exaggerate the angle of its lean. Who would ever believe it?

When Sam returned to the cabin with his dog and his pad and pencil, the room was quiet and dark. Thomas and Derek were curled together in the top bunk without a cover. Four pink feet hung off the end of the short bed and the ladder lay on the floor.

Sam put a log in the stove and warmed his hands and feet. He switched on the desk lamp and then moved it to the card table in the center of the room. Sparky went back to sleep beneath the table. Sam found a glass in the kitchen and poured himself another swallow of whiskey, which he put on the table without drinking. He quietly pulled a chair next to Sinclair's bed. You need to understand: It wasn't vengeance and it wasn't reverence. It was something like both. This had been, above all, an interesting day.

Sam took off Sinclair's glasses and put them beneath the bed. He gripped the two quilts from beneath the old man's chin and pulled them slowly to the foot of the bed. When Sinclair didn't stir, Sam sat down and began to work.

Every Knock Is a Boost

Dear valued customer, thank you for buying this Upton Sinclair title from Red Shovel Press. In order that we may serve you better, we ask that you take a few minutes to complete this information card.

What is your age?
- ☐ 11-13
- ☐ 14-16
- ☐ 17-20
- ☒ 21 and older

What is your yearly income?
- ☐ Nothing
- ☒ Under $10,000
- ☐ $10,000 - $20,000
- ☐ More than $20,000

How did you hear about this book?
- ☐ Friend or family member
- ☐ Internet
- ☐ Unfavorable review
- ☐ Graffiti
- ☐ The Last Folksinger
- ☐ RSP catalogue
- ☐ Bookstore publicity
- ☒ Other: YOUR MAMA SHOUTED IT OUT WHILE WE WERE HAVING SEX BACKWARD

How many Upton Sinclair novels have you read?
- ☒ 1-25   THERE IS ONLY ONE UPTON SINCLAIR NOVEL!
- ☐ 26-50
- ☐ 51-75
- ☐ 76-100
- ☐ More than 100

Would you recommend Upton Sinclair novels and RSP to a friend?
- ☐ Y
- ☒ N

Why not? I LIKE MY FRIENDS

Do you have any suggestions for Red Shovel Press?

DIE, PLEASE !!

THANK YOU! We value your feedback and your support of RSP.

•

5 March 2002

Dear Sinclair,

I hope this letter finds you alive and well. I read about Tacoma in the capitalist press. What a circus! I'm anxious to hear your version of the story, which is to say I'm anxious to find out what really happened.

It pains me to be writing you with bad news. You know that we love your books and that we appreciate your ongoing financial support, but I'm afraid that we can't publish ANOTHER RETURN OF LANNY BUDD! As I've told you before, I read all the Lanny Budd books when I was a kid and I loved them. He's an important American literary figure. But Lanny was born in 1900 and his story is fundamentally a story of major events in the early- to mid-twentieth century. In your new novel, Lanny would be 102 years old! That's rather old for a protagonist. Lanny has a gold-tipped cane in chapter 1, but it is never mentioned again. In chapter 4 he plays tennis and by chapter 9 he's outrunning terrorists on the roof of a moving train. He seems to get younger as the novel goes on. It just didn't seem realistic to our editors that this ancient man could still be traveling around, witnessing important historical events, meeting famous figures, and acting heroically. There was an unintentionally comic element to the whole novel. I think it's a mistake to bring Lanny back, Sinclair. Let him rest. Give us a younger hero, a hero for these new times.

We can't wait to see the novel on mercury poisoning. Send it as soon as you are finished.

All best,
Morris

P.S. We're pretty strapped over here. It's amazing what a bomb and two fires will do to insurance rates. We'd appreciate anything you can send.

The Camera Eye

It is the late summer of 1968 and my sister lisa is five and I am not born yet and muckraker upton sinclair will die in a few months on november 25 at age ninety having lost three wives having lost his fame having lost it is true his radical dreams having supported the military aggression in vietnam having patched things up a bit with his first son having given well sold all of his letters to the library at the university of indiana and if you go there and read one letter per minute for eight hours a day it will take you five hundred days to read them all and the street is dark with rain

the sidewalk and the frontwalk make a perfect T and the small lawn is cut short and neat and across the street there is a tree or at least a telephone pole and the car is a neighbor's brandnew 1968 volvo and this is america with white children playing safely in the frontyard they don't need to wear shoes even and the thing is is that the children hold signs in the air they are picket signs signs of protest little white poster-board signs maskingtaped to sticks these white children protesting some-thing in the suburban frontyard on a rainy day but you can't see the front of their signs because the photographer who is my father is behind the children and you want to see

when I am older than my father was then I say dad do you remember this day he says of course I do and dad what was written on those signs

194

lisa says she can't remember and my father says nothing there was no writing on them they were blank the kids were playing protest just imitating it's what they saw all around them this was 1968 it's what people did

just ten years later what we played is war in the neighborhood the arm of the chair was loose it looked like a rifle and I pulled it off and snuck it out of the house I shot you no you didn't you missed no I got you you're dead

•

History

History repeats itself
History repeats itself
History repeats itself
History repeats itself

The first time as tragedy
The second time as farce
The third time as tragedy
The fourth time as worse

Halley's comet came in 1910
But Sinclair was too busy with his pen
To notice
It came back in '86, the spring
But again he could not bring
Himself to look up from the muck
When the world is fair
He'll look up there
Maybe 2059, when Halley's back

And the world is Socialist
And metric too!

History repeats itself
History repeats itself
The fifth time as publicity stunt
The sixth time as tax write-off
The seventh time as pilot for a one-hour courtroom
     drama
The eighth time as another tragedy

All the copies of Robin Hood *were banned*
Taken from the libraries in a van
And driven to an underground warehouse
In Colorado
Then Sinclair and his merry men stole them back
And returned them to the library stacks
Under the cover of darkness!
The National Guard was called out in the night
Sinclair found himself in another gunfight
Without a gun
He died and the merry men were tarred and
     feathered
The books were put in an armored car
And hauled back to Colorado,
near NORAD

It's just history repeating itself
History repeating
The eleventh time as a joke
The twelfth time as dirty campaign tactic
The thirteenth time as pay-per-view event

The fourteenth time as sickening reminder of all the
    other times before

At the end of a bloody millennium
Everyone said the world would die
Sinclair went to bed early
He knew it was a lie
And he was right
The bloody world was here to stay
There was work to do the next day
And the day after that too
History repeats itself
History just repeats
The twenty-fifth time as a bullet point
The thirtieth time as tragedy that receives little or no
    media attention
The fifty-eighth time as boring repetition
The seventy-fourth time as nothing you can do
    anything about anyway, so what's the point?

Sinclair was dead but now he's back
With a Bush in the White House and bombs in Iraq
The generals and anchors have cool names for the war
But Upton's been shocked and awed before
Oil by any other name would well as sweet
Oil!
It's a rerun
It's Operation History

The hundredth time as your daily routine
The hundredth time as your daily routine
The hundredth time as folk song

The hundredth time as news of the sorry world
When the world is fair
Maybe then he'll gaze up at the heavens

It's history, history, history, history

One more time now

PART TWO!

The Greenville
Anti-Socialist
League
Fourth of July
Book Burning

*If you take this book rightly you
will consider it a textbook of
military strategy.*
　　—I, CANDIDATE FOR GOVERNOR:
　　　AND HOW I GOT LICKED

1

It was a fine morning, the second Saturday in June, and so most of the citizens of Greenville walked to the meeting. The women wore long summer dresses in optimistic colors. They carried coffee cakes, muffins, and loaves of banana bread beneath sun-dazzled tinfoil. Their purses, worn with straps over the shoulders, were large and shapeless, more luggage than accessory. The men wore blue work pants and short-sleeved button-down shirts with ink stains in the pockets or sweat stains under the arms or grease stains on the shoulders. Their shoes were creased black leather, roomy, with worn soles. Over the years, the cuffs of their pants had gradually crept up to reveal their tube socks. Their wives noticed this, but the men did not, for there had been a day long ago when they had tried the pants on and they had fit, and if the pants fit once, they must fit now. Children tagged behind their parents or ran ahead, wearing shorts or skirts. Some fell and scraped knees and elbows; if they were young, they sobbed inconsolably, then stopped and ran ahead once again. Their inhalers were nestled in the mothers' purses.

Neighbors called out to one another on the walk. The men shook dry hands, occasionally left-handed if a right thumb was missing or a right hand was bandaged. The women hugged as well as their baked goods allowed.

"Whatever that is under there, it smells fantastic."

"Bob, dammit, I still have your ladder."

"How about that Huntley?"

It was agreed that they saw each other too rarely. They lived just a couple blocks apart! Lives got busy. There were the children and there was overtime at the plant, if you were lucky. And yet they really should do better.

Others, the ones who lived farther away and the ones who were not well enough to walk, drove to the meeting in light blue American cars with patriotic bumper stickers. The men drove slowly, as if in a parade. One had to watch for bouncing balls; one had to watch for kittens. The drivers nodded and waved from the open windows. Their forearms were thick and tan, and the backs of their hands were hairy. They never talked about Vietnam. In many cases a woman in the passenger seat clutched a warm crumble or crisp in her lap, but she could not be seen behind the gleaming windshield.

Arthur Rudkin stood at the base of the steps of the elementary school, welcoming his neighbors to the meeting. His son, Stephen, stood close beside him, wearing a small nylon backpack and rubbing his ears and the back of his neck. His father had cut his hair earlier that morning without placing a towel around the boy's shoulders.

A fat, kind man named Hollis Michael shook Arthur's hand. "It's been a long time, Art. How's your back?"

Arthur told Hollis that most days it was just fine.

"Any luck finding work?"

Arthur shook his head. "But I have some good leads."

Hollis said, "Well that's great, Art. Good luck." He looked down at Stephen. "Goodness, this one's getting big. You'll be, what, in the sixth grade?"

Stephen scratched his neck and looked at the ground. "Eighth."

Arthur put his hand on Stephen's bony shoulder. "Boy's on the *honor* roll."

Hollis said, "Is that right? Got yourself a bookworm?"

Arthur said he sure did. Stephen tried to line up his shoes perfectly. If he got the tips just right, the heels seemed a little off. He traced the inside of his ear with his index finger.

"They do grow up fast," Hollis said. Arthur agreed. "Hey," Hollis said to Stephen, "Looks like someone got after you with a scissors." He laughed. "Looks like someone cut your hair on a *bicycle.*"

Stephen stared at the weeds that grew in the sidewalk cracks. He tried to smile at the joke. His father had told him he could wear a hat if he wanted, but Stephen was worried that it would hurt his feelings. It was a bad haircut, spiky and uneven.

Hollis said, "Come by sometime, Art. Bring Stephen. The kids have rigged up a waterslide in the backyard. Just a hose and some trash bags. They're out there for hours." Arthur thanked Hollis and shook his hand once again before Hollis turned toward the stairs. Arthur said quietly to Stephen, "Can you go get me a chair from inside?"

Stephen jogged up the stairs and into the school. Inside a classroom he found an old, heavy wooden chair. He had trouble lifting it, so he dragged it down the hallway and out of the school. While his father shook hands and tickled babies and peeked under tinfoil, Stephen lugged the chair down the steps one step at a time. He set the chair beside Arthur and took off his backpack. He was out of breath and he tried to think about calm things, like clouds or a dog asleep in the dirt. Stephen's former teacher asked Arthur how he'd been feeling and Arthur said just fine. Everyone was talking about Huntley, though in truth there was little to say. In the nylon backpack there was an inhaler and two science fiction books from the town's one-room library. Stephen had already read the books, but he needed them in the backpack to give it some bulk and heft. He didn't like carrying the inhaler in his pocket because it was lumpy and uncomfortable, and everyone could see it. So he carried it in his backpack along with books or a balled-up jacket. He used his inhaler and his breathing returned to normal.

The meeting was held in the cafeteria, where the cinder block walls were covered with sun-faded posters of milk and food. Blocks of cheese cavorted with fish sticks and tacos. All of the food items had wide eyes and big black shoes, and they spoke zealously on behalf of the industry. "That's right, Sloppy Joe! Meat DOES make you strong!"

The townspeople sat at long cafeteria tables with their coffee, juice, and baked goods. At the center of each table was a full roll of paper towels on a wooden holder. Once everyone was seated, Arthur stood up and addressed the group, nervously at first but gradually becoming more comfortable. "I want to welcome everyone to our summer meeting of the Greenville Anti-Socialist League." His neighbors whistled and applauded, and Arthur waited for the noise to die down. He continued, "It's great to see a few new faces. I think I know everyone, but just in case, let me go ahead and introduce myself. My name is Arthur and I'm the current president of the league." Someone shouted, "Arthur!" and there was laughing and more clapping. "There are some of you friends and neighbors I feel like I haven't seen since the winter meeting. We all just get caught up in our lives. I think we do a lot of great work through the GASL but I've always thought one of the best things about these meetings is that they just bring us together and keep us connected and remind us of important things." At their tables the people nodded, blowing on their coffee. "Once we finish with our official business this morning, I hope we can all just stick around for a while and catch up."

Stephen sat in the back corner of the cafeteria at a table he shared with nine senior citizens who had been bused in from the nursing home. He was proud of his father. He was happy to see him in front of all of these people, speaking with confidence. He liked it when people yelled "Arthur!" Most days Arthur did not see anyone and he spoke very little. He rarely left the house. Stephen had taken to doing the grocery shopping and the laundry.

Arthur said, "In terms of news, there's no change in Sinclair's status. He continues to be alive as of February. He was last seen a few days ago in the Midwest."

Many people booed, but they were happy and excited. In past years, when Sinclair had been dead, the meetings were poorly attended and the membership was listless and glum.

"The big news, I guess, and I'm sure all of you know this, is that Joe Gerald Huntley was paroled on June 7."

Some people cheered and clapped.

A man whispered to his friend, "Washed up."

The friend whispered, "Twenty says he ain't," and the two men shook hands across the table.

Arthur said, "We have several items on the agenda today. You'll remember that we discussed putting an Anti-Socialist League billboard at the town limits on Route 87. We've gotten the OK to do that and I'm told that construction will begin on that real soon."

A bald man named Chester, a former GASL president, stood up and said, "I was by there yesterday, Art. They've already started it."

Arthur said, "Have they? That's great. Thanks, Chester." Chester gave a mock salute and sat down. "Nancy, do you want to report on the league's litter pick-up campaign?"

Nancy, the GASL secretary, reported that the campaign was a success but that the league was always looking for more volunteers to help pick up litter on the third Saturday of every month. She enlisted three more volunteers on the spot. Reports followed on the pet-adoption program, the library fund drive, the child care facility, the parenting classes, and the winter-coat donation center, all of which were succeeding if not thriving. It was a matter of pride in this town that while many Anti-Socialist Leagues across the country had faded away, gone underground, faddishly shifted their opposition to some other, more timely threat, or become purely ceremonial or festive, the Greenville chapter had remained strong, active, and determined.

When these matters were concluded, Arthur stood up again. "Now, in the winter meeting I promised that we'd revisit the issue of whether the league should send cards and care packages to Sinclair assassins." People murmured as they recalled the debate. Arthur explained that with the parole of Huntley, there remained five men and one woman currently serving time for the assassination or attempted assassination of Upton Sinclair. "I think everyone here knows how I feel about this," he said. "I believe we are united by our hatred of Socialism and our love of the free market and the American way of life, but I personally don't advocate assassination. I believe we should stop short of shooting

Sinclair and supporting those who do. Individuals can of course act on their own, but I don't think the league should sanction this. I know that past presidents have felt differently"—here Arthur glanced at Chester—"but I'd rather see anti-Socialists use more peaceful means."

One of the senior citizens at Stephen's table whispered, "Imagine just sitting in that cell all day."

Arthur said, "Does anyone want to speak on this matter?"

Several young plant workers, tireless volunteers in the pet-adoption program, gave impassioned, loosely organized speeches about eradicating Sinclair and his ideas. Saliva accumulated at the corners of their mouths. Others said that sending a care package was not a political gesture and hardly tantamount to supporting assassination. Others warily defended Arthur's comments, taking care to emphasize their own seething, implacable hatred of Sinclair and Socialism.

Eventually, Arthur called for a vote, which was taken by a show of hands. Nancy counted and Arthur reminded people to keep their hands up where Nancy could see them. Stephen, not old enough to vote but too old to be down the hall with the children, stood on his bench and counted, as well. A slight majority of members voted not to send league-sanctioned cards and care packages to the prisoners. Stephen noticed that some who had spoken for it had voted against it, perhaps out of a fear of committee work. Stephen was pleased that his father's position had been vindicated.

Arthur said, "Well, that just about does it, I think. If anyone—"

Chester's wife, Margaret, interrupted Arthur. "Arthur, what about the book burning?"

Arthur put both hands on top of his head. "My goodness," he said, glancing down at his notes and then at Nancy, who grimaced and then began flipping through her minutes. "I have to say, I forgot completely about the book burning."

"For the Fourth," Margaret said, pointing in the direction of the school softball field, the traditional location of the event.

"Yes, of course," Arthur said. "I just plain forgot. Who was in charge of the burning this year?"

The cafeteria was quiet as everyone looked around. A few took the opportunity to get another muffin. Don, the GASL treasurer, knocked over a full cup of coffee on his table and then scrambled to sop up the mess with paper towels. Nancy checked her records and said, "Miles."

"Oh. Miles."

Miles was a housepainter in town who had fallen off a roof in April and broken both of his legs. He was at home recuperating and he was not, according to the reports of friends and well-wishers, doing well at all. The hospital bills were piling up and Miles was said to be considering selling the bullet from the Madison Miracle, which he kept in a locked glass case in his home.

A friend spoke. "I offered to bring Miles this morning, but he just wasn't quite up for it. He wanted me to tell all of you that he was thankful for the food and all the other nice things you've done. Arthur, I have to say that I just don't think Miles is going to be able to handle any league responsibilities right now."

Arthur nodded. "I should have realized this situation before. That's my fault. We've still got a little time and we've got a nice budget this year because of Mr. Ames. Would anyone..." Arthur trailed off and looked around the room. The anti-Socialists stared at the brown crumbs on their paper plates.

The GASL Fourth of July Book Burning had at one time been an important social event in the town. People Arthur's age and older fondly remembered the raging bonfires of their youth. The mountain of gas-soaked books, garlanded with sparklers and strings of firecrackers, burning deep into the summer night. The children, permitted to stay up late for this one special night, dancing circles around the inferno of leftist literature. The burning, however, had fallen off in recent years. Three years ago it had been cancelled by rain, and the last two years nobody in the league even bothered with it. But then the previous January old Miller Ames died and left the GASL some of his money, a significant portion of which he earmarked for the book burning. It was his wish that the event return to its former glory and significance. Oh, did Miller Ames hate Socialism! You just don't see that kind of fervor much these days. Miller, by the way, claimed to have wounded Sinclair from a moving taxi in '76, but the details of the story shifted enough in his constant retelling that it was regarded by most of his neighbors as fantasy.

Arthur said, "Rodney?"

"I'm not volunteering," Rodney said. "I just want to say that whoever does it, they should stay away from the mall. I have a friend who runs a burning in Kansas. He left things to the last minute and then he went to the mall. They only had a few Socialist books and he had to buy a lot of non-Socialist books just to fill out the pile. The thing to do is order directly from Sinclair, in bulk. He's got a small publisher, very friendly and efficient. His books are available, they're cheap, and they burn well."

"Thank you, Rodney." Arthur tried to make eye contact with a potential volunteer. "I know it's a lot to take on at this point, people. But is anyone willing?"

Rose Middleton, the pretty librarian who was unable to conceive, stood up. Her hands were clenched into fists and she held them against her chest.

Arthur said, "Oh, Rose, yes. I don't suppose you're volunteering."

When the laughter died down, Rose gave an abbreviated version of the speech she had given in years past. Her voice quavered, as it always did, and a red splotch bloomed on her neck. She said she didn't expect her words to change anything, but she felt the need to speak out against the book burning. Couldn't the league celebrate in some other way? Thank you. Rose's husband, Bobby, stared at the floor while she spoke and he did not look up when she returned to her seat. He would hear about this at poker.

The cafeteria was uncomfortably quiet after Rose sat down. Arthur said, "Well, Rose, thank you for that viewpoint. That's an interesting angle. And we are, after all, a democratic organization. So. OK. Do I have a volunteer to run the burning?"

"I'll do it." Stephen's voice was so faint that Arthur did not quite hear it.

"Did someone volunteer?"

Stephen stood on the bench of his table at the back of the cafeteria, while below him the senior citizens sipped their black coffee. They of course remembered when the GASL meetings were held at night at the Elks Lodge, with booze and violent agendas. It was not unusual in those days for chairs to be thrown over doctrinal conflicts.

"I'll do it, Dad."

"Stephen?"

Stephen had trouble catching his breath. "I can do it," he said. "I hate Socialism." He took a shot of air from his inhaler. "I can do it."

Before Arthur could say anything, a man named Frank stood up to speak. He had trouble getting his legs out from beneath the table and past the built-in bench. "Now just hold on," he said. "Look, Arthur, I know that Stephen is a good kid. A heck of a speller, we all know that. But he's just too young to be in charge of the book burning. The book burning is a big responsibility—it is a *large* responsibility—and it requires an individual who is older and more mature than Stephen is at this point in time." Frank looked around, hoping he had stirred his comrades. "That is all."

Someone said, "So are you volunteering, Frank?"

"No," Frank said. He sat quickly and tried to get his legs back beneath the table.

Another man, named Richard, stood and said, "I agree with Frank. How old is Stephen? Nine?"

"He's twelve. Almost thirteen."

Richard said, "That's still too young."

"Wait a second, Richard," said Nancy, the GASL secretary. "How old was your Mary when she made the effigy doll?"

People murmured and calculated. That had been six years ago. Mary would have been eleven, and it was the best effigy doll anyone could re-member. Richard had nothing else to say.

"I say let him do it."

"Me too."

"Yes, let him do it!"

"Why not?"

Mrs. Whitaker turned to her neighbor and asked, less discreetly than she perhaps imagined, if there was money in the book burning budget for a proper haircut.

Stephen stood on the bench and clutched his inhaler, trying to keep his knees from shaking, trying not to scratch at his neck or dig in his ears. The senior citizens at his table stared up at him and clapped. Arthur, visibly proud of his son, called for a vote. All in favor raised their hands and held them high. Nancy stood and began to count but there was no need. The majority was overwhelming, the will of the people was clear. In this way it was decided that young Stephen Rudkin was in charge of the Greenville Anti-Socialist League Fourth of July Book Burning.

2

Upton Sinclair walked briskly through the woods, his left arm tightly wrapped in a sling beneath his shirt, the shirtsleeve dangling empty. He felt tired but refreshed, happy to be out walking once again. He swelled with a sense of hope and possibility as he considered that in ten days, the world might be a very different place. Red Shovel Press was set to publish his new novel, *A Moveable Jungle!*, an exposé of corporate outsourcing and of the wretched working conditions of foreign employees. The last three chapters were nothing less than a roadmap to international Socialism. Reviewers would be forced to take notice. The American working class would be moved and outraged, stirred to action. It was all there in the book, and it was the truth. It was not possible that people who knew the truth could just ignore it. America was ready for this book, ready for revolution. America would lead an international movement for social and economic justice. Sinclair would be celebrated in the songs of one hundred languages.

A magpie hopped through the branches of a tree with a shingle in its mouth. Old shotgun shells dotted the path, packed with dirt, their once vibrant colors faded to pastels. Sinclair was just beginning to regain his strength. For months he had overworked himself on the book, and then seven weeks ago (on May Day), while recuperating on a fishing trip, he had been shot in the shoulder by Francis Scott Billings, the cocky, seventeen-year-old savant whom the media had quickly dubbed Billings the Kid. Eighty yards out with a stiff crosswind. Sinclair fell to the bottom of the boat and his new secretary, Nick, threw his pole in the water and dove down next to him. The boat rocked and swayed. Nick whispered, "I quit." Sinclair stared up at the clouds, shapeless and racing. He said, "Huntley." He knew of no one else who could make that shot and he was wrong.

Sinclair arrived back at the cabin at the same time that his new secretary, Paul, returned from town. At twenty-six, Paul was older than the typical Sinclair secretary. His name had languished on the waiting list for nearly six years, and by the time he got the call, in the middle of a rainy spring night, his life had acquired some shape and stability. By that time he had a history degree, an apartment without roommates, a decent job, a car payment, and a cat. He was even getting along fairly well with his parents. There had been a moment of indecision, holding the phone, sitting on the edge of his new bed while the rain blew against his windows and his cat stared at him from the top of a chest of drawers.

He hesitated, it was true, but when he spoke, he spoke with conviction. He left the cat with a neighbor, sent a contrite e-mail to his boss, and the next morning he was on a crowded, sour-smelling bus, headed for Sinclair.

Paul unloaded plastic bags of groceries from the back of the station wagon. "How are you feeling, Mr. Sinclair?"

"Don't try to carry all of those at once." Sinclair peeked inside each of the bags that dangled from Paul's hand. "Were you able to get the ginger root?"

"Yes." Paul shut the back door of the wagon and took the groceries into the cabin.

Sinclair walked close behind. "Did anyone follow you?"

"No."

"Did you wear the hat?"

"Yes.

"Did you wear it?"

"Yes, I wore it. And I looked ridiculous."

Paul was not carrying the large canvas sack that Sinclair had used for many years to transport his mail. "Say," Sinclair said, "where's the mail? Is it still in the flivver?"

"I have it. I just put it all in one of the grocery bags. There wasn't that much."

Sinclair sat at a wooden table. "Perhaps you didn't get it all."

While Paul put away the groceries, he noticed that a cabinet door was loose on its hinges and made a mental note to tighten it when Sinclair napped. "I got it all, Mr. Sinclair."

"Did you," Sinclair said, "buy any sweets?"

Paul turned toward his employer and leaned against the counter. He knew he was being tested. Sinclair had begged him to return with sweets, but had also said upon Paul's arrival that the purchase of sweets at any point was grounds for immediate dismissal. Paul shook his head slowly. "No," he said. "No sweets."

Sinclair made his free right hand into a four-fingered fist and pushed his knuckles into his forehead. "I wish," he said, "that you wouldn't mix the mail with the groceries."

After a light lunch—during which Sinclair explained that some smaller pieces of mail can slide all the way to the back of a post office box, which is deeper than it seems, and go unnoticed by an inattentive or distracted secretary—Sinclair and Paul sat down at their desks to handle correspondence. Sinclair had allotted three hours for the task, but given that Paul had in all likelihood returned with only a portion of the day's mail, he conceded that they might finish in an hour.

One of Paul's duties was to open the mail, read it, and take dictation for replies. He pulled a yellow padded envelope from the plastic grocery bag. "Why don't we begin," Paul said, "with *this*." Paul opened the envelope from Red Shovel Press and presented to Sinclair the first copy of *A Moveable Jungle!* Sinclair snatched the book with his right hand and studied the cover intently. He examined the spine, the back. He flipped through its pages one-handed.

"I see that Mr. Doctorow did not provide the blurb that he promised. He'll likely regret that."

Paul said, "It's a handsome book, Mr. Sinclair."

"It's still a thrill," Sinclair said. "After all these years and all these books, it's still a thrill to hold a new book in my hands for the first time." He put the book down on his desk, but then picked it back up and handled it once more. "This one is going to be big, Paul. This one is going to change everything."

"How many books is that? How many total?"

"Gee, Paul, I'm not even sure. I lose track."

"One twenty-five?"

"One twenty-seven."

Paul said, "There's a note here too, from Morris. 'Upton, hope you like the look of the novel. Everyone here is excited about the publication. We're set for an initial printing of a thousand copies. We'll need more money if we're going to do a second run. Best, Morris.'"

Sinclair said, "Paul, take a letter to Morris. Ready? 'Morris, the novel looks beautiful, but we can't very well start a revolution with one thousand copies. Enclosed please find a check for a second run of five thousand copies. I'll soon send you more. Yours, Upton.'"

"Five thousand?"

"You think we should do more?"

"I'm worried about the money."

"It's not your job to worry about money, Paul. Continue."

"This one's from the Gladiator Tennis Company."

"Ah, yes," Sinclair said. "This might very well take care of some of our problems."

"'Dear Mr. Sinclair, thank you for your nice letter and photograph. Looks like you've still got a pretty swing, old-timer! We are glad that you enjoy Gladiator rackets, the best rackets on the market. I am sorry to say that we are unable at this time to accept your kind offer to allow us to sponsor you. It is not our policy to sponsor recreational players, no matter how talented or infamous. Sincerely, Ross Tower, public relations. P.S. Socialism will never work in this country.'"

Sinclair said, "Well, it was worth a try."

"Do you want to respond?"

"No. We'll follow up later. Go on."

"This is a package from T. Russell from Missouri. There is a letter and . . . something else." Paul studied the enclosed object and set it on his desk. "The letter says, 'Dear Upton Sinclair, I have read seventy-three of your novels. When people ask me if I went to college, I say yes. I say I studied JUSTICE at Sinclair University, where there is no summer vacation or spring break!'"

"Indeed, yes! Ah, that's good, no spring break. Keep reading, Paul."

"'Your books have been my classroom and I want to thank you. I read on the Internet about your new novel, *A Moveable Jungle!* I don't have the money for the book, Mr. Sinclair, but perhaps you would accept barter. I, too, am an artist. I am a whittler. I am a political whittler in an abstract mode. The enclosed piece is called *The Downtrodden.* Would you accept it in trade for your new novel? Yours in the struggle, T. Russell.'"

Paul handed the block of dark wood to Sinclair, who turned it in his free hand and held it up to his eyes. "I don't know anything about whittling, Paul. But this looks poor."

Paul nodded. "Not a good trade."

"Sinclair University! I rather like that. Let's send him a book when they arrive."

"But Mr. Sinclair."

"Just do it. I can't very well ignore this T. Russell."

"You give away half your books. Morris is not—"

"And include a note," Sinclair said. "'Mr. Russell, thank you for the inspiring letter and the abstract wood. My tastes in whittling run more in the realist vein, but I appreciate the spirit of your art. Enclosed please find *A Moveable Jungle!* I hope that it is an enjoyable course of study.' I'll sign it 'Professor Sinclair.' You got that?"

"Yes," Paul said.

"Next letter."

"This is from a Derek Bittle. It's from overseas."

"Oh, a former secretary. Nice boy."

"He writes, 'Sinclair, I'm recovering well in Switzerland, though I still have the limp and the nightmares.' What happened to him?"

"Nothing. It was a misunderstanding."

"'Rest assured that your reputation here is as strong as ever. They love you in France, Germany, and the UK. They follow your lives and deaths closely. Your books are widely available, and you are considered an artist of the highest rank. If you ever tire of American guns, art, and politics, you could live well here, Sinclair. But I'm sure you know that. In less democratic areas of the globe, you are less popular, of course. Presently, nineteen of your translators are imprisoned worldwide. I am involved with a Swiss organization that works to free these men and women, or at least to improve their conditions. It keeps me busy and it feels like important work. (And it's also out of the line of fire!) I hope this letter finds you safe and well. Yours, Derek.' Did he get *shot*?"

"It was a freak thing. We must send his organization some money."

Paul stared at Sinclair. "There's no money."

"I'll think of something. Hold off on this one. Perhaps I should write another diet book."

"This is a letter from Jack Crump in Utah. 'Dear Mr. Sinclair, my wife is the possessor of strange and wonderful powers. She can move small objects with her mind and also bend items (see photograph!). Your work has been important to us. The neighbors used to have us over some, but not anymore. Please visit us and write something about the amazing powers of my wife, which are true.' Signed 'Jack Crump.'"

Paul looked at the photograph, which showed a woman in a red bathrobe gripping a fork with bent tines. Her eyes were squeezed shut in effort. Paul handed the photo to Sinclair, who studied it carefully. "We'll be in the West in September. Make a note of this. We'll stop by and see the Crumps."

Paul said, "Are you joking?"

"No. I am not."

"But he's lying."

"Why would he lie, Paul?"

"So he can shoot you when you show up outside his trailer."

Sinclair waved the photograph. "Would you have me just ignore this evidence?"

Paul got up from his chair and walked the short distance to the kitchen. He took a spoon from a drawer and bent it in half. Then he held the spoon out in front of him and squeezed his eyes shut in concentration. "I have powers of the *mind*!"

Sinclair said, "Sit down this moment."

Paul placed the bent spoon in the sink and returned to his seat.

Sinclair said, "Paul, I realize that this is an age of cynicism, but I do not appreciate the quality, and I simply won't abide it in my secretaries. Do you understand?"

Paul said yes.

"Chances are, these people, the Crumps, they are fooling me or fooling themselves in some fashion. They are perhaps using trickery. But I will not assume that to be the case until I have compelling reason to do so." Sinclair stood and moved to a window. He parted the dusty curtains and looked out. "My wife, Mary Craig, had a gift. I know what it is to be mocked and disbelieved. I know what it is to try to convince someone of something about which he has quite made up his mind. How rare it is for a man to keep himself open to those ideas that the world tells him are impossible!"

"I understand," Paul said. "I'm sorry, Mr. Sinclair."

Sinclair remained at the window for a moment and then returned to his seat. His left arm itched inside its sling and he tried to scratch it with a pen. The cabin, of course, was bugged. "I meant to tell you," he said. "On my walk earlier I saw a bird with a roofing shingle in its mouth. It was the kind of bird that we called a tuxedo bird when I was a boy."

"A magpie?"

"Yes, a magpie."

The next letter was from the leader of a leftist puppet troop that was stranded in Oregon. The tour bus had been stolen and one of the puppeteers had developed gangrene from a knife wound. They needed money to get home and didn't know whom else to ask. There was a letter threatening a libel lawsuit. And another. There was Francis Scott Billings on the cover of a glossy weekly, flashing his gold tooth, holding up ten fingers. There was a zealous letter from a woman who advocated an all-grass diet. Paul hid the credit card offers. There was zero percent interest on all balance transfers for six months. A New York poet needed cash. The studio was not interested in the screenplay. The utilities bill was due. *Babbitt* was awesome. Little League pitchers were way too old, which was not fair. Albert looked forward to seeing his father in July. The chain bookstore regretted that it would not be able to carry his new novel.

Sinclair slumped in his chair and doodled in the margins of a manuscript page. "For God's sake," he said, "I used to correspond with Jack
London and Sir Arthur Conan Doyle. Albert *Einstein.*"

Paul had saved a few ominous pieces of mail for the end. The letters
did not have names or return addresses. Some of them didn't even have
postage. Paul knew they were death threats and he knew, moreover, that
they would cheer the old man. He opened them to find that they were indeed terse and ungrammatical promises that Sinclair would be shot
dead if he published *A Moveable Jungle!*

Sinclair was giddy. "I've struck a nerve, Paul! By God, every knock
is a boost! They're scared. They know what could happen if the truth
comes out. They've called out their goons."

The last letter, however, was different from the rest. It was one sentence and Paul read it to himself twice.

Sinclair said, "What is it? Read it."

"This one's bad."

"Read it. My skin is plenty thick by now."

"'If you publish the novel,'" Paul read, "'Albert dies.'"

Sinclair asked Paul to read the sentence again, and then for a third
time. He stood and paced the room, his empty left sleeve dangling.
He asked if there was a return address on the letter. There was not. He
walked to the small kitchen and stared down at the bent spoon in the
sink. He cleaned his glasses on his shirt. "Does the letter say anything
else?"

"That's it."

"Probably just a lunatic."

"Do you want to see it?"

Sinclair said, "I'm sorry I was short with you before, Paul. And I'm
sorry I lectured you on how to collect mail. You're a good secretary."

Paul said, "Think nothing of it. Please." He balled up the plastic bag
and discovered that there was one more letter inside, from a Stephen
Rudkin of Greenville. Sinclair paced the room and did not see Paul remove the letter from the bag. Paul considered what to do with it. He put

it in the top drawer of his desk, but then a moment later he took it back out. Sinclair stopped in front of the window and again parted the curtain with his free hand. Paul said, "There is one more letter, Mr. Sinclair."

Sinclair did not turn from the window. "Go ahead."

Paul read: "'Dear Mr. Sinclair, my town is having a Fourth of July celebration. Everyone here is interested in your writing and we want to have your books here for the celebration. I have sent you a check for 500 books. It doesn't matter which ones you send. We like them all. We need them by the Fourth. Thank you. Sincerely, Stephen Rudkin.'"

Sinclair turned from the window. "Five hundred books?"

"How about that?"

"And there is a check enclosed?"

"Yes." Paul removed a calculator from his desk and tapped in the numbers. "And it's enough to cover shipping."

Sinclair returned to his desk and read the letter himself. He studied the check, held it up to the light. He put his head down on his right arm and kept it there for several minutes. Paul thought he was asleep and he worried that Sinclair would bend his glasses again, but then the old man raised his head. "Let's send the books to this Mr. Rudkin. Five hundred copies of the new novel. The movement will start there, in Greenville. It will be the cradle of American Socialism."

Paul took notes. He said nothing.

"And," Sinclair continued, "we will go there for the Fourth."

"Where?"

"Where the celebration is. Greenburg."

"You want to go to Greenville?"

"I want to be there for the celebration. I want to meet Mr. Rudkin and his comrades. It is fitting that I be there for the start of this. I'll give a speech. You'll drive me there, Paul, and we'll surprise these good people."

Paul nodded and thought of Derek Bittle. He knew better than to say anything. He made a note to himself to check the RSP mailing list to see if there were, in fact, any Sinclair sympathizers in Greenville.

"I'm going to take my nap now. I'd appreciate it if you could keep the noise down for an hour or so. And I need you," Sinclair said, "to write a letter to my son. Tell him two things. First, I regret that I'll be unable to see him in early July, as we had planned. Tell him the truth. Tell him I've been invited to a celebration in my honor and that I cannot in good conscience refuse."

Paul wrote down the instructions.

"And second," Sinclair said, "tell him to be careful." He lay down on the lower bunk. He took off his glasses and closed his eyes. "Tell him that these are dangerous times and that he should be very, very careful."

3

Lionel T. Pratt parked the Lexus at the end of the long, dirt driveway and began walking through the woods to the house. The walk was familiar to Pratt, though he had not been here in a number of years, and he noted that the dirt road at its edges was being reclaimed by the forest floor, and branches of trees now hung low enough to brush passing cars. There seemed to have been an increase in wildlife. Birds and squirrels jabbered in the trees. Chipmunks darted and rustled. The trees blocked the afternoon sun, but the day was hot and the road was dry and dusty. Pratt reached for his handkerchief and realized with surprise and dismay that he was not carrying one. This was unusual. Had he misplaced it during the day or had he just forgotten it while getting dressed? He could not remember using it or noting it at any point that day, and he concluded that he had left his condo that morning without a handkerchief. Pratt scolded himself for this forgetfulness, not simply because he missed the handkerchief now in the heat, but because it suggested that he had become careless and impatient in his excitement. He reminded himself to relax. He tried to release the tension from his shoulders and hips. He was a tall man, and trim, with thick, wavy gray hair. He was sore from yoga and uncomfortable in his suit. He walked quickly, carrying a leather briefcase. Without consulting his watch, he knew he was early.

As Pratt neared the house, he heard the barking and soon they were upon him, five large dogs with tangled fur and yellow teeth and bloodshot eyes. They circled Pratt in the dusty road, hackles up, growling and barking, bouncing on their front legs. They smelled awful. Pratt was prepared for the dogs. He took from his jacket pocket a bag of chicken livers and tossed one onto the road. Three of the dogs lunged for the liver, snapping and growling. Then all five dogs sat down politely, wagging their tails in the dirt and drooling. Pratt distributed the livers to the dogs, making sure they all received an equal share. When he was finished, his thumb and forefinger were greasy, and he again thought of the missing handkerchief. He continued his brisk walk to the house, the dogs trotting beside him, their expired rabies tags jingling.

Everyone knew that Joe Gerald Huntley grew up poor, but most just assumed that he had become wealthy during his long and successful career. This was not the case. He had had a bit of money once, but it had disappeared through a series of unwise business decisions, periods of profligacy, and two expensive, well-publicized divorces. The house that Pratt now approached used to be a hideout, a quaint forest getaway, but for some time now it had been Huntley's main and only residence. Even from a distance Pratt could see that the house was in poor condition. A section of the roof was covered with a plywood patch. The paint was cracked and peeling. Gutters sagged. There was a missing stair leading up to the front porch and the yard had long ago been worn to dirt by the dogs.

Pratt stood at the bottom of the stairs, holding his briefcase and thinking about his breathing.

"You must be Mr. Pratt."

Pratt flinched and turned to see a woman standing inside a small fenced garden to the right of the house. Her gloved hands rested on the fence. Pratt walked to the garden, wondering how long she had been watching him. "You must be Carla. It's nice to finally meet you."

She took off a glove and shook Pratt's hand. Huntley's third wife was a small woman, pretty but hard, and much younger than Huntley. She thanked Pratt for the flowers he had sent but she did not smile at him. She had written to Huntley in prison several years ago and after an eight-month epistolary romance, they had been married in the prison chapel.

"I see you know how to handle the dogs," she said.

"I've been coming here for years. Where's the big one?"

"Baxter?"

"The big black one."

"He died a while ago," Carla said. "When Joe and I were first married."

Pratt looked past Carla into the garden. There were three rows of staked tomato plants, two rows of lettuce, and two rows of something else Pratt did not recognize. "Those tomatoes are doing well."

"Mr. Pratt, I don't mean to be rude, but maybe you can tell me why you're here."

Pratt coughed into a fist. He set down his briefcase and took off his glasses, which he cleaned cursorily on the sleeve of his jacket. It occurred to him to tell Carla that he had known her husband since before she grew the first hair on her cunt, and that furthermore the legendary man she had fallen in love with was largely his own creation. One should be able to visit one's creation without explanation. He felt the tension pool in his hips. "I'm here to congratulate Joe," he said. "We're old friends, as you know." He put his glasses back on. "Is he home?"

"He's home."

"Is he out in the range?"

"No. He's inside."

"I imagine you're happy to have him home."

"You have no idea."

"May I go say hello to my old friend? He's expecting me."

"Door's open."

Pratt thanked Carla and picked up his briefcase. The dogs, he noticed, were gone.

"Mr. Pratt," Carla said, "Joe's having a hard time right now. It's an adjustment. It's just going to take some time."

"Of course, yes. I've seen this before, Carla."

"The thing is—" She stared up at Pratt violently. "The thing is, Joe is retired. You need to know that, Mr. Pratt. He's through."

Pratt said, "Is that right?"

"He's too old for it."

"Your husband and I share the same birthday, Carla. I am aware of his age."

"The same year?"

"Yes." It was not quite the truth, but not far from it.

"I'm sorry. I didn't mean to say that he was *old*. Just that—"

"I understood you well." Pratt walked away from the small fenced garden toward the house, the treacherous stairs. "It was nice to meet you, Carla."

"Mr. Pratt."

Pratt kept walking. He said, "When a man reaches a certain age, he values the old friends."

The house was dark and hot inside. Curtains were pulled across the windows, blocking the light and any afternoon breeze. Carla, Pratt could see, had decorated well. He paused in the living room to examine a series of black-and-white photographs of an old brick warehouse, tastefully framed. There were pieces of furniture that Pratt had never seen: a simple beige loveseat, an antique cabinet, a narrow coffee table with glass panes. The flowers he had sent were in a vase on the cabinet. There was no television. The rug, too, was new.

Pratt knew where to find his old friend. He walked the length of a dark hallway to a half-open door. He knocked twice and then pushed the door open.

Huntley's study contained a wooden desk, a worn leather chair beneath a stand-up lamp, and three tall bookshelves. The room was much the same as it had been, though Pratt sensed small changes. The light blue curtains that covered the windows, for instance. There had been blinds previously.

Huntley sat in the leather chair beneath the lamp with a book in his lap. He still had that glorious mane, but it was almost completely gray now. He wore loose cotton pants, sandals, a black T-shirt, and a pair of reading glasses attached to a red string around his neck. Pratt had not seen Huntley since a prison visit eighteen months ago, and in that time Huntley had lost weight. His face was stubbly, pale, and lined.

"You're not the terror you once were, Joe."

"Nice to see you, Lionel."

"What are you reading?"

Huntley held up the new Upton Sinclair novel, *A Moveable Jungle!*

"How is it?"

"Same as ever. Hysterical, irresponsible. He hasn't bothered to learn a bit of economic theory in the last century. He doesn't have a single original idea. He has never had one."

"He got a decent review in the Baltimore paper."

"The hometown kid," Huntley said. "I will say that the writing isn't bad, for him. It's his best book in a while, though I'm sure the end will be terrible."

"I hear he's going on the road again. Another revolution tour."

Huntley stared at the novel in his hands. There was a proletarian image on the cover and a plot synopsis on the back. Sinclair was described as "the Pulitzer Prize–winning author of *The Jungle*," which struck Huntley as a misleading statement. There were no blurbs on the outside or inside of the book. There wasn't a writer alive who would dare blurb a Sinclair novel. "It's hard for me to get too worked up about that," Pratt said. "I just got home, Lionel."

"You don't—"

"Plus, look, I just don't see that he's much of a threat anymore."

"People are starting to say the same about you."

Huntley put the book on the oak side table next to his chair. "Listen—"

"Is that new? That's a nice piece."

Huntley looked at the table and nodded.

"Your wife has improved the place."

"You met her."

"Outside. She's nice."

"She's incredible," Huntley said. "I'm not getting married again, I can guarantee you that. This is the last time."

"She's no doubt trying to improve you, as well."

"If anyone can, it's her."

Pratt stared at the blank wall behind the desk. "There," he said, pointing at the wall, jabbing. "It was there. Where is it?"

"Carla hates it."

"Has she any idea of what it's worth?"

"I'm sure she does."

"And does she know who gave it to you?"

Huntley shrugged. "She hates it. Hell, I never really liked it all that much, either."

"Joe, it's not a thing you like or don't like."

"It's in the attic."

Pratt placed his briefcase on the desk. He continued to stare at the blank wall and resolved to himself to buy or steal the painting. The framed and autographed movie poster was missing too. "How are you doing, Joe?"

"I'm fine."

"Your wife said you've been having a hard time."

"Like I said, I'm fine."

Pratt clicked open his briefcase. He took out a bottle of whiskey with a red ribbon around it and stood it on the desk. "I brought you this. Are you"—Pratt motioned his head to the window, to the garden beyond—"allowed to have it anymore?"

"Fuck off, Lionel."

"What are you doing with your time, Joe?"

"Reading. Walking with the dogs. I can't watch TV anymore. It's too stupid. I thought I might start writing."

"Have you been shooting any?"

"Not much."

Pratt leaned against the edge of the desk and again thought of his handkerchief. It would have been a good prop now. He might have used it like a magician. He worried that he could not do what he came to do without the handkerchief. "Are you depressed, Joe?"

"I got some pills. I feel OK."

"Many people report feeling depressed and aimless when they retire."

Huntley gently squeezed the arms of the chair and smiled at Pratt. "Like I said, maybe I'll start writing. I was doing some in prison."

"They report not knowing what to do with themselves. Suddenly. It's a question of identity and purpose."

Huntley said, "Lionel, if Sinclair walks down my driveway and makes it past the dogs, I'll get my rifle and shoot him. But I'm not going out again. I'm just not."

"I respect that."

"Thank you for the whiskey, by the way."

"But I do think you should have all the facts." Pratt took three glossy magazines from a bundled stack in his briefcase. Francis Scott Billings was on the cover of each one, smiling, flashing his gold tooth. His hair was short, tousled, and gelled. His eyes were close together, his nose was long and sharp, and his lips were thin. On the covers he wore silk shirts, unbuttoned to show his pale bony chest, his tattoo *(#1 KILLER)*, and a bullet on a chain around his neck. He wore flared pants and black leather boots. The covers of the magazines said, "PHENOM!" and "FROM THE GUNS OF BABES" and "MEET THE NEW SHERIFF."

"You seen these?"

Huntley glanced at the magazines, turned away, and then looked back. "Carla hides them. She throws them out. I don't want to see it."

"It's pretty interesting stuff, Joe."

"I heard about this kid in prison."

"He's a big deal now. I don't know if you realize."

Huntley grabbed one of the magazines and stared at the photo of Billings kissing the barrel of an automatic rifle. "Christ, look at him. He's ridiculous."

"You were brash too. When you started out, you were a skinny little punk too."

"Not like this."

"The times are changing, Joe."

"How old is he? Twelve?"

"He's seventeen," Pratt said. "And he's got quite a mouth on him too." Pratt flipped through a magazine to the lead article. "Here we go. Interviewer: 'Are you really this arrogant or is this part of an act, a publicity stunt?' Billings: 'Arrogant? I ain't arrogant. I'm just the best. Period. I'm just who I am. Ain't no act. Sinclair got lucky the first time. I put one in his shoulder from a hundred out and my eye was swelled shut from a bee sting. From now on he won't get lucky anymore. See these bullets? Ten bullets. That's all I need for my career. Just these ten. That's all I carry. I'll kill him ten times with ten bullets. Then I'll go lay on a beach on an island with blue water and dolphins and shit.' Interviewer: 'What do you know about Socialism?' Billings: 'I know I hate it. That's all I need to know.' Interviewer: 'Why do you want to kill Sinclair?' Billings: 'Because he hates America. Because I'm the best there ever was.'"

Huntley got up from his chair. He moved more slowly, but he was still an imposing man, tall and erect. "This kid is brain damaged."

"Interviewer: 'Which Sinclair book do you hate the most?' Billings: 'They all bad. I hate them all. All that socializing. I'll kill him. Then I'll write me a book and then I'll kill him again.'"

"That's enough, Lionel."

"Interviewer: 'Did you pattern yourself after other assassins? Did you grow up watching Huntley or reading his books?' Billings: 'I'm my own man. Hunter did his thing, but that ain't nothing to me. I don't need some coach or role model. I'm the best. Hunter might have been good, but he's old now and he needs to stand out of the way. Even in his prime he couldn't do what I can do with a gun. Nobody can do what I can do with a gun. Ten bullets. I'll kill Sinclair ten times, then I'll go visit Hunter in the old folks' home, then I'll go lay on a beach.'"

Huntley stared at the books in one of his bookshelves, his back to Pratt. Pratt had made up the "Hunter" error and the final part about the old folks' home, but everything else was word for word. He said, "You're in here too, Joe. Page forty-six. There's a little sidebar about your parole."

Huntley said, "He hasn't even done anything yet."

"Yes, Joe, he has. He's gotten himself on the cover of all these magazines. He's gotten his picture taped up in boys' bedrooms in every state. He's negotiating for his own clothing line. He's done something."

Huntley sat back down. "I did what I did, Lionel. I did it well. So he's on posters. I was on a stamp."

"How many years ago? And I can tell you, those stamps aren't going for what they used to."

"It's difficult for me to get all that worked up about any of this, Lionel."

"Where are the flowers, Joe? Just tell me that."

"Big deal, flowers."

"After parole this place usually looks like a goddamn florist shop. And the mail? Where's the mail?" Pratt looked among the framed photographs on the wall behind Pratt's chair—there was a famous shot of this very office covered wall to wall with bulging canvas mailbags, but he saw that this too had been removed from the office.

"It's a relief."

"You miss it. I know you do."

"I could get used to things out here."

"We're slipping, Joe."

"What do you want? Why did you come out here?"

Pratt parted the curtain and looked out to the garden. He didn't see Carla. "Let's go out to the range. Can we?"

Huntley cleared the cobwebs off of the lock and tried three keys before he found the right one. "It's one of these," he said.

Pratt pointed above the door. "That's a nasty wasps' nest, Joe. You should take care of that."

Huntley pushed open the door to the range and it squealed on its hinges. Both men could hear the scurry of mice. Huntley flipped a switch and the lights blinked on. "It's been a while," he said. The room was as hot and stuffy as an attic.

Pratt took a pair of ear protectors from a pegboard hook and told Huntley to show him what he had.

Huntley chose a dusty rifle from a rack and loaded it. "I don't have my glasses."

"It doesn't matter," Pratt said.

Huntley took aim down the long narrow room. His breathing was slow and even. He held still for thirty full seconds and then he fired six quick shots. Pratt turned the crank on the pulley, reeling in the target— a life-size outline of a small man—down the length of the range. When the target approached, Pratt squinted through his bifocals and said, "Not bad, old man. Not bad at all."

Huntley put the gun back on the rack. "You should leave now," he said.

Pratt said, "In this briefcase I have a check. It's an advance for a book from our publishers. It's the largest advance ever given for an assassination book."

Huntley said he didn't understand.

"On the Fourth of July, a small American town is having an Upton Sinclair celebration."

"The whole town?"

"Greenville." Pratt had received confirmation that five hundred novels had shipped from the Red Shovel Press office the previous morning. "The whole town. An American celebration on Independence Day. And Sinclair is going to be there to announce the start of the revolution."

Huntley said he still didn't understand.

Pratt said, "I have an advance to write a book about Upton Sinclair's dramatic assassination on the Fourth of July during a celebration in his honor."

"You have an advance to write a book about an event that hasn't happened yet?"

"A very large advance," Pratt said. "Half of which is yours if it's your dramatic bullet that dramatically kills Sinclair."

"How did you do this?"

"They know it will be a good book, Joe. They know it will be a best seller. It's a great American story. The crafty old-timer picks up the gun one more time to thwart Socialism and to teach the cocky upstart a thing or two."

"They're still paying for this? Don't you think Socialism has already been thwarted? What about thwarting terrorism? The spread of Islam?"

"But it's a town, Joe. A whole town of reds. Could be the cradle of American Socialism."

"It won't go anywhere and you know it."

"The Left may be dead, Joe, but the fear and hatred of the Left will never die. It's an American passion. Sinclair could write cookbooks and run for dog-catcher in Alaska, and he'd still be picked off, and we'd still get six figures for the gripping account."

"Billings will be there?"

"In Greenville? Who knows? Probably."

"He fucked up my name."

"The wise old master comes out of retirement for a final challenge. A career-defining moment. Could be another movie, Joe."

"I don't care about the money."

"You could at least patch your roof. Get some new gutters. You'll need to be careful out there. These people love Sinclair."

Huntley stared at the target. All six shots hit the Sinclair outline and two were kills. "Give me a day to think about it."

When Pratt returned to his car, Billings was dancing in his seat with the radio turned up loud. Pratt put on his seatbelt and turned off the radio.

"What took you so long, Lionel? God*damn* I was bored."

Pratt started the car. "Shut up, Francis."

"What did he say? Is he going to come?"

"He'll be there."

"Did he *say* he was coming?"

"He'll be there, Francis. He wants what you want. Stop that dancing."

"I've got some moves."

Pratt turned the car around and pulled out onto the county road.

Billings said, "Was he all old and shit?"

Pratt chose not to answer.

Billings turned the radio back on. He said, "And I get half, right?"

"If you get him."

Billings made pretend pistols with the thumb and forefinger of each hand, and he fired both imaginary weapons out the window. "Pow. Pow. Pow."

In the rearview mirror Pratt saw the thick clouds of dust from the tires. He tried to release the tension from his lower back and his hips. "A great American story," he said. "The young phenom thwarts the spread of Socialism and dethrones the king. It's good drama."

Billings said, "Ka-pow!"

4

When Albert woke up, the young woman in the bed was applying a condom. She was not gentle, but neither was she rough. She was determined, matter of fact, unashamed; she treated his body as a nurse would treat it. They made love, slowly and sadly. He thought her name was Hannah. They made love on the mattress on the floor of her small apartment. The floors were swept clean and there was an orange flower in a vase on the windowsill. Albert said, "Is your name Hannah?"

She nodded and touched his face. She picked the sleep from his eyes. Her hair was smoky. She lived above a dance studio and Albert could hear the waltz below. He lay there with his hands on the slope of her hips, his feet flopped out to the sides. Her knees pushed the soft mattress to the floor. They moved subtly and well. The light was good and contributed to the sadness. She yawned and stretched, hands above her head, and Albert watched her stomach, her ribs, the way her belly-button changed its shape.

"Are your knees OK?"

"Yes."

Both of them were trying to make this work. It was a risk, of course.

Albert saw his guitar case by the door. He hadn't brought up the amps last night because he was tired and drunk. Now he decided that if they had been stolen from his van in the night, he would cancel the tour and stay here with Hannah. The matter would be settled. They would make simple pastas. He'd write more love songs.

She pushed down hard on him and he pushed back. It could not, after all, remain as it had begun, slow and solicitous. It moved faster now, and more selfishly, toward the end. Each took what was available. The inside of Albert's mouth tasted bad and he came inside the condom. His full bladder muted the orgasm. She came too, he thought, though she didn't make a big deal of it.

She said, "Don't worry, I'm not going to cry."

Albert took both of her hands. "*One* two three, *one* two three."

Hannah left the bed and returned with a bowl of hot water and a bar of soap and a pink plastic razor. Albert sat up and leaned his back against the wall while Hannah shaved his face. The hot soapy water ran down his neck and chest and onto the sheets. There was a little blood too. He said her name over and over. He imagined living together on a farm. On hot days she might weed the garden, wearing overalls with nothing underneath. There would be a black Lab lying in the shade.

Before she left for work, Hannah told him to help himself to fruit, bread, cheese, and juice, and he did. He showered, thinking, What if I was still here when she returned? Before he left, he tried to write her a note, but gave up.

He found his van on the bright street. The equipment was still inside and the tires were not slashed. There was no pink ticket beneath the windshield wiper. It was noon and his mother was expecting him at the hospital at four. He put his guitar in the van and fed the meter. He still had the dull ache in his groin, the empty feeling. He put on his backpack and walked ten blocks to Page Boys, an independent bookstore with an Upton Sinclair Reading Room.

On the bulletin board inside the store a small poster advertised the previous night's show. In pencil, lightly, someone had scrawled, "If you see the Last Folksinger on the road, kill him." Albert didn't know if the message was playful or hateful. It was a question of tone, and it was more and more a problem.

He went directly to the front counter, where a teenager with pierced eyebrows did not speak but indicated, by glancing up from his book, that he would consider Albert's question. Albert knew many of the store employees from previous visits, but this kid was new. He leaned over the counter and said, "How many kilometers to St. Louis?"

The kid glanced around the store. "Come on," he said. Albert followed him back behind the counter, through the store office, and then down a flight of narrow stairs. The employee took a key from his pocket and unlocked a door at the bottom of the stairs. He held the door open for Albert and said, "Enjoy."

There were now, across the country, more than forty Upton Sinclair Reading Rooms, which were known by their patrons as Red Rooms, Rad Rooms, Prop Rooms, or Sinks, depending on the region. Page Boys was one of three bookstores that claimed to have opened the original Sinclair Reading Room. The argument flared up periodically on the Internet, and was not likely ever to be settled, but the proprietors of Page Boys had won the case to the extent that their underground room was known throughout the network as Sink1.

Sink1 was a large, low-ceilinged room with rows of homemade bookshelves lining each wall. Two of the walls contained the works of Upton Sinclair, which were available for purchase or two-week loan. The other walls contained the works of other authors on the insurance companies' Do Not Cover list. The center of the room was filled with furniture, mostly stools, wooden crates, and beanbag chairs. In Sink1, as in most Sinks, the narrow points of access would not allow for couches, large chairs, desks, or tables.

There were four other people in the reading room, browsing or lounging in beanbags with books and cigarettes. Only a handful of the forty Sinks were nonsmoking, another issue that inspired chat room hysteria. Albert went straight to Sinclair's recent work and saw what he had come for—there were a couple dozen paperback copies of *A Moveable Jungle!* He took one from the shelf and flipped, as he always did, to the acknowledgments page. Upton thanked his secretary, a courageous librarian, and the good people at RSP. The book was dedicated to the *millions who toil in our outsourced jungles.*

Albert sat down on the worn carpet next to a row of books on levitation and telekinesis. He read *A Moveable Jungle!* in three hours. It was a good book, typically well-researched and passionate, with a few subtle and poignant passages. Some nice dialogue. Surprisingly few exclamation points. The ending, of course, was terrible.

He would see Sinclair soon and he would tell him that he enjoyed the book. He would tell his father that it was his best book in some time, which was true.

A kid with a shaved head, browsing the Sinclair titles, whispered to Albert, "Good show last night."

Albert looked up at the bald kid, whom he remembered seeing at the club because his head had a weird shape. Albert shelved *A Moveable Jungle!*, then pulled out another one that had not been handled. He said, "Well, it wasn't, but thank you."

The kid with the shaved head said, "I like the new stuff, but *Splitting Wood with a Razor* is my favorite. It's amazing."

Albert tried to be polite. What was the point in arguing with the people who bought your music and came to your shows? And frankly, *Splitting Wood* was Albert's favorite too. It was, he had to admit, his best work. But he hated hearing people say it. Shouldn't your most recent work be your best work? Shouldn't you be getting better each time out? *Splitting Wood* was five years old and soon it would be ten years old, twenty. What if it remained everyone's favorite? How could it be possible to write and play for twenty years and not get any better? Albert stood up and faced the bald kid. He said, "What do you like about it?"

"What?"

"What is it about *Splitting Wood* that you like so much? Why is it better than the other ones?" Albert could sense the desperation in his question. This was worse than telling the kid to fuck off. He wished he had just told the kid to fuck off, but Albert thought maybe this kid heard something that he couldn't hear. It was like the hitting coach who notices that small glitch in your swing and gets you out of your slump. This kid had listened to the CD a thousand times and he might know what's wrong. He could fix Albert's swing. Albert would thank him in the liner notes of the next one. I want to thank the bald kid in Sink1 who got me back on track.

"It's the songs," the kid said. "The songs are just really fucking great."

On top of a crate in the center of the reading room was a glass jar full of money. Albert put in a large bill and took out his change. He wrapped the paperback in an old shirt in his backpack and climbed the narrow stairs.

Out on the bright street, Albert called home from a sticky pay phone and Laura answered on the fourth ring.

Albert said, "How is everything?"

"How is everything?"

"Yes. How are you?"

"Everything is fine, Albert."

"Do I have any mail?"

"Mostly junk. There's a letter from Fenn and a letter from your illustrious father."

Albert stared at a pile of green ice cream, melting on the sidewalk.

"Do you want me to open them?"

"Yes."

"Fenn says, 'Al, can't remember if you're on the road now or not. Either way, hope you're well. Sorry to break bad news, but we can't put out the new CD with Brutal. It's not the songs. The songs are good. You know that all of us in Ezra are big fans of yours. But we've been catching a lot of shit from your last two CDs and our tour together last winter. We even had a bomb threat here at the office. We just—' Jesus, what a fucking coward. Do you want me to keep going?"

"That's enough."

"The songs *are* good, Albert."

"What does my father say?"

"Do you really want to do this?"

"Go ahead."

"Looks like his letter had already been opened when it got here. OK,

'Dear Albert, I'm sorry to tell you'—Oh my God, that fucker—'sorry to tell you that I won't be able to meet you here at the cabin in July as planned.' Now there's a shocker. 'I've been invited to an Upton Sinclair celebration on the Fourth of July in Greenville and I feel I must attend. It could be an important event.' Yes, yes, it might turn the tide, Upton! Greenville could be the cradle of American Socialism."

"Knock it off."

"I'm sorry, but he's infuriating."

"Is that all it says?"

" 'I hope that you're eating wisely, son. Please be very careful. These are dangerous times and I ask you to be very careful.' That is pathetic. That's so pathetic. Why do you even try anymore, Albert? He's never going to play catch with you in the backyard."

"That's all it says?"

"That's it."

A tall man with an eye patch waited to use the phone outside the booth. Weren't there other phone booths in this town? Albert held up a finger to indicate he'd be just another moment.

"An Upton Sinclair celebration?"

"Don't let him off the hook, Albert. He could have invited you to go with him."

"I played Greenville once and they threw bottles at me and made me play 'Smoke on the Water.' That was about the meanest place I ever played."

"Things are changing." She sang, " 'And he who gets hurt will be he who has stalled.' "

Albert noticed that the man with the eye patch was no longer waiting outside the booth. "I shouldn't have gone on tour, Laura."

"It wouldn't have made any difference. You know that."

"I'm not playing well."

"Have you seen your mom?"

"Not yet."

"I'm sorry, but Upton's a prick. He's unbelievable."

"I spent the night with someone last night."

"A woman, you mean?"

"Yes."

"That doesn't really surprise me, Albert. Nor does it bother me."

"I don't believe that."

"You're free to do what you like. Spread your seed."

Albert rubbed a patch of stubble on his throat that Hannah had missed. He knew this awful truth: The time he spent with her, the wonderful things they did with their bodies, would become a bad memory, a mistake. He said, "I'll call again in a few days."

"Eat wisely," Laura said. "And be *very, very* careful."

Albert arrived at the gigantic hospital complex at a quarter after four. As always, he had scheduled a night off on the tour so he could visit his mother. She lived in the main building, on the ninth floor, which was long-term care. She had lived there for more than three years and they still weren't sure what was wrong with her.

When he entered her room, his mother was in bed, sleeping.

"Mom?"

She opened her eyes and stared at Albert, her face retaining the blankness of sleep. She did not seem to recognize him.

"Mom, it's me."

Then she smiled and sat up, patting the mattress beside her. "You came."

He hugged her and kissed her on the cheek. He smelled her perfume above the sour smell of her illness and long-term care. "I always do, Mom."

The room was small, yellow, and hot. There was a sink and a mirror, a window overlooking a parking lot, and a low bookshelf with a portable CD player resting on top. A machine in the corner made loud breathing noises.

"My God," Albert's mother said, "I thought I was dreaming when I first saw you. You look more and more like your father."

Albert laughed. "Oh, no."

"No, not as he is now. That's not much of a compliment. I mean when he was a young man. The way he looks in those old photographs. He was handsome. He was almost pretty."

Hundreds of men and women claimed to be the children of Upton Sinclair, but most were lying or had been lied to. Nobody, however, could dispute Albert's lineage. He had the same high forehead, the same long Roman nose, the same full, pursed upper lip that in the father looked effeminate and moralistic, but in the son looked sensual and decadent. Albert was taller than his father, but he had the same slight frame. In his case it was the frame of a touring, pack-a-day musician, not an athlete.

Albert's mother said, "I can't keep track of him anymore. Is he alive?"

"As far as I know."

"Have you seen him?"

"No. He's too busy. I get letters once in a while. He doesn't approve of me."

"It's not that. I'm sure he's proud."

"Do you hear from him?"

"He sends money when he can. That's all. But I don't expect anything more."

Albert took the book from his backpack. "I brought you the new one."

His mother thanked him and told him to slide the paperback under the mattress. The skin hung loose down her face and her eyes were bloodshot. She appeared to have lost more weight.

Albert said, "How are you feeling, Mom?"

"Not too bad. Just tired."

"Are you eating?"

"I eat what I can."

"Have they figured out anything?"

"They're stumped. They come from all over to look at me, but nobody knows anything."

"Do you want to go outside? Can you? The sun might feel good."

They took the elevator to the lobby and walked slowly outside to a small courtyard. Albert held his mother's hand and they sat together on a bench in the sun and played Scrabble. While they played, a burn victim walked across the courtyard, arms held out to his sides. Each step was pain. A nurse walked beside him, offering encouragement, trying to maintain the same unbearably slow pace. The sun felt nice, Albert's mother said so.

She got cold when their table fell into shadow, and they returned to her room. An orderly brought dinner for both of them, and as he leaned over Albert's mother's bed to set up her tray, his shirt rode up and Albert saw the small red shovel at the base of his spine. The orderly asked them if they needed anything else, and when they said no, he smiled and left.

Albert said, "He seems nice."

His mother said, "I've never seen that one before."

Albert sat beside her bed with his tray on his knees. "The food is actually not that bad."

"The thing about your father, Albert, you have to share him. You know that. He thinks of Shelley as his father. That's his idea of fatherhood. He's trying to be a father to the whole world. He's got no time to be a real father."

"No. Because you can't get famous doing that."

"There's more to it than that, probably. He's just not cut out for it." Albert's mother often recalled the one night she spent with Upton. She had shared a house with a group of college students who offered to let Sinclair hide at their place after a rally for striking electricians. It was 1970, Sinclair was giddy to be alive again. In the middle of the night he came to her small room and mounted her with surprising energy, but when he finished, he was despondent. He paced the room, remorseful and ashamed. He talked about birth control and God. He said that God was watching him. During the day he clearly didn't even believe in God. He shouted. He said he was an artist and not a lover. He said he had tried to sneak through his work, but you can't sneak with God. She had tried to get him to return to her twin bed, but he wouldn't. He wrote for an hour and then fell asleep on the floor. She would never tell her son this, of course.

She said, "If you want to see him, you must go see him. You can't wait for him to decide it's important. That won't happen."

"I imagine it won't."

"How is Laura?"

"She's fine, Mom."

"Did you bring me some music?"

"I'll bring you something in the morning. I'll stop by before I leave town."

"Thank you for coming, Albert."

Albert's mother struggled to stay awake. She asked him if he had a place to stay and he said that he did. He hugged her again and then sat beside the bed, waiting for her to fall asleep.

Down in the lobby he watched muted TV with the other visitors. There were two empty seats between every seated person, so he stood and watched TV, not wanting to single out a person to sit beside. When a woman left with her small child, Albert sat down in a blue plastic chair beneath a framed poster for a drug company. There were no people in the poster and no drugs—just mountains, some elk, a rising sun.

He took his battered road atlas and his tour itinerary from the backpack. He wanted a cigarette. Tonight he might return to Hannah's apartment above the dance studio. Maybe the right-wing punks would slash his tires, steal his amps. He flipped back and forth between colorful state maps, made rough calculations of mileage. He could cancel his show on the fifth. He could play his show on the third and then drive all night through an orange state. There were roads from wherever you were to wherever you wanted to go. Even if he stopped for an hour or two to sleep, Albert figured he could make it to Greenville for the big Upton Sinclair celebration.

5

Stephen could not sleep on the eve of the book burning. He lay beneath only a sheet in his narrow bed, going through his checklist over and over again. In the garage he had the five gas cans, filled. He had a twenty-five-foot length of rope to use as a wick. He had yellow CAUTION tape to mark off the bonfire area. He had the firecrackers and the sparklers. He had a fire extinguisher and safety goggles. He had arranged with Myron Lewis for a big off-season delivery of firewood, which would give the pile structural support and a long-lasting center. (He had called Myron that morning to make sure Myron was prepared; he would call again the next morning, he decided.) And of course he had the books, five hundred Upton Sinclair titles, shipped directly to his front door from Red Shovel Press. Stephen had feared the books would not arrive in time. He had had nightmares of showing up at the burning, in front of the entire town, with two of his school notebooks and a green stick he pulled off of a tree. He had grown despondent, desperate. He paced the house, close to tears. He ran outside, night or day, when he heard a truck on the street. His father told him not to worry, though Arthur himself had become a bit concerned when the books had not arrived by the first of July. But they had come the morning of the second: *fifteen boxes.* Now Stephen lay in bed and thought of the books, arranged in four stacks along a wall in the dark garage. Fifteen boxes of Socialist propaganda in his own garage! Three stacks of four boxes and one stack of three. It was thrilling and terrifying to consider the number and proximity of those dangerous books. Yesterday Stephen had bought a second padlock for the garage door. He had considered whether to charge the four-dollar padlock to the GASL book-burning account, but in the end he decided the padlock was an extraneous expense, and he paid for it himself with his own lawn-mowing money.

Gas, rope, CAUTION tape, fireworks, fire extinguisher, safety goggles, firewood, books. Stephen had his book-burning clothes laid out on top of his pine dresser with his inhaler. It was best, the Internet articles agreed, not to wear anything long, baggy, or loose-fitting, such as bathrobes, ponchos, dresses, sarongs, or trench coats. To the best of his knowledge Stephen did not own any of these items; in fact, most of his clothes were uncomfortably snug after his recent growth spurt. He laid out the snuggest: jeans and a year-old striped shirt.

Gas, rope, CAUTION tape, fireworks, fire extinguisher, safety goggles, firewood, books, clothes. He also had instructions, printed from the Internet, for how to construct the book pile to achieve your desired effect. There was quick-burn methodology and slow-burn methodology. Many people (including Stephen, just a week ago!) assumed that you simply dumped your books on the ground and lit a match. You could do this, of course, but don't your friends and neighbors deserve better? There were very specific ways to create beautiful, safe, and memorable book burnings, specifically suited to your unique celebration. The arrangement of books and firewood and other flammable material was vital, as was the amount and application of gasoline, as was the wick mechanism. Why not create a book burning that is most appropriate to the mood of your occasion? (If you are unsure of the type of book burning you're looking for, turn to Worksheet 3 and take the short quiz.)

Stephen had done the research by himself on the lone computer in the Greenville Public Library. He had asked Mrs. Middleton for help—he had asked her three times, in fact. The first two times she told him she was busy and Stephen waited patiently. It was not like her to ignore him or put him off. They were friends, after all. When he approached the third time, Mrs. Middleton sighed and said, "Stephen, honey, what if we searched for something else? I'll show you how to use a search engine and I'll teach you how to get around the Internet, but I'd rather not help you look up how to burn books. Is that OK?"

Stephen shrugged. "I guess so," he said. "But why?"

Mrs. Middleton asked Stephen to look around him. "I have," she said, "a certain professional regard for books, regardless of their content."

That sentence stuck in Stephen's brain. It was an elegant sentence, regardless of its content. Mrs. Middleton, whose quavering speech at the GASL meeting still had people in town rolling their eyes, was emerging in Stephen's mind as an eccentric. They sat together and searched the Internet for sled dogs, Benjamin Franklin, and the lost city of Atlantis. Stephen was a quick learner and when left on his own, he quickly found dozens of sites on book burning. He selected the most comprehensive, highly regarded site (linked at BewaretheIdes) and printed it after Mrs. Middleton reluctantly showed him how to use the printer. Those pages, now stapled and filled with Stephen's marginalia and underline marks, lay on the pine dresser next to his clothes and his inhaler.

Stephen was wide awake. The weather forecast was good. It was very good. The forecast had been good all week and it was still good. Sunny and hot. From time to time he thought he felt something crawling across his foot or leg. He tried to concentrate on his checklist, which was not difficult.

Gas, rope, CAUTION tape, fireworks, fire extinguisher, safety goggles, firewood, books, clothes, instructions. There was, in addition to these items, Stephen's speech, which was handwritten on paper torn from a spiral notebook. Stephen did not want to give a speech and he had no specific reason to expect that he would have to. But he had, on occasion, attended functions at which someone, and once his father, was asked to give a speech. Not asked, really. Implored. "Speech!" people yelled. "Speech!" And the person singled out had to stand up and give a speech. Stephen could recall the terror he had felt on the speaker's behalf. If, as the director of this year's book burning, Stephen was asked to give a speech—if his neighbors and teachers began chanting "Speech!"—Stephen wanted to be prepared. The short speech, hidden in the top drawer of the dresser, was little more than a compilation of his father's favorite sayings and lessons, culled from the dinner table and the couch, about human nature, competition, hard work, and the survival of the fittest. The speech ended with Arthur's favorite homily: *Look out the window.* (Stephen did not write *window* because the book burning would be outside.) *Take a good look out there. The squirrels are chasing each other around the tree. The ants are hauling away the carcass of the beetle. The birds are stealing each other's nests. This is our natural world. Socialism ain't natural.* (After lengthy consideration, Stephen kept the *ain't.* He knew it was wrong, but he felt intuitively that it was forceful and persuasive. He hoped his English teacher would understand.)

Stephen got out of bed when he realized there was no use trying to sleep. This was worse than Christmas Eve. He turned on a football helmet lamp and checked the items on top of the dresser, then opened the top drawer to see his folded speech. He turned off his lamp and left the bedroom in his white underwear, sidestepping in the dark hallway a bucket that was a quarter full of old rainwater. His father slept shirtless on the couch in front of the television. The cushions were worn and soft, and Arthur's body sagged deep into the couch, as if he were in a hammock. The windows were open and a rattling box fan blew warm air into the room. Stephen turned off the television and removed the empty glass that rested precariously on the arm of the couch by his father's head.

In the kitchen he took a flashlight from a drawer because the fluorescent lights in the garage took forever to come on. He unlocked the door and opened it as quietly as he could. He imagined, with the terrible force of a nightmare, that the four stacks of books would be missing from the garage. His breath came short and he had to stop in order to concentrate. His inhaler was back in his room, and he didn't want to return for it. He thought about sled dogs to settle down. When you typed *sled dogs* into a search engine, a world opened up. His breathing returned to normal and he entered the garage, which smelled strongly of gas. The books were there, against the wall, next to the gas and other supplies. Or at least the book boxes were there. He walked across the gritty floor on tiptoes and inspected the boxes, which seemed to still contain the books. He felt nervous to be alone in the dark with books that were so wrong they had to be destroyed. The smell of the gas made him lightheaded and giddy. He pointed the flashlight at the shipping label on the side of a box: *Red Shovel Press. A Moveable Jungle! Upton Sinclair.* He tried to open a box, but he couldn't remove the heavy tape. The other boxes appeared to be similarly taped, so he put the flashlight on top of the box, picked it up, and carried it back into the house. The box was heavier than he expected it to be.

In his room, with the door shut and the lamp on, Stephen used the key to the new padlock to saw through the packing tape, stopping once to use his inhaler. On the quiet count of three he jerked open the flaps of the box, half expecting to see something horrible inside. A dead animal or a severed limb. But what he saw, when he opened his eyes, was just an invoice slip on top of stacks of identical paperback books. Stephen got up and checked to see if his door was locked. It was. He unlocked it and locked it again, then returned to the box on the floor.

He cautiously picked one of the books from the box, once more expecting a nasty surprise, a burn or a shock, but the book felt normal in his hands. He looked at the cover of *A Moveable Jungle!*, an image of two powerful arms clasping each other. There were no people, no bodies, just these muscular arms, linked. It was like a handshake, except the hands gripped the forearms, just beneath the elbows. The arms were drawn, not photographed. They were realistic, but the muscles and the creases in the rolled-up sleeves seemed stylized and exaggerated, like the figures in comic books.

Years later he would vividly remember this night, sitting in his white underwear on the floor of his room, holding *A Moveable Jungle!*, perched at the edge of something vast. He would say, later, that he had intended to build a miniature model of the book pile in his room. He would say he had intended to practice his burning technique, and this may have been true. It probably was. But instead of building the model pile, Stephen held the book in his hands, turning it over and over. He felt the sharp corners of the cover with his index finger and he flipped the crisp pages with his thumb. He lifted the book to his nose and inhaled as deeply as his anxious breathing allowed. He opened to the middle, closed his eyes, and buried his face in the crease, inhaling. The smell of the novel! Beneath the mild sweetness of the pages he detected the medicinal, antiseptic scent of the ink, the chemical tang of the glue. The object in Stephen's hands seemed to belong to some new and distinct category, some new species of object, not even distantly related to the soft-cornered, water-stained, dog-eared volumes at the town library or to the bleached and battered textbooks at his school. Stephen, it should be said, had never held a new book. Instead of building his miniature pile in preparation for the GASL book burning, he opened the novel to the first page and began reading, and he did not stop until he had finished it. By that time the sun was coming up on the Fourth of July and for Stephen the world was a very different place.

6

Poorly disguised muckraker Upton Sinclair and his twenty-six-year-old secretary, Paul, arrived in Greenville on the evening of July 3. Sinclair was not drunk, as the made-for-television movie would later depict. The son of an alcoholic, Sinclair was an ardent teetotaler and Prohibitionist, who had in all likelihood never tasted a drop of alcohol (though there are varying accounts). Needless to say, Sinclair was not wearing a tall Uncle Sam–style hat and leaning out the passenger-side window of the

station wagon, gripping a bottle and yelling "Vote for me!" to the
Greenvillians who had gathered on lawns and front porches on a beautiful summer evening. The true account of Sinclair's arrival does not
make for good television: Paul drove and Sinclair slumped low in the
bench seat. His left arm had healed well and was no longer wrapped in
the sling. He wore a large, unruly white beard that did not quite match
in color or texture the wispy strands of hair on his head. He looked
vaguely rabbinical.

The trip to Greenville had been, for the most part, uneventful. At a
rest stop in Ohio, Sinclair had wandered away from the car, and after ten
anxious minutes, Paul found him in the truckers' parking lot, talking to
the drivers about their working conditions, the possibility of unionization,
and the fraternity of international workers. As it turned out, Sinclair had
been invited inside one of the trucks and had toured the cab and sleeping compartment, which was, he told his relieved but angry secretary
once they resumed their trip, something he had always wanted to do.
Sinclair had shown Paul a drawing of the inside of the "rig" that he
made in his notebook. Paul glanced away from the road at the drawing
and grunted. "I admit I'm not much of a drawer," Sinclair had said
cheerfully.

There was one other tense moment when Sinclair got stuck inside a
locked gas station bathroom in Kentucky. The doorknob simply came
off in his hand; Paul had no reason to suspect foul play. While Paul
worked to pick the lock from the outside, Sinclair stood in the dirty
bathroom, holding the grimy knob in his hand, and speaking through
the door about the ways that capitalism, widely regarded as an efficient
system, in truth produces shoddy work, lazy workers, and waste. Paul
interrupted by opening the door. He took the doorknob from Sinclair,
fixed the door by replacing the knob on its post, then suggested that
Sinclair return to the car.

The driving was pleasant. The roads, the weather, and the car held
up nicely. Paul stopped at the library of a small college to photocopy the
mixed review of *A Moveable Jungle!* that had appeared in the Baltimore

newspaper. Sinclair read it for an hour, giddy with the critical acclaim. He talked, slept, predicted, and wrote. He speculated wildly about Stephen Rudkin, gradually generating, on the basis of nothing, a profile of a poet-revolutionary, a future ally and loyal correspondent. He insisted that Paul keep the radio tuned to a series of popular country music stations that played, at least once every hour, a new single titled "Sinclair Season," a reactionary smash hit that Sinclair chose to interpret as a necessary step toward the revolution. The chorus:

> *My camouflage is red, white, and blue*
> *You can't see me, but I can see you*
> *I'm cocked and loaded, got you in my sights*
> *It's Sinclair Season and I'm huntin' tonight*

The song had good production value, no doubt about it. There was a nice horn part in the middle, and some irresistibly sassy background singing.

Each time the song ended, Sinclair said, "Did you hear that, Paul? Did you *hear* it?"

Paul confirmed that he had heard it.

At one point Sinclair asked Paul what he thought of Albert's music.

"I like it," Paul said. "He's not that great of a musician. His harmonica playing is terrible, in fact."

"That's my sense."

"His voice is not that good, either."

"All those cigarettes."

"And he writes these rambling songs," Paul said. "But they're good. The songs are good. Both the political songs and the other ones. *Splitting Wood with a Razor* is one of my all-time favorites. It's like all the elements aren't very good, but they add up to something excellent."

"I fear he hurts the cause."

"I don't think he does."

"I should try harder to like it, I suppose."

"He wants you to like it."

"He's not a bad boy," Sinclair said. "Heaven knows I did not want another child, but he could have turned out worse."

Paul said, "He could have been a banker."

Driving through Greenville, Sinclair desperately wanted to sit up and study the town and its people, but Paul urged him to stay low. Didn't Sinclair want to make a surprise entrance at the celebration? Yes, it was true, he did. For his part, Paul suspected that Stephen Rudkin's enthusiastic letter was an exaggerated version of the truth. He imagined that something less than the entire town was participating in a Fourth of July celebration of Upton Sinclair. He suspected that the Sinclair celebration was in fact alternative and underground, that Mr. Rudkin had either overstated the facts to flatter Sinclair, or that he was inclined, like Sinclair, to let his idealism cloud his perception. There were not, Paul noticed, any Sinclair banners or signs in the town. Thus he drove warily through Greenville and did not regard every citizen he passed as a friend of Socialism.

"Tell me what you see," Sinclair said, slumped low in the seat.

"American flags," Paul said. "Smoking barbecues and grills. White people on crutches. High-water pants. Kids in sprinklers. A lot of flags. Tube tops."

"Yes," Sinclair said through his beard. "Yes."

Paul parked outside a hotel called the Greenville Inn, where a hand-lettered sign said GOD BLESS USA VACANCY. Paul said, "I'm going to check in. Please stay in the car."

Sinclair said, "I don't imagine there is any vacancy."

Paul pointed to the sign. "It says 'vacancy.'"

"You can't believe it just because you see it there, Paul."

"Will you promise to stay in the car?"

"Probably a lot of out-of-town visitors," Sinclair said. "There are not likely to be any rooms left."

There were in fact some out-of-town visitors for the holiday, mostly freelance journalists, operating on chat room tips and rumors, hoping for a big break. Some of the journalists sat in the small hotel lobby, drinking coffee and pretending to read magazines. When night arrived, they would sneak through the streets of downtown Greenville, talking into handheld recorders, hoping for a glimpse of an assassin who might jumpstart their careers.

There were a few vacant rooms, the desk clerk told Paul. He asked how many adults. He asked smoking or nonsmoking. He asked was Paul in town for the big celebration. He said the weather forecast was perfect. He said it sure was neat the league was resuming the book burning. It would be just like the old days. And to think, the whole thing organized by that skinny middle school kid with asthma! He said don't tell *him* that today's youths were lazy and disrespectful. He asked how Paul was planning to pay.

Paul stared at the bunting. He said he forgot his wallet in the car and he would be right back.

Out in the parking lot, Sinclair was talking to a kid holding a skateboard and wearing an Ezra Pound Postcard T-shirt. The sun was setting, but the night was still hot. Paul told Sinclair to get in the car.

When the doors were shut and the windows rolled up, Paul said, "We've got a problem."

"I just couldn't stay in this car," Sinclair said. "It was too hot. And I wanted to talk to that young man. He has some interesting ideas, but—"

"Listen," Paul said, "we need to leave."

"We can't stay here?"

"No."

"I told you it would be full."

Paul told Sinclair about the Greenville Anti-Socialist League Fourth of July Book Burning and Stephen Rudkin, the twelve-year-old lying capitalist bastard. "And you think having a folksinger son is bad?"

Sinclair said, "Surely there is a misunderstanding."

"No," Paul said. "There is not." Paul was mad at himself for getting tricked by a kid. He missed his cat and his own bed. "Get your head down."

"Mr. Rudkin is twelve years old?"

"Yes."

"What a precocious little guy."

"No," Paul said. "Listen to me. Are you listening?"

"Yes."

"He's not on your side. They're going to burn those books like they used to."

"Sinclair Season" came on the radio again and Paul turned it off. Sinclair took off his glasses and rubbed his eyes. He ran his dry tongue over his dentures. He scratched his face and broke loose a part of his beard. "Well, Paul? What shall we do now?"

"We have two options," Paul said.

"Good. Tell me."

"The first and best option, which you'll no doubt reject immediately, is to leave this town right now."

"Absolutely not. What's the second option?"

Paul reached past Sinclair to the glove compartment and pulled out a small scrap of paper, on which was written, in his own handwriting, the complete Red Shovel Press mailing list for Greenville. "The second option," he said, "is we find our one friend."

7

The Greenville Fourth of July celebration was to be held in a grassy park in the center of town. There would be music and food and games throughout the afternoon and evening; then, at dusk, the mayor would lead the townspeople five blocks to the softball field at the elementary school. The book burning was to take place after nine o'clock on the infield dirt of the softball field, which had been the home of the burning for as long as most people could remember. A few of the GASL old-timers could recall the days when the burning was held downtown, but the league changed the location after an ice-cream shop burned down one windy Fourth of July during the McCarthy era. Either an ice-cream shop or a jewelry store, depending on who told the story.

By July 3, all of the assassins who were attending the Fourth of July celebration had arrived in Greenville. The perfectionists and neophytes had shown up as early as July 1, while the more confident and experienced shooters trickled into town in the following days. Given the town's pro-Sinclair fervor, they took great pains to keep a low profile. They remained hidden during the day and scouted the town at night, gathering information and creating a kill plan. They had received word that the fireworks, bonfire, and Sinclair celebration would take place on the softball field at the elementary school. Thus the roof of the school was the most obvious place to set up; and because it was the most obvious, it was immediately ruled out. If the pinkos were to conduct a sweep for snipers, they would certainly begin on the school rooftop.

The softball field was hardly ideal as a kill spot. It was too open; there was very little cover. On the third-base side was a small equipment shed with a window facing the field, but you'd be crazy to set up there because you could not escape easily or secretly, and you'd be shooting at ground level. There were few assassins who would paint themselves into that corner. It was much easier, and much less of a risk to yourself and innocent citizens, to set up above your target and shoot down. This left few options, once you ruled out the school. The Greenville Bank, at three stories tall, was the highest point in the town, and it was four blocks away from the softball field. From the roof it would be a long and challenging shot, but it was clearly the safest and best location.

Late at night on July 3, there was a hushed and collegial atmosphere atop the Greenville Bank as the black-clad shooters claimed their spots, painted their bullets, and studied their sight lines.

"Is that you, Busby?" one man whispered.

"Hey, Rod.

"Nice spot. When did you get here? May?"

"Dedication, my friend."

Rod squinted into the darkness in the direction of the school. "This is not an easy shot."

"It's a tough one. Better eat your carrots."

"You working for the GOP again?"

"Nope, the other guys. They think the old guy is making them look bad. Who are you with?"

Rod named a large automobile manufacturer.

"You making pretty good dough?"

"Not enough."

"I'm telling you, we should go union."

"Jesus, don't even joke about that."

"Who else is here?"

"Roland's over there. He's with the corn guys again. Brooker. Let's see. Pearl's here. She doesn't even know who she's working for. There's another guy over there that I don't know. Someone said they saw Grady in town, but he's not up here."

"Is Collins coming?"

"No, he got another gig."

"How's his girl?"

"Not so good. She needs another operation."

Busby lowered his voice. "Huntley?"

"No. Haven't seen him. Or Billings."

"If Huntley shows up, you shouldn't give him your spot. I'm all for showing respect, but that's got to stop. How are we supposed to make a living?"

"I'm staying put."

Busby said he'd better get a spot or he'd be shooting from Walkerton.

"When you're done, go see Brooker," Rod said. "He's running the pool."

Three-time Upton Sinclair assassin Joe Gerald Huntley checked into the Trail's End Motel in Greenville at 10:45 P.M. The rooms had their own doors to the outside, so he could come and go without walking through a lobby. He paid cash and signed in as Lt. Frederick Garrison, a Sinclair pseudonym from his early career as a pulp writer. It's not the sort of fact that Billings would know. That gold-toothed fool had probably never read a page of Sinclair. In his room, he locked the door and called home because he had promised he would. Carla answered after one ring.

"It's me."

"I just kept hoping I'd hear your truck coming back up the driveway."

"I'm here. I made it OK."

"Every time the dogs barked, I went out there to check."

The television was chained to the wall. The carpet was dark, but Huntley could still see stains. The headboard creaked and the bed smelled like smoke. "This is the last time."

"I hate it here without you."

"Last time."

"I hate you for going, Joe. You should be here."

"I bought you some sparklers. They're in the closet on the shelf."

"I hope you miss."

"You like sparklers. Don't you like them?"

"Yes. I hope you miss."

"I won't, though."

"I hope you do."

Huntley changed his clothes and snuck out the door with his gear in a duffel bag. He walked downtown, past the grassy park. Greenville, like many other American towns, had been founded by a man on a horse, and this man, in all likelihood a Mr. Green, was commemorated by a statue at the center of the town. Red, white, and blue streamers were draped in trees and on fences; flags and Fourth of July banners hung in front of shops and municipal buildings. There was nothing, Huntley noticed, to indicate any pro-Sinclair sentiment. A black cat ran across the narrow street ahead of Huntley, who was, like many assassins, superstitious.

He walked the five blocks to the elementary school, seeing everything. He had long ago begun to see the world in terms of targets, escape routes, sight lines. His right knee ached from the long drive. His back too. He was aware of his body in a way he had never been as a young man. He stood in the center of the infield and turned in a slow circle. He ruled out the top of the school. He ruled out the roof of the distant bank, where he was certain all the amateurs and corporate goons would be encamped. From that distance he knew they would constitute a serious threat to the citizens of Greenville. They were probably up there now, Huntley thought, inspecting their weapons and daydreaming about what they'd do with the cash. A speedboat. Braces for the kid. The Italian Riviera. He did not hate those men. True, for most of his career he had been a snob about corporate work. He had considered it less noble than government work, which he had felt was in the interest of national health and security. But these days he no longer recognized a distinction; everything was corporate work. He wished he were in bed with Carla.

Huntley would not be bothered if one of these auto or pharmaceutical guys nailed Sinclair. He just didn't want Billings to get him. Anyone but that asshole kid.

Huntley picked the lock on the aluminum equipment shed on the third-base side of the softball field. He dripped lubricant on the track of the door so it would slide open without squeaking. Inside, the shed was hot and messy, and it smelled of gasoline and grass and old canvas. With his flashlight Huntley saw the riding lawn mower and dented red cans of gas; he saw the lumpy bags of softballs, the aluminum bats, the dirty bases; he saw the red rubber kickballs in a net bag, the rolled-up volleyball net, the incomplete croquet set; he saw the badminton rackets with broken strings hanging from hooks on the wall. He followed a path through the junk to the window. He applied lubricant and it easily slid open, but would not stay open, so he inserted a small block of wood he found on the dirt floor. He looked through the narrow crack in the window to the infield of the softball field and figured it was about twenty-five yards to home plate. A difficult line because it was ground level, but if he were patient and steady, he'd get a shot. When he got back home, he would tear down the shooting range and build the greenhouse that Carla wanted. He removed the block of wood and eased the window back down. He put the block of wood in his duffel bag, along with the lubricant. He assembled his rifle, loaded it, and looked for a place to conceal it in the shed. His plan was to go back to the motel to get a few hours of sleep before returning to the shed early in the morning, before daybreak. It was too risky to enter the shed in the daylight, so he would have to sit in the hot building all day and await the celebration. It would be a long and uncomfortable day, but he had had it much worse than this.

Looking for a place to stash his weapon, Huntley moved the bag of red balls from the corner, and that's when he saw the other rifle and the black satin bag. It took him a moment to realize what had happened. He had, remarkably, been beaten to this spot, which had happened before, but not often and not in many years. Huntley could not think of many in the business who would risk setting up in this shed, but then he saw again the sheen of the satin and he got a sick feeling in his gut. He knelt down in the corner with his flashlight and closely inspected the gun. He saw, along the barrel, an engraved cursive logo: THE KID. In the black bag he found a silk shirt, a thick gold chain, a large bottle of water, an apple, a sandwich, a Little Debbie snack cake, binoculars, ammunition, a stack of glossy magazines (women, cars), a cell phone, and an envelope containing a promissory note signed by Huntley's own biographer, Lionel T. Pratt.

It was a dark night, by all accounts. The moon was just a sliver. It would have been difficult for the assassins on the roof of the Greenville Bank to see the figure of a man, out on the softball field at the elementary school, splashing gasoline in a line from the center of the dirt infield to the dry summer grass leading up to the equipment shed on the third-base side. Nobody saw it. Nobody, later, claimed to have seen it. The men on the rooftop were busy with their preparations. They painted their bullets, managed the pool. They gossiped and bitched about their work. The man called Brooker fashioned a crude pulley system, by which means he hauled a large cooler of beer up the side of the bank, plenty enough for everyone.

Huntley placed the empty gas cans back beside the riding mower. Before leaving and locking the shed, he removed all of the bullets from the rifle and from the black satin bag. There were, he noticed, considerably more than ten.

8

Years later, of course, hundreds of people would claim to have been at the Last Folksinger's last show, where, they would say, they definitely felt something ominous in the air. There was undeniably an eerie mood, they would say, you could just sense it. But the truth is, the tiny bar had a maximum occupancy of sixty-four, it was only about half full on the night of July 3, and those in attendance reached a level of inebriation that would call into question later reports that relied upon their subtle discernment of mood.

Albert played and sang well, for the first time on the tour. The small crowd was, if not attentive or knowledgeable, at least festive and appreciative. Albert did not talk or even take advantage of the free beer from

Frank at the bar. He just played and sang. He played almost all of *Splitting Wood*, and in his second set, when the blitzed divorcées began bellowing requests, he honored them and played what he could. He became a jukebox, and then, as the evening degenerated, he became a karaoke machine and he was loved by the people. They wanted classic rock and radio fluff and he gave it to them, with good faith and sincerity and a few playful references that went unnoticed by everyone except Frank. Albert did not need to know the words because his audience did. They sang and they threw bills in his guitar case. It was the kind of show Albert generally detested. He had done it before for rent money, but he would always lace the vapid pop songs with minor chords, he would scornfully sabotage the lyrics, and he would brim with contempt for his audience and for himself. But on this night, he surrendered to the mob and he had a nice time. His guitar proclaimed, *This machine exhumes dead radicals*, but tonight, on the eve of Independence Day, in Albert's final show, this machine exhumed only your favorite smash hits from the '70s, '80s, and '90s. There was really nothing very eerie about it. The old man would not have approved; he would have pursed those lips and shaken his head, just as Frank behind the bar was shaking his head as Albert tried to pick up a Van Halen song on the fly. The people in the bar were not so much singing as yelling, but still Albert could hear the steady voice of the father in his head, patiently explaining the true and noble function of art in a capitalist system. Albert, though, was too weary to fight.

Nobody in the room had health insurance. The father had once written that wherever you find millionaires, you also find Socialists, for they are cause and effect. But that was not even true anymore. It was more true to say that wherever you find millionaires, you also find aspiring millionaires. Albert knew that art must not turn its back on the world. He felt deeply that art—his songs—must address inequity and cruelty and suffering. What was required, he knew, was a poetics of engagement. And yet what was also required was that Journey song, you know the one. And Albert played it as well as he could, resisting the ironic impulse. He was giving the proletariat a good night out, and he tried to see that as a worthy political act.

Two young women stood near the back of the bar, pierced and tattooed and serious. They clapped for Albert's first set, then left quickly when he started playing requests. He saw them leave out of the corner of his eye, but he did not look directly at them. He knew they were fans who had driven a hundred miles. He knew they would drive back home and go directly to some chat room to provide a lengthy and nasty report on the latest sellout.

Late in the evening, when those remaining in the bar were passing out or groping a new acquaintance or getting sick in the dirty bathrooms, Albert returned to a few of his own songs. He had planned to play a brand-new song after midnight, to bring in the Fourth, but instead he played an old one, an anxious love song called "Leave the Key Under the Buddha." Frank, the bartender and owner, sang along and clapped when it was over. He was a Vietnam vet with a plate in his skull and a nice voice, who had in recent years drifted toward anarchism. Albert waved to Frank and smiled. Then he played a Credence song about the rain and packed up his guitar.

In the dark hallway by the bathroom, Albert leaned on an Assassin pinball machine and called home. He hung up when he heard his voice on the answering machine, but then he called back and left a long, sloppy message that he knew, even while he was leaving it, he would regret.

He sat at the bar and drank two cups of strong coffee, while Frank counted out the money for Albert and gave him an extra twenty, as usual. "It was like damn karaoke out there."

Albert couldn't look him in the eye. "I know."

"You're too good for that."

That was true and not true. Albert didn't say anything.

"Next time you come through, all these people will come and bring their friends and you're going to play shit that doesn't rhyme very good and get drunk and pissed off at all of them for not liking it."

That sounded plausible to Albert and he nodded into his black coffee.

"Are you driving tonight?"

"Greenville."

"Greenville. Jesus. Better stick with your covers."

"I don't know, Frank. Things may be starting to change a little bit."

"Not in Greenville they aren't."

Albert packed up his equipment by the back door, shook Frank's hand, and walked out to the dark and empty parking lot. His feet crunched the broken glass and he could hear the roar of the trucks up on the interstate.

Albert had loaded everything in the back of the van before he noticed that the left back tire was completely flat. Then he saw the left front tire was also flat. He walked around the van and saw that the right tires were flat, as well. He looked around. Someone was reclined and passed out in the front seat of a rusty Malibu. A man and a woman left the back of the bar with their arms around each other, weaving. The trucks that rushed by on the interstate left behind silence and a humid breeze. Albert hauled his amps, microphone, and monitor back into the bar and told Frank he'd come back for it all in a couple of days. He gave back the money Frank had just given him and asked if Frank would call someone about getting the tires on the van fixed.

"Tomorrow's a holiday."

"The next day, then."

Frank agreed, but would not accept the money. Albert stuffed half of the bills into the tip jar on the bar, and left once again. He took his backpack and his guitar and he climbed the weedy bank toward the interstate. The moon was just a sliver. Up on the highway, the billboards were brightly illuminated but the exit signs were difficult to read. He took a minute to figure out which direction he was headed, and then he began walking the gravel shoulder, thinking not of the slashed tires, which happened at least once every tour, but of his performance that evening, the abandoned set list. He didn't want to feel proud about it, but neither did he want to feel ashamed. Those two girls who had left—were they right? He could call them immature, but he's the one who had played Journey. At one point years ago he had been like those girls, resolute in his determination of the Good and the Correct. Had he, since that time, gained something or lost something? Had he matured or surrendered? He walked alone and sober along the highway, early morning, Fourth of July, USA. It was, after all, a good time and place for an epiphany. It would be a good story to tell—the dark hot night, the crunch of gravel and glass beneath his boots, the sudden flash of earned insight about the theretofore irreconcilable obligations of the artist and the entertainer. The beginning of Wisdom, the golden mean. But he didn't realize anything. He didn't know anything, even after these many years. The old man knew and the knowing made his lives easier.

He walked in the direction of Greenville and was not visited by the truth. He wore his backpack and carried his guitar and smoked cigarettes. When he heard the first rumble of a truck behind him or saw its headlights grope across the dark pavement, still warm from the sun of the day, he turned into the glare and stuck his thumb out across the white line.

9

Stephen sat on a stool at the kitchen counter, staring at the swirling pattern of the countertop. He wore his tight clothes, but no shoes, and the tips of his socks were floppy. Box fans rattled the windows and blew warm air and dust across the house. His father was talking to him. Stephen wondered who made the countertop and who made the stool and who made the box fans. These products were made by people, he knew that now. He supposed he had always known it. If someone had asked him yesterday who made that box fan, he would have said that a person made it. Of course a person made it. It was not harvested from the earth; it was not born of another box fan. And yet he hadn't understood the answer—a *person*—as he understood it today. A person made that box fan. A person in a hot workshop, or a cold one. A person who rode a bicycle with a basket on it. A person with curly hair and large front teeth, in love with a girl from the neighboring village, the one with the pretty eyes. A person who worried about his sick mother or sick sister or sick uncle. A person with secret things hidden in the small room he shared with all the other persons, and whose life—whose capacity for joy and pain—was fully as large and wondrous as Stephen's. A person made that box fan, even though he would rather not have made that box fan. The person had other unexplored interests, aptitudes. Mathematics! Piano! Soccer! The days were long and hot (or cold), and the person was not rewarded well for all of the box fans that he made. And then there was the CEO of the box fan company—Stephen knew about him now too. Stephen's father was still talking, saying Stephen's name impatiently. The CEO was a shrewd businessman, a good father, a lover of fine Scotch, a scratch golfer. He had never made a box fan or met the people who did. He was not a bad man—he acted in the interests of the box fan company and of its stockholders. The CEO's box fan competitors made their box fans cheap—that is, they used persons in the hot (or cold) workshop to make them cheap. And so—this is just good business—the CEO of the company that produced that box fan in Stephen's kitchen window had to do the same. But the whole point— Stephen now knew this and would never forget—is that the *company* did not produce the box fan. A person produced the box fan. A person who sold his labor because he had no other way to survive. A person, ultimately, not very interested in producing box fans, whose daily pay for producing many box fans was significantly less than the retail value of a single box fan. This is the sort of day it had been.

It was six o'clock in the evening of the Fourth of July. Arthur told

Stephen he was going next door to borrow Mr. Garrity's minivan. He told Stephen to put his shoes on and get ready, but Stephen did not respond. Arthur thought the boy was nervous, which was understandable. He was a bit nervous himself.

Arthur left and the screen door slammed shut. Stephen slid down from the stool, knelt on the linoleum, and looked beneath the stool to see where it had been made. It was just as he suspected!

When Arthur returned, the boy was sitting on the kitchen floor with no shoes and floppy socks. Arthur suddenly wondered if Stephen was on drugs, which is not a suspicion he had ever had before. "Stephen," he said, "did you put that extra padlock on the garage?"

"Yes."

"Do you have the key?"

"Somewhere."

"Look, what's wrong with you? You've been weird all day long."

"Nothing."

"Can you get the key? We've got to load the stuff and get over to the field."

Stephen got up off the floor and walked listlessly to his room. His pants were too short. Arthur watched him carefully. He knew that there were drugs in Greenville. "Get your shoes on, son. Hurry up. We're late. And get those burning instructions."

Stephen returned with the key and the instructions and his inhaler, but not the speech. He left his speech in the top drawer of his dresser. There was no way he would give that speech now.

"Here, give me the key. Tie your shoes. We've got to get going."

Stephen helped his father load the fifteen boxes of books into the back of Mr. Garrity's minivan. He began reluctantly, but then he saw his father wince when he lifted a box.

He said, "Watch your back, Dad."

"It's fine."

"Here, I'll pick them up and hand them to you."

The boxes were heavy for Stephen, and he struggled, as he had hours earlier, to lift them from the garage floor. One by one he handed the boxes to his father, feeling like a worker.

"This one looks like it's been opened. Did you open this?"

Stephen shook his head.

"What else needs to go? The gas?"

Stephen nodded.

"Come on, what else? This rope?"

Stephen nodded again.

"Stephen, dammit, this is your big day. Come on."

Stephen's father was the president of the Greenville Anti-Socialist League. What could Stephen say to make him understand what was in his mind and in his heart? He could say nothing! In a few years he would learn that there were places he could go. He would leave Greenville, leave his father. He would come home for two days every Christmas and they'd eat a dry turkey and argue about politics. His father would leave the table, slam doors. Eventually they'd just take their meals in front of the television. Eventually they wouldn't even bother with the tree. The old man would drink too much, and he wouldn't get help for his back or his depression. Stephen would clean the house. He'd empty the overflowing bucket in the hallway and put a fan in front of the mildewed carpet. The whole house smelling like mildew and rot. Stephen would return to the city, to those beautiful dreadlocked dissidents, and he'd lie about where he was from.

Stephen shuffled through the garage and collected the CAUTION tape, the bags of fireworks, the fire extinguisher, and the safety goggles. Arthur didn't think marijuana would kill you, but twelve was pretty young. And there was harder stuff out there, as well.

"Did you call Myron about the firewood?"

"He'll remember."

"You ready?"

"Yes."

"You OK, son?"

Stephen nodded.

"I'm proud of you," Arthur said. "I want you to know that. I'm proud of all the work you've done. It's going to be a good night."

Stephen tried to smile for his father. He felt dizzy. It was clearly not going to rain.

Arthur put his hand on Stephen's head. "Hair's starting to grow out some. I really butchered you last time."

"It wasn't that bad," Stephen said.

Arthur closed the garage door and locked it. He started the minivan, but then shut the engine off. "Hold on," he said. "Forgot my camera." He got out of the minivan and when he shut his door, Mr. Garrity's keys jingled in the ignition.

Stephen had only slept three hours, and when he awoke, on the floor with the novel on his chest, he found that nothing in his life was the same. He felt that the book had been a strange dream and that he was still trapped within it. Before getting dressed that morning, he read the labels on his clothes. The people who made them were like him and his father. One was a shy young girl, Stephen's age, with shiny hair. She made Stephen's shirt because her family needed the money. Everyone in her family worked hard, and yet nothing good came of it. It was awful what they suffered and what they lost. It was not fair—this was the childish but bone-hard truth that Stephen could not dismiss or assimilate, not now and not in the disobedient years to come. This was the beginning and the end of a political philosophy. He could have been her and she could have been him. Stephen had stood at his bedroom window that morning and prayed a selfish prayer for rain. He had actually put his hands together and closed his eyes. He figured he had a better chance to influence the weather than the global economy, though here now was the bright sun, the cloudless holiday sky.

Overnight, everything had changed—his father, his hometown, the GASL. Every article in every section of the Greenville *Echo* looked different today, the Fourth of July, than it would have the day before. Even the sports and human interest stories. But it was Upton Sinclair and his novel that had changed the most. The thought of burning even one copy of *A Moveable Jungle!*, much less five hundred, made Stephen sick to his stomach.

When his father returned to the house, Stephen scooted over to the driver's seat and started the minivan. It did not even feel like a decision. Sitting as far forward in the seat as possible, he clumsily shifted from Park to Drive and stretched the tip of his shoe to the accelerator. The minivan sped from the driveway, and when Stephen quickly stretched his foot to the brake, he could hear the boxes of Socialist literature shift and tumble in the back. He held the wheel with two hands. He had trouble with his breathing. Stephen knew now who had made this minivan and who had profited. He drove, slowly, a mile and a half through the tree-lined streets of Greenville, stopping twice to use his inhaler. Most Greenvillians were already downtown, so few were in their homes to see Mr. Garrity's burgundy minivan swerving and jerking down their street.

Stephen parked in the alley behind the small house belonging to Rose Middleton, the librarian, and her husband, Bobby, the honest if unimaginative mechanic. He ran to the back door and knocked before he heard the yelling inside. It was Rose and Bobby, mostly Bobby. He knocked again, louder, and through the door Rose said, "Who is it?"

"It's Stephen."

Rose parted the curtain and peeked out at Stephen. "What do you want, Stephen?"

Bobby yelled something that Stephen couldn't make out. "I need to talk to you."

"It's not a good time, Stephen."

"It's about tonight."

Rose unlocked the door and opened it. She glanced around the alley and pulled the boy into the kitchen.

Bobby leaned against the kitchen counter, wearing a white tank top and blue work pants, holding a bottle of beer. His face and neck were red. He laughed when he saw Stephen. "Well," he said, "if it isn't the young master of ceremonies. Got those books ready to burn, son?" Bobby said this much louder than he needed to.

Stephen ignored him. "Mrs. Middleton, I need to talk to you." He had never seen his librarian in shorts before. Her hair looked different too, though he couldn't have said exactly how.

Rose said, "Did you *drive* here?"

"Yes."

"Is that Mr. Garrity's minivan?"

"Yes."

Bobby said, "*Big* fire tonight."

"What do you want to talk to me about, Stephen?"

"Yes, Stephen, what's on your mind?"

Stephen looked at Bobby and then at Rose. "Alone, please."

Rose put her hand on Stephen's shoulder and led him past Bobby, out of the kitchen and into the hallway. Bobby glared at them. "Goddammit, Rose."

In the hallway, Stephen said, "Remember how you told me you were against burning books?"

"Yes, but there's nothing I can do about it now, Stephen."

"Well, I'm against it now too."

"You can't be against it, Stephen."

"I am."

In the kitchen Bobby made the noises of explosions and raging fires.

Rose said, "It's too late to be against it. You have to go through with it now."

"No, we can't burn the books. We can't." Stephen pointed toward the kitchen door, the minivan, the world outside. "I have them with me. You can help me." He struggled with his breathing again.

Rose had always wanted children and she liked Stephen. He was one of very few children in Greenville that she liked. Sometimes when he visited the library, Rose would imagine that Stephen was her son. She imagined just the two of them living together in a tiny apartment in the city, far away from Greenville. No Bobby and no Arthur. No neighbor with a bumper sticker that said, I HATE UPTON AND I VOTE. She imagined giving Stephen a decent haircut in the kitchen and introducing him to the Romantic poets. She still had the Norton Anthology from college with her giddy notes. *Art as mystical. Art as religion!!* And when Stephen checked out his science fiction books and left the library, she always felt both sad and guilty. It was a terrible thing to imagine.

"Come here," she said. She opened a door in the hallway and Stephen saw that it led downstairs. "Wait here a minute. Don't move."

Rose went back into the kitchen and said something to Bobby that Stephen could not hear. Bobby said, "Rose, goddammit, do not go down there."

Rose said something else and Bobby said, "*Five minutes.* You better take care of this mess, Rose."

Rose took Stephen's arm and led him downstairs, closing the door behind her. At the bottom of the steps, Stephen could see that the basement had been converted into a den. The walls were wood-paneled and the floor had wall-to-wall red shag carpeting. A dilapidated plaid love seat and a leather recliner were situated in front of a giant-screen television, which was off. There were shuttered closet doors on the far wall. Two high, small windows gave little light; on the outside they were covered halfway to their tops by the mulch in Rose's flower beds in the front yard. Stephen felt strange being in Mrs. Middleton's basement. He had once had a dream in which his father married Rose and they all lived together in the one-room library. It had been a good dream.

"Sit down, Stephen," Rose said. Her voice was firm, but not unkind. Stephen sat in the plaid love seat, his feet dangling above the floor.

Rose stood in the middle of the room. "You can come out now."

The shuttered closet doors opened outward, revealing two men, one of whom was startlingly old. Stephen had seen the billboards and talk shows. The old man emerging from the laundry closet appeared to be muckraker and folk hero Upton Sinclair, author of *A Moveable Jungle!* Stephen reached for his inhaler.

Sinclair did five deep knee bends and five windmill toe touches. He said, "Hello, young man."

Stephen could not speak. He sucked on his inhaler and nodded.

Rose said, "This is Stephen. Stephen, this is Mr. Sinclair and his secretary, Paul."

It had never occurred to Stephen that a man could be a secretary. He nodded again and waved at Paul.

Paul said, "Stephen *Rudkin*?"

"Yes," Rose said.

"This is the kid who got us into all of this. This is the little shit who wrote the letter and invited us."

Rose said, "Stop. Listen."

"Did you frisk him?"

Stephen considered saying that he hadn't actually invited anyone, but he thought it best to remain quiet. Also, he wasn't breathing well at all.

"Easy there, Paul," Sinclair said. "The child is having some trouble."

"This is the kid, Sinclair. This is our Mr. Rudkin, man of the people. He got us into this."

Sinclair sat on the arm of the recliner. "I'm sure there's an explanation."

Stephen said, "I loved—your—book."

"He's lying."

"Thank you, young man."

Rose said, "All of you, sit down and listen to me." Sinclair got up from the arm of the recliner and sat down on the love seat next to Stephen, who looked as though he might get sick. He had never met an author; he had never really considered that it was just regular people who wrote books. Paul sat in the recliner.

"Now," Rose said, "Stephen is a good kid and he's not lying. At least not now. He has your books, Mr. Sinclair, and he does not want to burn them. Isn't that right, Stephen?"

Stephen nodded.

"What I suggest—and you didn't hear this from me—is that you transfer the books from Stephen's minivan to your car and get out of town right away."

Paul said, "Stephen has a minivan?"

"They've paid for those books," Sinclair said. "We can't very well take them back. They're not my books anymore. And we can't leave now. We've made inroads here. There is good work to be done tonight."

Paul said, "I think those books will fit in the station wagon."

"You need to get out of here right now," Rose said. "Deal with the books or don't, but you need to get out of here. I do not want to be involved in any of this."

Paul said, "You're not acting like a friend of the cause, Rose."

"I'm *not* a friend of the cause."

"You're on the RSP mailing list."

"That was seven years ago and I made one order. I was curious. I'm not a Socialist."

"You're just so broad-minded that you don't like to see any books burn, is that it?"

There was a rumbling noise upstairs, as if someone with bad intentions were dragging something heavy across the floor.

Sinclair said, "I'm convinced we should go downtown tonight. We have momentum. We've converted one already and we can convert the others. They will be reasonable. The people here just need a new way to interpret their circumstances. They've sent us money and we owe them books. I intend to deliver their books."

Rose said, "They'll burn them."

Paul said, "It's half the press run, up in smoke."

Stephen began to say something but was interrupted by the sound of a slammed door upstairs in the kitchen. Everyone stopped to listen. Rose walked up the stairs, already knowing, as she walked, that the door would not open. She was right. There was a bookshelf in the hallway, pushed in front of the door. The really terrible thing was that Rose had married Bobby because she had been pregnant. She miscarried two weeks after the wedding at Greenville Baptist and had never been able to get pregnant again. She didn't much care for Bobby as a life partner. She stood at the top of the stairs and called his name through the door. She called several times, but it was no use because Bobby was gone, as was the minivan full of gasoline, fireworks, and Socialist novels.

Downstairs, Paul and Stephen realized what had happened. Paul slumped over and put his head on his knees.

"I'm sorry," Stephen said.

Sinclair stood up from the love seat and clapped his hands. "Come now," he said. "I didn't spend three months of my life on that novel just to watch it burn."

10

Francis Scott Billings had never in all of his seventeen years been so bored. Or so hot, for that matter. During the heat of the day, the aluminum shed turned into an oven, and Billings, forced to spend the entire Fourth of July inside it, was miserable. There was nothing glamorous about this lifestyle. Nothing at all. The kids in the suburbs with the Billings the Kid posters on their bedroom walls had no fucking idea of what it was really like to be an assassin. He received hundreds of letters and e-mails a day from kids who thought it was all about guns and fast cars and cool clothes and pussy. There were people who handled the mail, who sent back the form letters and glossy, autographed photos. But Billings decided he was going to start writing personal letters back. He was going to write letters that described the sitting and the waiting, the heat and the cold, the bumfuck towns with no nightlife.

He wished he were lying by the pool with Melissa. Melissa had a killer body and was sexually adventurous.

Billings stripped to his boxers and reclined on a coarse canvas bag. He spent the day napping and flipping through his magazines, bending the corners of pages that had clothes, cars, or women that appealed to him. He decided there was probably no way he was going to write personal letters to the kids. It would take forever and he had never written a letter before in his life. He masturbated while thinking of Melissa, and also of other women. He wished he could call his friends, but Pratt had told him that under no circumstances was he to call anyone except Pratt. He waited and sweated it out. He drank plenty of water and pissed in the dirt in the corner of the shed. The gas fumes gave him a headache.

At a little after five, a man drove onto the infield of the softball field in a pickup truck full of chopped wood. Billings watched from the window of the shed. This man was the only person he had seen all day. Things, he felt, were moving forward now. He got dressed and took some speed, but then nothing happened, the man just stayed in his truck full of firewood. It looked to Billings like he was sleeping. The early evening had cooled off only a couple degrees, and the shed remained staggeringly hot. Sweat soaked Billings's silk shirt. He cursed and stripped again. All of his friends were at barbecues. He wanted to smash his head through the window.

At six o'clock the man climbed into the back of his truck and began tossing the pieces of firewood onto the softball field. Billings had to admit that this job looked worse than his. It was hot and dusty on the field, and there had to be all kinds of splinters and spiders in those logs. Hell, snakes even. When the man finished unloading the wood, he drove off and then returned with a second load, which he added to the pile on the infield. This was becoming an impressive mound of wood. The man left again and returned with yet another big load.

At 7:15, Billings saw a burgundy minivan park next to the pickup truck on the softball infield. A man in a white tank top and blue pants got out of the minivan and talked briefly with the driver of the truck.

Then the two men began to empty the third truckload of firewood onto the pile in the center of the infield. Billings raised the window an inch, but it fell back down. He searched the shed for something to prop the window open. All he could find was a softball, which was too big, he decided. It was way too big.

Twenty-five yards away from the equipment shed, Bobby Middleton was trying to think his way through this sticky situation and Myron was making it difficult. Myron was chatty. He was in business with his father, who never said a word. Myron's old man just grunted or nodded, and then went about his work, so Myron liked to converse when he got the opportunity. Bobby liked Myron's father better.

Myron said, "So where's Stephen?"

Bobby had seized the opportunity to become the new director of the book burning. This was good. This would not go unnoticed by the people of Greenville or the staff of the *Echo*. He said, "Hm?"

"Where's Stephen?"

"Stephen's not going to make it."

"Why not?"

Bobby might have just called the sheriff, who was a good guy and a poker buddy. It had crossed his mind. But if he had called the sheriff, he would have had to explain why Upton Sinclair was in his basement. It was a small town and word traveled fast. He was lucky if the news wasn't already spreading.

The two men worked slowly in the lingering heat of the evening. Working together, it took them longer to empty the truckload than it had taken Myron to do it himself. Again Myron said, "Why not?"

Sinclair in his basement! Bobby could not believe it. He had to think this through. The book burning had to go on as planned. He was seeing to that. This was good. He said, "Stephen just realized it was too big of a job for a kid to handle."

Myron said, "I can see that. I had that thought myself. But wouldn't he still come?"

The truth was, too, that Bobby loved his wife. It pained him to know that she was unhappy. He shouldn't have trapped her down in the basement with Sinclair and Stephen and the male secretary, he could see that now. That wasn't going to help anything. But he hadn't had time to think it all through. He had had to act fast and he had been upset. Any man would be upset if Upton Sinclair came to his house late one night, and his very own wife told him to put down his gun and get the extra set of sheets from the closet. Bobby said, "Just don't worry about Stephen, Myron."

Myron took another armful of firewood from the truck. "It's mighty hot."

This was OK, this was good. People would notice that Bobby had saved the book burning. This night would become known as the Fourth of July that Bobby Middleton rescued. He'd tell his story to the *Echo*. He'd leave out the part about harboring a Socialist in his basement and he'd leave out his wife's involvement. He wouldn't mention his wife, other than to say that she was a constant joy and comfort to him. He loved his Rose and wished she could be here. It would be the first Fourth of July they had not spent together in many years. Ten, maybe.

Myron regarded the tall pile of firewood on the infield dirt. "Is there any kind of system to this?"

"System?"

"Or is it just a big mound?"

"What are you talking about, Myron?"

"Is there, like, any special way you're supposed to arrange the wood and books? I've just been throwing the wood on."

Bobby stopped working and stared at Myron. Oh but Jesus he was dumb! "It's just a pile, Myron. There's nothing to it."

Later, after the burning, Bobby would go home and free all of the people in his basement. That was his plan. He hoped Sinclair wasn't sitting in his recliner. He should not have locked Stephen down there, he could see that now. But a few dolphins always ended up in the tuna nets, that's what he told himself. He'd let them go. Sinclair and his boy secretary could leave town in the dark and nobody would have to know they were ever there. He'd give Stephen a ride home and he'd make sure that he kept quiet about it. Then there was Mr. Garrity's minivan. He could see now that there were some problems. But he had had to act fast. Any man would have made mistakes. He'd lie in bed with Rose and apologize for pushing the bookshelf in front of the basement door. That had been an accident. Well, not an accident, a mistake. He'd tickle her naked back with the tips of his fingers and call her his dolphin.

When Bobby and Myron finished unloading the wood from the truck, they began to take brown cardboard boxes from the back of the minivan. Billings watched through the window of the shed. There was just no telling what these communists were up to. The shed smelled strongly of gasoline and urine. The men on the softball field opened the boxes with pocketknives and then began to toss what appeared to be books on top of the wood. Two other men showed up and helped throw hundreds of books on the pile. Billings used his binoculars—he could see that all of the books were identical, but he couldn't make out the title. He speculated that they were copies of Huntley's diary or biography. That was fine with Billings. Let them burn.

Myron said, "How's that look?"

"That looks good," Bobby said. "Now let's do the gas, boys."

Billings got dressed again and took some more uppers. He liked the looks of Myron's pickup truck. It was shiny, and it had an extended cab and a big bed. He'd like to get one of those maybe. He took his rifle from the corner of the shed and it felt nice in his hands. He felt uncomplicated and purposeful, like a one-celled organism. He imagined Melissa sucking on the gun barrel and his heart beat faster. Yes, it had been an awful, boring day, but it would all be worth it in the end. He felt lucky and ready. The only problem, he now noticed—and it was really quite a serious problem from an assassin's standpoint—was that there were not any bullets in his rifle. Or in his bag.

The men on the infield splashed five cans of gasoline on the wood and the books. Other men arrived and helped add three large bags of firecrackers and sparklers to the tall pile. The man in the white tank top directed the action. They all drank cans of beer from a metal tub in the back of a truck. They finished by setting out yellow CAUTION tape on the dirt around the pile, and then they shook hands and patted each other on the back. They were proud of their work. They were dusty and their shirts were soaked with sweat. One man set the small fire extinguisher on the ground next to the huge pile, and all the other men laughed. People began arriving in cars and on foot, setting up their lawn chairs and blankets in the outfield grass. Soon the mayor would lead a large group of celebrants from downtown.

As the sun went down, the rooftop of the Greenville Bank was buzzing. Down in the equipment shed on the third-base side, Billings called Pratt on his cell phone and told him the unfortunate thing about the bullets.

11

It is not easy to follow someone who is hitchhiking, but Collins had done it before and he stayed with his man throughout the night and the following day. There were long stretches where the folkie was walking, so Collins had to stop along the shoulder, far enough back so he wouldn't be noticed. If he ran the air conditioner, his car would begin to overheat, so he shut the car off and suffered in the July sun. He popped pills to stay awake and reminded himself why he was doing this. He flipped the sun visor down to look at the picture of his eight-month-old daughter. He flipped the visor back up, then flipped it down again. Charlotte Anne.

Collins had never seen or heard of the Last Folksinger, and he did not know or care that the singer was related to Upton Sinclair. He did not generally have strong or murderous feelings about Socialism or folk music. What he had was a sick child and a crushing hospital debt. He had told his wife when she was pregnant that he was finished, but when the offer came in—he did not know from whom—he could not refuse it.

Albert's fourth ride dropped him off at the exit to Greenville, on Route 87, and he started the two-mile walk into town as the sun was beginning to set. He was exhausted; his feet and shoulders ached, and he switched his guitar from hand to hand every few steps. He began to wonder why he had come. It would not be, he knew, a joyous reconciliation. He could imagine his father's face when he arrived, dirty and tired, at the old man's big celebration. He could already feel his father's embarrassment and he could hear the lecture about hitchhiking and smoking, about diet and hygiene. He knew his father would not hug him; he'd shake his hand. He'd see the guitar and he'd worry that Albert wanted to sing some of his songs around a fire.

And yet Albert knew that this is why he had come. He had come to upset his father, to make a scene. He had not come so that they might spend some quality time together and catch up. He had not come to take part in a rare celebration of Upton Sinclair or to engage in heady discussions of art and politics. It was ugly but it was true: He had come to spoil the old man's party. He had come to say, *Here I am. I am real and I am yours. Do anything but ignore me.*

Albert wasn't hitchhiking when Collins pulled up behind him on the shoulder. It wasn't pleasant, doing what Collins had to do. He didn't enjoy it and he never had. Albert turned his head around to the approaching car. Collins had studied the photographs that were sent to him and he knew this was his man, no doubt about it. He unrolled his window and stuck his head out. "Going to Greenville?"

Albert thought the man looked familiar, but he wasn't sure why. He was almost delirious with fatigue and dread. "Yes."

"You want a ride? I can probably get you there before the fireworks show."

Albert put his backpack and guitar in the backseat, then got in beside Collins. He thanked the driver, leaned his head back on the rest, and closed his eyes.

A few hundred feet past a gaudy Anti-Socialist League billboard, Collins turned off on a gravel road that passed over a creek and by a Christmas tree farm. The dusty road went gradually down into a valley, and the leaning mailboxes became less and less frequent in the ditches. Collins was aware of the jab of the pistol in his waistband. He turned again, and the road led into heavy woods. Albert felt the jolt of potholes and heard the low-lying branches brushing the windshield. When he opened his eyes, he could barely see the road that led through the dark trees. The driver should have had his headlights on. Albert said, "You should turn on your headlights."

"I can still see pretty good."

"Where are we going?"

"Right here."

Albert had wanted to shame his father among his fans and disciples. Look, the father of American Socialism has a son who smokes and drinks too much, who sleeps around and eats fast food, who plays harmonica poorly and sings snide, messy songs about the revolution, the resurrection, bad love. He had come here to be a bedbug. He had come to part the crowd. *I am here. This is me. I am yours.*

The driver said, "Why don't we take a little walk."

12

Escaping the basement proved more difficult than its inmates expected. Sitting on Paul's shoulders, Stephen was able to slide open the top half of one of the high windows. Mulch from the flower bed fell into the basement and onto Paul's head. It was fragrant and warm from the sun, and it reminded Paul of previous summers spent working for a small landscaping company, dreaming of the revolution. He had hated it then, but it seemed like good work to him now. Stephen gingerly swept the mulch out of Paul's hair. He stood unsteadily on Paul's shoulders, his knees trembling in his snug bonfire pants, and he squeezed his head and shoulders through the tiny opening. Paul grabbed his feet and helped push him through the window, though not as gently, Rose thought, as he might have. Rose was worried about her flowers, but decided it was inappropriate to say anything to Stephen. Stephen banged his shin on the window and he got mulch in his mouth and in his shirt, but he eventually squirmed out of the basement and into the flower bed without much difficulty. Sinclair paced the shag carpet, mumbling and strategizing, providing no practical help at all. "Good people of Greentown," he muttered. "Fine citizens of Greentown."

Paul suggested that it was the last they'd ever see of Stephen, but in a moment they could hear him in the hallway, outside the basement door, where he faced the challenge of moving the bookshelf. Sitting together at the top of the stairs, Rose and Paul could hear Stephen grunting and wheezing. Paul's knee was touching Rose's. He hadn't touched a woman in months. Rose was pretty and tough, and she really was trying to help. Still, it was a dumb time to want to kiss her neck. He said, "I'm sorry about what I said to you."

"It's fine," Rose said. "Just be nice to Stephen."

Behind the door, Stephen said, "I can't move it."

Rose said, "Try again."

Stephen tried again.

"Is it moving at all?"

"It's heavy."

Sinclair said, "I would very much like to share with you some thoughts about what Independence Day means to me."

Stephen said, "Mrs. Middleton, are all of these books yours?" There were four full shelves and Stephen had never seen so many books in a private collection.

Rose said, "Yes."

Paul said, "Try again."

Rose said, "No, Stephen, don't. Why don't you take the books off the shelves? That will make it easier."

Stephen began removing the books from the shelves, which turned out to be a lengthy and painstaking process because he felt compelled to examine the cover of each book before he placed it in a neat stack at the end of the hallway. He was trying to memorize the titles and authors. He wanted all of these books to be inside of him. He wanted to be that big on the inside. Through the door he said, "Mrs. Middleton, are all of these books good?"

"I guess most of them are. At least I think so."

"As good as Mr. Sinclair's book?"

Rose looked at Paul. "You need to hurry, Stephen."

Stephen could not reach the top shelf. He dragged a chair in from the kitchen and asked Rose if he could stand on it. When he had unloaded the books into neat stacks on the floor, Stephen tried again to move the bookshelf. "It moved, I think. A little."

Paul rubbed his temples. Sinclair said that true independence meant the freedom to engage in meaningful work. Rose told Stephen to remove the shelves, as well.

Stephen noisily removed the shelves and was then able, with great effort, to slide the bookless, shelfless bookshelf out from in front of the basement door.

What followed was a brief meeting around the kitchen table. Rose said she wasn't going downtown and nobody else should, either. She would take Stephen home, and Sinclair and Paul could get out of town and consider themselves fortunate. It would not be difficult to get away, since it was growing dark outside and the entire town was at the burning. Paul agreed heartily: They could return to the relative safety of the cabin and Sinclair could begin a novel about the whole experience. They'd come up with a few hundred dollars to send Morris for another press run to replace the burned books. Nobody would die! When it was his turn to speak, Sinclair said he was going downtown and Stephen said he was doing whatever Mr. Sinclair was doing.

"That's a good lad," Sinclair said.

13

The Fourth of July! As the sun went down on Greenville, the residents gathered outside the elementary school to celebrate their fine town and honor the birth of their nation. Hundreds of townspeople congregated on the softball field, while many others packed the two small stands of bleachers. The outfield grass was covered with blankets and lawn chairs, as was the grassy bank on the first-base side. Flags were planted in the hard ground. Middle-age women wore red, white, and blue earrings.

Old Man Garvey, at 101 the town's oldest citizen, sat in a wheelchair in shallow right field, surrounded by his three remaining children, his nine grandchildren, his sixteen great-grandchildren, and his twenty-one great-great-grandchildren. Garvey had been a resident of Greenville his entire life and he was still sharp as a tack. It was Garvey's secret, and he would take it to his grave, that he had voted Democrat in four of the previous six presidential elections.

Big Nate was there with his mobile barbecue shack and business was brisk. Nate had hired a few of Mrs. Pearson's best drama students to dress up in pink pig costumes and work the crowd. It was the first time he had used pig mascots, but it would not be the last.

Members of the Greenville Fire Department had parked a big truck behind home plate. They sold raffle tickets and let children climb on the truck and turn on the flashing lights and pet the dalmatians.

A group of high school girls went to the bathroom inside the elementary school to put on the makeup their mothers disallowed. A group of boys smoked cigarettes out behind the equipment shed on the third-base side. One of them had stolen some wine in a box from his father, and the boys passed it around inside a backpack, holding the box above their heads and pouring the wine into their mouths. The boy said his dad drank a box a night and he would never notice it was gone.

Coworkers sat together and compared injuries and tried to avoid eye contact with the recently laid off. They felt sorry for them, but they knew that if they themselves had gotten laid off, they wouldn't want anyone's pity. Turning away was a form of respect. The recently laid off set up their blankets on the fringes of the celebration, deep in centerfield, halfway to the Greenville Bank, out by the children of migrant workers and Chief Omar, the crazy Indian.

The sun had set and the daylight was fading. The low moon was little more than a sliver.

In the center of the diamond, illuminated by a bright searchlight mounted to the fire truck, a mound of wood and books stood twice as tall as a man. Bobby Middleton, the mechanic and the husband of the unusual librarian, stood proprietarily nearby, dirty and quite drunk. Rumor had it that Arthur Rudkin, league president, had never even shown up, and neither had his son, Stephen, the nominal director of the burning. Many people agreed that the boy should never have been given such a great responsibility and that is why they had voted against it at the June meeting, while everyone else got swept up in his eagerness and youthful spirit. Ah, the perils of democracy! The word was, too, that Bobby had taken over, and by the looks of things, had done quite well.

This is what happened next: Bobby Middleton, sensing that the time was just about right to begin his book burning—and sensing, furthermore, that Chester Stutt, former GASL president, would soon seize power if he waited much longer—borrowed a bullhorn from the boys in the GFD. "Happy Fourth of July, Greenville!" Bobby shouted, but the bullhorn was not turned on. Bobby had drunk seven cans of beer at this point. His white tank top was brown from the dirt and dust of the field.

A volunteer firefighter ran over to Bobby and helped him switch on the bullhorn. "Happy Fourth of July, Greenville!" Bobby shouted. The crowd cheered and whistled. The assassins on the roof of the Greenville Bank searched the crowd for Sinclair, occasionally glancing up from their rifles to see if anyone else had spotted him. They shook their heads and shrugged at each other.

"I just want to say a few things before we light this sucker up." Bobby began a slurred speech, but as it turned out, nobody was listening. Everyone had stood and turned toward right field, where something clearly was taking place. This definite but vague knowledge that something was happening rippled outward like a wave. People murmured and exclaimed and pointed because the people beside them had murmured and exclaimed and pointed. The epicenter, the direction that most of the murmurers and exclaimers were pointing, was right field.

Bobby continued his incoherent address. "I am *not* a hero, people. I did what any of you would do under circumstances that were similar to my own."

While most of the people gathered at ground level on the softball field could not yet determine what was happening, the rooftop assassins had a good view of three people parting the right-field crowd and walking toward the infield. There was a young man, a boy, and, holding the boy's hand, an old man who appeared, through binoculars, to be Upton Sinclair. Who was, in fact, Upton Sinclair. But the assassins held their fire. None of them had the guts to fire into a crowd at dusk from this distance. If they missed, they'd surely pick off a youth pastor or a Little League coach or someone's sweet granny. Maybe the boy. They had seen it happen before. They had seen it finish many promising careers. Why, they wondered, was the crowd not cheering Sinclair's arrival?

Paul walked behind Sinclair and Stephen. Nobody watched him, so he was free to watch the people of Greenville as they stepped aside to let the trio pass. In '34, barnstorming California as a gubernatorial candidate, Sinclair had met the poor and desperate people who, Sinclair had told Paul on numerous occasions, had crowded up to the platform to shake his hand. They would catch at him and try to touch him as he went past. He never forgot their hands—the big hard-crusted hands of farmers, the hands of mechanics with fingers missing, the thin, skinny hands of toil-worn women. He could still see the blur of faces, tens of thousands of California's people. He could see them rise to their feet as he came upon the platform. He had told Paul that it felt, eventually, as if he were no longer a person. He felt that he had become a symbol of the hopes and longings of millions. And now, as Paul walked through the outfield grass, he saw the same people that Sinclair had seen decades before. He saw the same hands, though they weren't reaching out for Sinclair. The hands were wrapped tightly and protectively around children and spouses. They were raised to point or utilized for obscenity. Paul could see that Sinclair was still a symbol, though not a symbol of hope. He knew too that if he survived this Fourth of July, he would not stay on as Sinclair's secretary for much longer. This was a young man's job.

Over on the left-field side, unnoticed by the crowd or the assassins, Lionel T. Pratt, Huntley biographer and best-selling author, crawled along the dry grass in the dark, carrying a rifle. Pratt had purchased the rifle from a deer hunter whose gun rack he had spotted in the parking lot of a fast-food Mexican restaurant that remained open on the Fourth. The hunter had no intention of selling his gun to the ridiculous man in the linen suit. He named an absurdly high price as a joke and promptly received a check from Pratt, who was now attempting to deliver the gun to Billings in the shed. He had already worn holes in the knees of his linen pants.

"Don't thank me," Bobby said through the bullhorn. "There is no need to thank me. I did this for you. I want to dedicate this fire to you, my friends and neighbors. And to my wife. I love you, Rosie!" Bobby groped in the pocket of his pants for a lighter.

Sinclair, Stephen, and Paul made their way past the Garvey clan and reached the infield. By this time everyone on the field was standing and word was rapidly spreading that Stephen Rudkin had arrived with two other people, one of whom was the detested Socialist Sinclair Lewis. Everyone grew quiet as the old man took the bullhorn away from Bobby, who was clearly intoxicated and confused. An assassin with extortionate child support payments took a shot at Sinclair and missed. From the field the gunshot sounded like a distant firecracker.

Sinclair held the bullhorn with two hands. "People of Greenston," he began. The audience in the infield slowly backed away from Sinclair, which was confusing but advantageous to the assassins atop the bank. There was a safe distance now between Sinclair and the townspeople, but he was a small man, very far away, still flanked by the boy, the secretary, and the drunk guy. Sinclair said, "I have had the opportunity today to befriend this young lad standing to my right." The entire town looked at Stephen. In a few years he would run away from home and few would be surprised. "And I tell you, you should be proud to live in a community that produces such bright and clean and decent young people."

Three more shots were fired from the rooftop of the Greenville Bank and the bullets lodged in the gas-soaked firewood. Soggy novels slid down the pile to the dirt. Paul looked around anxiously. The firemen behind home plate did not seem friendly. He had a bad feeling about this night. He wasn't, of course, as optimistic as Sinclair, but who was? Sinclair believed that things got either better or worse. Many people believed this, it was an American belief. But things did not get better or worse, Paul thought. Things got worse slow and worse fast. You might claim you were struggling for peace, justice, and equality, but in truth you were struggling for the pace of their inexorable decline. It was all that remained to fight for. You lay down on railroad tracks, dreaming of a new railroad. Paul was afraid of getting shot.

Sinclair continued, "We're going to hold off on this fire for the time being." Some of the children began to whine and weep. Their parents did not stop them, nor did they try. "I'd like to talk to you folks for a little while," said Sinclair, who was lit up by the searchlight. "I'd like to begin with an analogy."

The rooftop assassins shot dirt, wood, and books. Bobby patted all of his pockets again, but he couldn't find his lighter. Along the left-field side, Pratt heard Sinclair speaking and realized he might not make it to the shed in time to give Billings the rifle. Since the townspeople had backed away from Sinclair, Pratt had a straight shot at the muckraker from ground level. He had never fired a gun before. All those visits to Huntley's shooting range and he had never picked up a gun. Lying on his stomach, he squinted along the sight and tried to steady his hands. Sinclair, standing with the other two men and the boy, was drenched in white light. He looked unreal, dreamlike. Pratt tried to release the tension from his shoulders, forearms, and hands. It was good drama, it would be a great story. He concentrated on his breathing and aimed for Sinclair's heart.

Sinclair said, "How many of you here have horses?"

Pratt squeezed the trigger and Bobby Middleton fell to the ground, bleeding from the thigh. The assassins fired another round of painted bullets from the Greenville Bank, blasting the bullhorn from Sinclair's hands and extinguishing the searchlight in a shower of sparks. A few young children squealed happily and applauded what they mistakenly took to be fireworks. For a moment, the field fell into silence and darkness. Then someone screamed—a shrill, stricken cry from shallow right field—and the panic set in. Celebrants sprinted in all directions from the infield, knocking over neighbors, carrying infants like footballs. Others jumped to the ground from the top row of the bleachers, spraining ankles and calling out to loved ones. Families abandoned blankets and holiday coolers as they chaotically cleared the field in every direction. Many ran directly toward the guns at the bank. Dogs barked and yelped when stepped on. The burly Garvey twins, Mike and Mark, picked up their great-grandfather from his wheelchair and carried him in a dead run to the parking lot. Two firefighters hauled Bobby behind their truck, out of the line of fire. Pratt dropped the weapon in the dry grass and ran with the rest of the mob. Paul grabbed Sinclair and Stephen, and tried to steer them toward cover. Someone lit the bonfire. In its July 5 edition, the *Echo* reported that Bobby lit the fire, but as much as he would have liked to take credit, Bobby had, by the time the gas-soaked pile exploded in flames, passed out from the pain. In the hastily produced made-for-television movie, Chief Omar lit the fire from deep centerfield by shooting a flaming arrow into the pile, but few if any people in Greenville gave credence to this version of the event. For reasons that the editor of the *Echo* could not discern, the fire chief turned on the siren on the fire truck, which increased the panic and chaos in the dispersing crowd. The investigation that the editor called for never came about.

The fire jumped as high as the Greenville Bank and also scorched a bright path to the aluminum equipment shed on the third-base side. Witnesses later claimed to have seen someone in a "shiny shirt" scrambling out of the shed just as it was engulfed in flames.

Paul led the geriatric and the asthmatic up a small hill to the elementary school, while the firecrackers in the pile exploded like gunshots, and the huge fire illuminated the night. Past the front door, Paul took them left down a hallway and into a dark classroom, closing the door behind them. At the back of the room, past rows of wooden chairs with the built-in desks, he found an open closet and they all went inside. The closet smelled like Elmers glue. Both Sinclair and Stephen were breathing heavily. Sinclair soon recovered, but Stephen could not catch his breath. Paul reached out in the darkness to calm the child, and he accidentally struck his face with the side of his hand. Stephen's cheeks were wet with either tears or sweat. Paul moved his hand down to the boy's shoulder, which he gently squeezed and patted.

Sinclair whispered, "I may have miscalculated."

Paul said, "Did you get hit? Are you OK?"

Sinclair whispered, "All those books."

Stephen said he was sorry. He said it over and over again, hyperventilating in the dark.

Paul said, "Shhh."

Sinclair said, "It's OK, lad. We lost five hundred books, but we gained another soldier. I'd say we came out on top." Paul didn't think Sinclair sounded very convincing. "And it will be all over the news tomorrow. I call that a step forward."

Paul said, "Shhh."

Someone entered the classroom and turned on the light. In the closet Paul could see the thin strip of yellow light beneath the door. Stephen used his inhaler, but he could not stop wheezing. Paul put his arm around him and whispered, "It's OK. Relax." Paul thought of Derek, the former secretary with the limp and the bad dreams. Switzerland sounded nice. He did not want to use the gun, but he was glad he had brought it.

According to Sinclair's journal, it was while he hid in the dark supply closet in a classroom at Greenville Elementary School that he received the telepathic messages from his dying son. They had a conversation in their minds, at a distance of several kilometers.

"Dad?" Albert's voice sounded weak and garbled in Sinclair's mind.

"Albert?"

"It's me. Can you hear me?"

"It's not a good time, Albert."

"Dad."

"Albert, are you hurt?"

"Yes."

"Is it bad?"

"It's bad."

"I told you to be careful. I warned you, Albert."

"I accepted a ride from a stranger."

"I warned you." When Sinclair closed his eyes he could see a blurry image of his son in his mind. Albert lay on the ground, in the dark woods. His guitar was there too, by his feet. "Did you get my letter?"

"I don't know how you do this over and over, Dad." Albert's voice faded away like a radio station at the edge of its range. Then it came back. "Don't know how you do it."

"There was always so much to do. There were so many people who wanted things from me. Do you understand me, Albert?"

"And you were dead a lot of the time, Dad." Albert's laugh turned into a wet cough. "I understand. It doesn't matter now."

"My God, why didn't you listen to me? You should have listened to me. Don't die, Albert."

"I hope you had a good day."

"Albert."

"You in a closet, Dad? I can sort of see you."

"We've suffered a setback."

"Every knock. Right?"

"Don't say that."

"The new book is good. It's your best in a while."

"I think so too."

"I have to go now."

"I just couldn't do everything, Albert."

"I know."

"I am not by nature very personal, Albert. It is not in my nature. But don't die now. Please, listen to your father. Don't die. Be careful, like I told you."

"I have to go."

"I sent you a *letter*."

Albert's voice began to grow faint again. Their connection was fading.

"Albert."

"Don't mourn," Albert whispered. "That's my line, right?"

"No, Albert."

"Don't mourn."

"Albert."

"Organize."

"Listen to me now."

Albert said good-bye and the conversation ended.

There were footsteps across the classroom and Stephen gasped loudly.

Arthur Rudkin opened the closet door and pointed the rifle at Sinclair, who held his head in his hands. "Get out of there. Give me my boy back."

Paul and Stephen came out of the closet. Sinclair sat slumped, unmoving, the palms of his hands over his eyes. Arthur said, "Get out! Now!" Paul started to help Sinclair up, but Arthur told him to stand still. Sinclair got up slowly and emerged from the closet. Arthur backed up a few steps and kept the gun pointed at Sinclair. "Come here, Stephen. Right now."

Stephen stared down at his sneakers and shook his head. He whispered, "No, Dad."

Arthur pointed the rifle at Sinclair with his shaking hands. "Look what you've done to him. You've ruined him."

Sinclair didn't say anything. Paul looked at Stephen and noticed for the first time how poorly his clothes fit. He said, "Stephen, it's OK. Go with your father."

Stephen looked up at Paul and then at Sinclair, who stared directly ahead, at the wall, at nothing. Paul said, "It's OK. Go ahead, Stephen."

Stephen walked slowly to his father with his head down. Arthur held the gun in his left hand and with his right hand he pulled a paperback from his back pocket. "I find *this* under my son's mattress. I think maybe the kid's on pot and I find out it's much, much worse than that." He threw the creased copy of *A Moveable Jungle!* at Sinclair. Remarkably, Sinclair caught the book with two hands, then placed it on a wooden desk. "But I'm taking him back. You can't have him. I'm taking him back. And you," Arthur said, pointing the gun at Sinclair, "will be lucky to get out of Greenville alive."

Some time later, in a book about his six months with Sinclair, Paul would write that this was the only moment he had ever thought of Sinclair as old. In that classroom, Paul thought, Sinclair did not look like a folk hero or a symbol. He looked like an old and devastated man. It seemed to Paul that he had given up, that he wanted to die forever.

Sinclair did not appear shocked or even interested when Paul pulled a small pistol from the waistband of his jeans and told Arthur to put down the fucking rifle and get against the wall. The gun was unregistered and certainly represented a breach of contract.

Arthur said, "If you leave right now and never come back."

Paul said, "That's what we have in mind."

Arthur put down the rifle. He took Stephen by the shoulder and they moved against the wall.

Paul said, "Turn around. Face the wall."

Paul leaned down to pick up the book off the desk. Here was one, at least, that hadn't burned. He took Sinclair's hand and led him toward the door. Stephen peeked over his shoulder to watch them go. He wanted to say something and he tried to speak. He concentrated on forming the words. He said, "Hope and shovels, Upton." It came out as little more than a whisper.

Paul tried to hurry Sinclair from the room, but Sinclair stopped and turned around. "What did you say?"

Arthur stepped closer to his son. "Keep quiet now, Stephen."

Stephen still faced the wall. He stared at the hard coins of pink and gray gum stuck to the cinderblock wall. His legs trembled and he felt as if he might fall. He said, allegedly, "Hope and shovels forever."

Sinclair stared across the classroom at the back of Stephen's head. Behind Stephen on the wall were bulletin boards from May. Construction paper bees flew in dotted lines over construction paper flowers. The scale was way off. The bees were huge, larger than the flowers. The look on Sinclair's face was horrible. Paul had never seen it before and he never saw it again.

Sinclair cleared his throat. "Oh to hell with shovels, boy," he said, quietly and allegedly, staring at the back of Stephen's head. "Get yourself a gun."

Paul left with Sinclair. Out the window of the exit door he could see that the fire was still burning strong. The volunteer firemen had found themselves in a difficult position. To allow the fire to burn could be considered to be in poor taste. A man had been shot, after all. But to extinguish the burning novels could be construed as a pro-Socialist action, so they decided to monitor the fire and to make certain it burned safely.

Paul guided Sinclair down the hallway, past banks of blue and orange lockers, away from the softball field. He said, "Are you OK, Upton?"

Sinclair shook his head. "It's Albert. He's dead."

"Dead?"

"He didn't listen to me and he died."

"How do you know?"

"I know. I saw him. I spoke to him in the closet."

Paul believed him and knew it was true. "I'm sorry, Upton."

Sinclair said, "Everyone can be a great father after the revolution, Paul."

Paul nodded. His own father had once stolen money from Paul's buffalo bank. He had broken the ceramic buffalo and taken the $7.46 for a malt liquor and some smokes.

"There was nothing left over."

"It's not your fault, Upton."

Sinclair stared at Paul. He had not suggested that it was. "All these years," Sinclair said. The words came slow and faint. "All these years." But he didn't continue and Paul wasn't sure what he meant.

Joe Gerald Huntley, recently paroled, stepped quietly from a classroom and met the two men at the end of the hallway. He was not immediately recognizable, both because the light in the hallway was dim and because he had aged considerably in recent years. When the newspapers and television networks showed his image, they used a dated photograph. He would always be remembered as a young man. Nobody cared to see the great figure in his middle years, the famous mane gone gray.

Paul recognized him first and stopped cold. "Huntley," he whispered. He felt a shock and a thrill to see this man in person, and he forgot momentarily about the danger. Paul had grown up during the peak of Huntley's notoriety. He had spent his childhood watching Huntley on television, reading about him in magazines. His fame had transcended morality or politics. In 1986, when Paul was in junior high, Huntley had been named the fourth most outstanding person in the world by a poll of newspapers. He trailed only Ronald Reagan, Mikhail Gorbachev, and Chicago Bears defensive lineman William "the Refrigerator" Perry. Upton Sinclair, gunned down that year by Huntley in the so-called Madison Miracle, did not crack the top one hundred. "Huntley," Paul whispered again. Down the hall, Arthur and Stephen left the classroom and hurried from the school, holding hands.

Huntley said, "Did you see the Baltimore review, Sinclair?"

"Bourgeois reviews don't concern me," Sinclair said.

"Right. I don't imagine they do."

Sinclair had never been this close to Huntley. In fact, these two men, whose careers were so tightly intertwined, had never met, never spoken. They had defined one another from the opposite ends of a gun. They were conjoined symbols. Sinclair took off his glasses and his dentures, which he placed in the pocket of his khakis next to a copy of the Baltimore review and a wrinkled, yellowed letter from physicist and humanitarian Albert Einstein. The letter, written after Sinclair's failed gubernatorial campaign of 1934, said, "As I read that this cup had passed from you, I rejoiced even though it had not gone exactly according to your wish." It said, "In economic affairs, the logic of facts will work itself out somewhat slowly. You have contributed more than any other person." There was an analogy about Einstein's son attempting to split wood with a razor.

"Well," Sinclair said. "Not a tough shot from here, Joe." He closed his eyes and waited, his arms at his sides. Paul reached behind his back, but Huntley, who was not holding a weapon, told Paul to keep his hands in front of him or he would shoot them both dead. "And you," he said, nodding to the secretary, "won't be coming back." Paul did as he was told.

According to Lionel Pratt's commercially disappointing account, *The Coward of Greenville*, now out of print, Huntley instructed Paul to lead Sinclair out the other end of the hallway and to leave town immediately. Billings was here, Huntley said. He was outside waiting, expecting Sinclair to leave from the other side of the school. Go now, he said. Be quick.

Sinclair opened his eyes and raised his arms. "You're not going to shoot me?"

Huntley, according to Pratt, shook his head. "I'm retiring and you should too," he said. "I'm building a greenhouse. Now get out of here. Go." Editors wouldn't touch Huntley's manuscript and it remains unpublished, though he allegedly ignored a query from RSP.

There was an awkward moment between the men. Sinclair said nothing. He replaced his glasses and dentures. He slumped at the waist and the shoulders, and he looked nothing like a folk hero or a revolutionary. Paul nodded to Huntley and gently took Sinclair by the arm, which felt bony and frail. They walked together slowly back down the hallway and Paul looked back twice to see Huntley's silhouette in the corridor. At the far end of the hallway, Paul opened the door and looked around. He didn't see anyone near the school, but he feared guns in the bushes, guns on the rooftops. Down the small hill he saw the fire truck still parked behind home plate and the fire still burning on the diamond. A small crowd had reconvened around it. A young fireman roasted hot dogs and marshmallows from a long, barbed projectile weapon he had earlier pulled from a burning log. In the outfield, the dalmatians ran loose and wild, picking food from abandoned coolers and picnic baskets. Paul shut the heavy door quietly behind them, and he began to lead Sinclair in the direction of the car, which was fuelled up and parked close to the interstate. He would drive them all night. He wouldn't stop. He put his arm around the old man, both to steady him and to keep him moving. Both men jumped when they heard a firecracker. "It was just a firecracker," the secretary said, and Sinclair nodded. Charred, feathery scraps of paper floated down from the sky.

On the infield, the bonfire had died down, but it continued to burn well. The pile had apparently been constructed with great care and foresight. A few more families returned to the field and gathered by the fire once it became evident that the gunshots and the panic were over, that the muckraker had either been killed or chased off. There were plenty of blankets and chairs, there was plenty of food and drink. The boys in the GFD spread out and kept a careful watch over the blaze. The children of Greenville, permitted to stay up late for this one special night, waved sparklers and danced wildly around the pyre of burned books.

PART THREE:

Faith in Spades

The men with the muck-rake are often indispensable to the well-being of society, but only if they know when to stop raking the muck.

—THEODORE ROOSEVELT

Item Number: 09201878
Item Title: Last Folk Song
Item Location: Greenville, USA
Starting Bid: $35
Time Left: 1 day, 14 hours
History: 2 bids
Shipping: Ships anywhere in U.S. Buyer assumes all postage or shipping costs.

Description: LYRICS OF UNRECORDED SONG HANDWRITTEN IN PENCIL ON RED SHOVEL PRESS INFO CARD. FOUND IN LAST FOLKSINGER'S GUITAR CASE (LFS WAS SUPPOSEDLY THE SON OF UPTON SINCLAIR). FAIR CONDITION. CORNERS WRINKLED. COFFEE STAIN. WRITING IS LIGHT AND DIFFICULT TO READ IN PLACES. DOESN'T PHOTOGRAPH WELL. LYRICS BELOW.

ANOTHER DIGGER SONG

Come carry a spade in the Digger Parade
We're a bit out of step, it's true

Your shovel can double as a muckrake
Or just something to hold on to

We don't try to let a sleeping dog lie
And we don't try to teach him new tricks
He may be a runt but that old dog will hunt
And we're proof that he's never been fixed

Baby, good night and sleep tight
Welcome to the shovel brigade
Where the bedbugs always bite
And we still have faith in spades

Like the frogs and the worms, the dolphins and terns
Red-Breasted Diggers are at the brink
We've got kilometers to go and our numbers are low
We're endangered but not extinct

Baby, good night and sleep tight
Dream the dream that never fades
Even though we're in their sights
We still have faith in spades

So come carry a spade in the national charade
Just like it's 1649
On St. George's Hill those Diggers were killed
But in Greenville they're still alive

Baby, good night and sleep tight
Dream the dream that never fades
And when the fireworks and bullets fly
We'll still have faith in spades

With spades and hoes and plows, stand up now
Stand up now, Diggers all

Acknowledgments!

I made use of about a dozen of Upton Sinclair's eighty-seven books, particularly his autobiography and his nonfiction account of the 1934 EPIC campaign in California. Occasional short passages of the novel are taken more or less verbatim from these two works, and I am grateful to the estate of Upton Sinclair, which granted permission for their use. Leon Harris's fine biography *Upton Sinclair: American Rebel* was extraordinarily helpful. I was inspired by the work of E. L. Doctorow, whose interviews—pieces of which I stitched together in "Professional Messiah"—are collected and edited by Christopher D. Morris in *Conversations with E. L. Doctorow.* I offer my gratitude (and apologies) to all of the novelists, poets, and songwriters whose work I borrowed, stole, and twisted.

A special thank you to my agent Lisa Bankoff and to everyone at Bloomsbury, particularly Gillian Blake, Mike Jones, and Marisa Pagano.

  Friends of the cause: Greg Meyerson (political adviser), Wesley Stace (songwriting consultant), Kevin Leahy (handyman), Neale Reinitz (man of letters), and my terrific colleagues in the English Department at Colorado College.

I'm happy to thank my family for their love, good humor, and general support of picketing and other modes of dissent.

And for her strength and intelligence, her clairvoyance and constancy, I am profoundly grateful to Jenn Habel, wise dealer from the deck marked Truth.

A Note on the Author

Chris Bachelder is the author of the novels *Lessons in Virtual Tour Photography* (an e-book) and *Bear v. Shark*, which has been published in five countries. He lives in Colorado Springs and teaches writing and literature at Colorado College.

BY THE SAME AUTHOR

Bear v. Shark

Who would win if a bear fought a shark? People all over America would cut their own arms off to attend the Bear v. Shark II fight in Las Vegas but it is the Norman family who are driving across the country with four tickets in their hands, besieged by a dizzying barrage of TV and radio personalities, Freudians, theologians and more, as the whole country bets, debates and argues over who is going to win.

'The cult book of the year. It's *No Logo* meets *Fight Club*.
It makes you want to blow up your TV'
Sunday Telegraph

'Sabre-sharp ... hilarious' *Arena*

'Think Pynchon, think George Saunders, but most of all
welcome a new, achingly funny voice of dissent' *Metro*

'Like DeLillo on acid' *Publishers Weekly*

'Bedazzling ... playfully referential, ostentatiously smart'
Los Angeles Times